Promise & Honor

Kim Murphy

*To Lynn,
Best wishes,
Kim Murphy*

Published by Coachlight Press

Published by Coachlight Press 2003

ISBN 978-0-9716790-2-3
Library of Congress Control Number: 2002109185

Coachlight Press, LLC
1704 Craig's Store Road
Afton, Virginia 22920
http://www.coachlightpress.com

Printed in the United States of America

This is a work of fiction. Names, characters, places, and incidents either are the product of the author's imagination or are used fictitiously, and any resemblance to any actual persons, living or dead, events, or locales is entirely coincidental.

Cover design by Mayapriya Long, Bookwrights Design
Front cover battle scene photo © 2001 Charles Holley Photography,
http://holleyphotography.com/

For Pat,
who never stopped believing, and all of the brave men
and women of the Civil War—on both sides.

Prologue

Near Manassas Junction, Virginia
July 21, 1861

WHEN THE CANNON ROARED TO LIFE, spectators sent up a round of cheers. They had spread checkered cloths and baskets filled with fried chicken and fine pastries across the grass. Children romped. Champagne corks popped. Women shielded delicate skin with gaily colored parasols. Eager to witness the deciding battle, congressmen had brought their families for a picnic. The first men in blue started falling, and mouths gaped at an unexpected sight—blood.

Lieutenant Samuel Prescott wiped a sweaty brow in the stifling heat. Nerves—no, it was the heat. After hours of waiting in the relative safety of the woods, the regiment marched across a blackened field. Charging men before them had trampled the summer grass. As they advanced, the spectators applauded and shoved fists to the sky for triumph.

What Sam wouldn't give for a cool Maine breeze. Through the smoke all he could clearly see were the feet of the man in front of him.

Guns pounded and ghostly figures rushed here and there. The boys hustled over a snake-rail fence. One private fell from the top rail, landed on his canteen, and dented it. The other boys gathered around and roared with laughter.

Less than amused, Sam failed to share their enthusiasm. Certain they would see the elephant soon, he shouted for them to keep marching.

At the top of a gentle rise, bullets whirred over their heads. A mass of dead and dying bodies sprawled across the field below. Rebels fired from the woods. Without the benefit of cover, many of the boys were caught in the open as easy targets.

Sam motioned for them to lie low. Minutes of more waiting passed.

When the Rebels formed a line, the spectators finally comprehended the danger and jammed the road with their carriages in a chaotic retreat.

The order arrived, and Sam shouted for the boys to fall in line. Face to face—a few hundred yards apart. So this was the enemy. The colonel signaled with his sword.

"Ready!" Sam commanded as if it was nothing more than a drill.

The men in blue readied their muskets.

"Aim!"

Muskets snapped to attention and sighted the targets in gray.

"Fire!"

Through the deafening volley, canister whistled overhead and sprayed the ground with balls of deadly lead. It tore through the ranks, and a number of men went down.

The Rebels moved toward Sam's line, and an unearthly yell rose above the frenzy. In spite of the heat, a chill of cold terror ran down Sam's back. He ordered the boys forward.

A sobbing private rammed his musket barrel with bullet after bullet without firing. A Rebel shot tore through the boy's chest, and he fell dead at Sam's feet.

The otherworldly yell sounded again, and blue and gray merged in hand-to-hand combat. Sam briefly thought of Kate. She had died over a year ago after giving birth, and he was ready to join her. The ground rippled beneath him, throwing him off his feet. He tasted blood in his mouth and checked himself. His arms and legs were firmly attached. He appeared to be unharmed.

A cold, sharp blade ripped through his left sleeve and grazed his arm. A wild-eyed Rebel loomed over him with a raised bayonet ready for another try. Sam rolled to the side and fired his Colt pistol into the scraggly bearded face. Blood spattered him, and the faceless Rebel fell.

The blue line gave way. Some boys clutched muskets as if they were part of them. Others threw down weapons, turning tail.

He needed to get behind them—keep the remaining boys from running. Regroup the others, and keep the line from breaking. But through the smoke, the Rebels swarmed their flank like bloodsucking flies.

Sam got to his feet, and a bearded Rebel officer with a sword in one hand and a pistol in the other charged toward him. He aimed the gun at Sam's head.

At first Sam failed to recognize him, but the gunpowder-blackened face belonged to Colonel Graham, one of his commanders before the war. The Colonel's uniform was covered in blood, and his eyes remained fixed in the other world of battle.

Sam sucked in his breath. He accepted death, but friends didn't meet as enemies on the same bloodstained battlefield. Unable to pull the trigger, he threw his pistol to the ground in surrender. Ready to die by the hand of a friend, he straightened to attention. His first battle would be his last.

Sam's eyes burned from the smoke, and he blocked out the fear of death with thoughts of home. A cool ocean breeze blew gently in his face as he inhaled salt air. He held a glass filled with ice water. Ice was scarce in Virginia. But Virginia was where he had left his daughter in the caring hands of the Colonel's wife, Amanda Graham. After Kate's death, she had taken his daughter and cared for Rebecca. She would see to the child's needs once he was gone.

The fatal bullet didn't come. Sam looked over at the Colonel as he lowered his pistol. Friendship registered in his former commander's eyes. Between them there was no blue or gray. But sympathy for the enemy could get a man killed, and the Colonel vanished in a cloud of smoke.

Cannon pounded, and muskets exploded. The field reeked of gunpowder and death. Sam retrieved his pistol and took his position at the end of the line. An exploding shell muffled a scream. Dirt and gunpowder showered the ground.

Sam shielded his eyes. When the veil lifted enough for him to see, a soldier in blue writhed from a belly wound.

Something struck him square in the ribs, and he was eating dirt once more. A Rebel swung his musket and struck him in the forehead. Blinding pain. Not ready to let go, Sam fought to remain conscious. Willful pride kept him from calling for Kate.

Someone was aiding him. Hands went underneath him and helped him up. The face was blurred, but he wore gray. When the face came into focus, Sam was comforted to see a friendly face—Colonel Graham.

The Colonol drew Sam's arm over a broad shoulder.

Dizzy. The light grew dim.

The Colonel staggered. His free hand went to his chest. Blood spurted between his fingers.

The company corporal stood across from them with his mouth agape. They must be quite a sight. Gray helping blue on the battlefield. Light narrowed to a dot, and Sam felt the Colonel slump. Small but strong hands caught Sam before he hit the ground a third time. What would he tell Amanda? Friends didn't meet as enemies. Too tired to think. Then blackness.

Chapter One

Near Fredericksburg, Virginia

MORE THAN A MONTH HAD PASSED since the Colonel made the final wagon ride home. Amanda had buried him on the grassy knoll behind the farmhouse. There, underneath the expansive limbs of an old oak, he joined her papa. One day it would be her resting place as well.

Lieutenant Colonel William Jackson had stopped by late in the afternoon to pay his respects. In the cool evening breeze, he covered his heart with his hat and lowered his head. She was grateful for his company. With John gone, the nights had been lonely. After a brief moment of silence, he said in his thick Charleston accent, "He died bravely, Amanda."

Instead of bringing her comfort, his words had the opposite effect. "Bravely? This whole war is foolish—a foolish waste." Raising the skirt of her black mourning dress, she stepped past Wil and started down the hill.

He caught her arm. "I beg forgiveness. I only meant . . ." His eyes showed sympathy.

"I know. The morning the two of you set out was overcast. John even said goodbye. He had never said goodbye before. I suppose I knew then that he wasn't coming back."

Wil dropped his hand and fidgeted with the brim of his hat. "I shall see to your needs. John would have wanted it that way."

Under a different set of circumstances, she would have considered Wil's offer suggestive. His reputation with the ladies was a well-known

fact, not to mention his gambling and drinking activities. Below prominent cheekbones, a neatly trimmed moustache lined his upper lip,
and the waves in his hair matched the black depths of his eyes. Even
Amanda couldn't deny a certain attraction. "I thank you for your kind
offer. My land is fertile for growing and grazing. We shall manage."

She strolled down the hill, and Wil joined her with the sword at his
side clanking.

"Amanda, this war won't be short. Virginia will be a wasteland before it's over."

They neared the farmhouse, and Wil opened the gate of the white-
washed picket fence. The breeze hinted at autumn. With a shiver,
Amanda realized she should have brought her shawl, but the cool air
wasn't the reason why she had suddenly grown cold. "The Colonel said
one battle—"

"Manassas was only a beginning." Wil's jaw tensed, and his gaze
grew distant. "I haven't seen anything like it since fighting the Mexicans."

John and Wil had fought side by side in the war against the Mexicans. Wil had even taken a bullet meant for the Colonel and barely
survived. Now he stood beside her, ever so proud and handsome in
his gray uniform with shiny brass buttons and fine gold embroidery
on the sleeves of his jacket. But John was gone, and she was no longer
misled by war's glory. Many more brave men would die.

"How long can it last?" she asked.

"At least three years."

"Three..." Amanda suddenly felt faint, took a deep breath, and
calmed herself. "Wil, where are my manners? We have a big pot of
stew simmering for supper, and Frieda will make tea."

Wil held out his arm, and she hooked hers through it. Next to him,
she detected the sweet aroma of cigars. When they went up the steps,
the wood creaked under their weight. With a slight bow, he opened the
door.

Amanda smiled in appreciation. "Thank you." Once inside the parlor, she gestured for him to make himself at home in the green velvet
wing chair. She fluffed a cushion and placed it behind his back. "I shall
tell Frieda that you're here."

"I appreciate your hospitality."

In the the kitchen, a whiff of hearty beef mixed with fresh garden vegetables drifted her way. For the first time since the Colonel's passing, she felt hungry. Maybe Wil's appearance had been a blessing.

The blind, slightly stooped form of her servant hovered over the cookstove, stirring the stew in a Dutch oven. The meal smelled so heavenly that Amanda's mouth watered. "Frieda, we have a guest."

"I make da tea." The old Negro woman waved a wooden spoon. "Miss Amanda, you watch yourself with dat one."

"Wil? But he's been a family friend for years."

"But da Colonel gone now." The wrinkles etched in Frieda's face became pronounced with worry. "He be thinkin' of you as a woman, and he da type to take what he can and run. Ain't never bin married. Must be nearin' forty."

"Wil is thirty six."

"Don't make no difference. A man his age should be married."

"I shall be careful," Amanda promised.

When Amanda returned to the parlor, Wil stood. She seated herself on the tapestry sofa across from him. One rumor had him courting a Carolina girl from a respectable family, but another tale was less flattering. Some folks even spread the story that he had taken up with a married woman. On previous occasions, she had ignored idle gossip, but with Frieda's warning she would pay more heed.

He reseated himself in the wing chair.

"Wil . . . " She cleared her throat. "I was wondering if you have heard anything from Sam Prescott? With the mail being erratic lately, it's not surprising I haven't received a letter, but I hope he remained in New Mexico."

"Prescott was at Manassas."

Not Sam too. Amanda closed her eyes. The war had already touched all those close to her. In the year that had passed since Sam's transfer to the New Mexico territory, she had come to think of his daughter as her own flesh and blood, but the feeling went deeper. He never said as much, but she knew she was the reason for his transfer. She would have never betrayed John's trust. And Sam wouldn't have respected her if she had, but after Kate's death, she had encouraged his friendship. As time went on, and his grief faded, she had noticed a gentle kindness return to his blue eyes—one of longing.

"Amanda?"

At the sound of Wil's voice, she blinked. "Is he . . . ?"

"I wouldn't know. The Yankees don't tend to send me casualty reports. He should be fine. After all, we sent the bluebellies scurrying . . ." Wil snorted a laugh. " . . . all the way back to Washington."

"Wil!" Amanda waved at his inappropriate gaiety. "Good men died there—on both sides."

He bowed his head slightly. "Forgive me."

His dark eyes sobered. Familiar with the look, she knew there was something he wasn't telling. "Wil, what do you know?"

"I don't *know* anything, but I have heard things—about Prescott."

"What sort of things?"

"Amanda, there was a lot of confusion that day. That's normal with unseasoned troops. To make matters worse, some Confederates wore blue."

"And?"

"My source says that John spent his last few minutes among Yankees, specifically Prescott."

Skeptical of the report, Amanda sent him a stare. Friends didn't go meeting one another on a battlefield. "Why didn't you tell me this earlier?"

Wil leaned back in the wing chair. "I didn't know whether you would believe my source. She has been prone to exaggeration in the past."

She. That likely explained his hesitation in bringing the matter up. At least one rumor was apparently true, and Amanda doubted his source was a proper Carolina girl. "Who is this *source?*"

The stooped form of Frieda entered the parlor, guided by a cherry walking stick. "Tea is ready, Miss Amanda," she said.

Wil watched Frieda, and an unexpected urgency entered his voice. "Amanda, I have another matter to discuss. The Yankees are making moves to cut off our supplies. You have a good, strong horse..."

Confused by his sudden topic shift, Amanda said, "The army has taken several of my mares and plow horses. Don't even suggest it. I'm not selling Red, and the mares that are left have foals at their sides."

He tugged on his moustache. "I wasn't suggesting that I take your horses. But I think we should continue this discussion outside." He pointed at Frieda.

"Why, Colonel, I detect some embarrassment in discussing your *source*. I hope I haven't contributed to your discomfort. I gathered you were well acquainted."

An amused grin formed on his face but quickly vanished. "My source is a traitor and a spy—in more ways than one."

"I see."

"Would you rather I lied?" Wil grasped her elbow and escorted her to the front porch.

A cool breeze blew, hinting at summer's fading, while crickets chirped a chorus. She remembered other summer evenings, sitting on the porch swing beside John. Now she dressed in black, and those days seemed so long ago.

"Think of me what you will," he continued, breaking the stillness. "But she is married to a Yankee captain."

Her hand flew to her collar. Ill at ease with his confession, Amanda twisted the fabric between her fingers. "Quite frankly, Colonel, I'm appalled that you would share the details of an illicit affair."

"Amanda, I have never pretended to be a gentleman."

Suddenly uncomfortable by his presence, Amanda looked out at the fields in the darkening sky. In the lengthening shadows her Negro servant, Ezra, led a mare and foal to the barn.

"On the night before Manassas," Wil said softly, "John told me that he wasn't coming back from this one. Many times, men get a feeling, and they think of home. He would have given anything to see you again. Whether Prescott was with John, I don't know. I wasn't with him when he died, but I trained Prescott in New Mexico. He's a professional soldier. I have no doubt he carried out his duty under the stress of battle. On the day of Manassas, he fought for the opposite side."

His insinuation was abhorrent. "Are you suggesting Sam was responsible for John's death?"

He studied her a moment. "No."

A ring of hesitation carried in his voice. Was Wil trying to spare her from further grief? After all, anything was possible under battle conditions. But Sam and John had been friends. A lump caught at the back of her throat. What if Sam had fired the fatal shot? "Wil—"

"Amanda, I need someone to run medical supplies."

Flustered that he kept evading her questions, Amanda narrowed her eyes. "I don't believe you! One minute you insinuate that Sam may have been involved in John's death, the next you ask me to smuggle medical supplies. Why, you're more like a timber rattler."

"Forgive me. I wouldn't have brought up Prescott's name if you hadn't asked, but I would feel more comfortable discussing the event if I knew the facts."

He was still neatly sidestepping her concerns. Amanda clenched her teeth before saying something she regretted. Once calm again, she asked, "Why would you want me to carry medical supplies?"

"Because a woman can slip through the lines more easily, and if captured, the punishment is less severe." His eyes grew piercing as he took her hand and lightly kissed it. "But Amanda, I will do my utmost to see that you are not captured."

On that account, she believed him, but doubt remained to what his true intent might be. "You'll guarantee that I shall carry only medical supplies?"

"Possibly other supplies, but no arms, if that's your concern. I won't risk having you branded as a spy, and you have the right to refuse anything you don't approve of. I will pay in gold, which should help you through this troubled time."

With the Colonel in his grave and no pension to be claimed, she certainly could use the money. "If you can give me a day or two to think it over—"

"I would prefer your answer sooner rather than later, but send a servant with your message when you have decided."

Running medical supplies might give her a sense of purpose. She needed that right now. What's more, by assisting Wil, she might relieve some needless suffering. "Wil, I can give you an answer now. I will run supplies. It shall help me heal if I can give comfort to others."

"I understand. I'll make the arrangements as soon as I return to camp."

A most confusing man, Wil Jackson had nearly laid down his life for John, and she trusted that he would do the same for her if the situation ever arose. But what could be gained by smuggling medical supplies? Weapons or spying would be of more value to the Confederacy. "Why medical supplies?"

His face darkened. Was it pain? But the expression was fleeting. "I shall try to tell you what you want to know—in good time. Please accept that for now."

He lifted her hand to his lips once more and gently kissed it. Bowing slightly, he turned. As he went down the porch steps, his sword clanked and spurs jingled. When he reached the bottom step, he glanced over his shoulder.

Their gazes met. Amanda knew the look and recalled Frieda's warning. His attention began to make sense. He hadn't visited to pay his respects to John but as an excuse to see her.

Within a fortnight, Amanda wondered what she had let herself in for. She brought the stallion, Red, to a halt in a forest glade next to a hundred-year-old oak with a distinctive branch in the shape of a dipper. The tree marked the spot where she was supposed to meet a man by the name of James. Wil had described the man as heavy-set and riding a black horse, but he failed to mention whether James was a surname or his given.

Although she had arrived early, she checked the map to make certain she waited in the right spot. No two trees could have identical branches. Satisfied she had found the proper location, she folded the map and stuffed it in her saddlebag.

So far, so good. But what was she to do while waiting? Sitting idle in the saddle played on her nerves. On her next supply run, she would time the pickup a little better. Next run? She must get through this one before thinking of the next.

A chickadee scolded from the ancient oak, and her hands tensed on the leather. She'd much rather be home tending farm chores than waiting alone in some distant Maryland forest. With the tight rein, Red pawed the ground.

Amanda loosened her grip, and the stallion relaxed.

The chickadee stopped scolding, and a cool breeze rustled through the leaves changing from summer green to shades of autumn red and yellow. Wishing she had brought her cloak, Amanda checked her pocket watch. How long should she wait if James didn't show? Wil had given her few guidelines beyond being careful. Then again, smuggling supplies was probably new to him as well.

A lone rider on a black horse with a white blaze on its nose trotted from an outcrop of trees. The horse was weighted down with several canvas bags over its withers. The burly man tipped his hat and halted a few feet away. "Mrs. Graham . . . ."

"Mr. James?"

Without answering, he reached a pudgy hand into his frock coat pocket and withdrew a handkerchief. He wiped his sweaty brow with the fresh white linen.

"Colonel Jackson—"

"First rule—no more names."

Though he was out of breath and wheezing, Amanda detected a distinct Northern accent.

"While the Yanks won't hang you, they wouldn't give a tinker's damn about me. Clear?" He reined the black across from Red and transferred a canvas bag. "I get the supplies out of Washington. Your concern is across the river."

Another bag was slung across Red's withers. The stallion bobbed his head.

Amanda opened the first bag and checked the contents—laudanum, quinine, bandages. Exactly what Wil had said she would carry. She reached inside the bag to make certain nothing else had been slipped in. Bags of medicine, but no weapons or cartridge boxes. The second bag held more of the same. Satisfied no arms or ammunition had been slipped in, she handed James an envelope.

He looked inside, and a smile crossed his face. "Pleasure doing business with you, ma'am." He reined the black horse around, but halted. "Tell the colonel that our Washington contact is weary of pretending to nursemaid sick soldiers. Next shipment will cost more."

The husky man spurred the black in the side. The horse groaned in protest, and they cantered off.

Doubtful that Wil would take kindly to the message, she focused on the job ahead. Her primary concern was crossing the Potomac. Only a couple of miles from the river, she cued Red to a trot. Wil had wanted her first run to be short—undoubtedly to make certain she wouldn't bow under pressure. Avoiding the roads, she trotted Red along an animal path through the forest.

She ducked to miss an overhanging branch and slowed Red to a walk. Up ahead, she heard the rushing water of the Potomac. On the other side, Wil would be waiting for her. She halted Red at the edge of the forest.

A gentle slope of waving grass dipped down to the ford in the river. The Confederate picket line would be watching for her. So why was she suddenly uneasy?

Red tugged on the bit to be moving.

Still, she waited.

She squeezed Red to a brisk trot. Once on open ground, Amanda focused on the swift running water a few hundred yards away. Nearly home free, she heard hooves pounding behind her. A quick glance over her shoulder confirmed her fear. Yankee soldiers—two scouts in hot pursuit.

The leather reins slid through her fingers, and she urged Red to a gallop. She neared the river. A soldier from the picket line fired a warning. Weighted down with supplies, Red was unable to outdistance the Yankees.

A corporal on a moth-eaten buckskin pulled even and seized the reins. Nearly twisting Red's head around, he brought the stallion to a halt.

Amanda reached into her saddlebag and leveled a pistol at his chest.

He let go of the leather and raised his hands. "I wouldn't hurt a woman."

Trembling, she lowered the gun slightly. "Then why have you stopped me?"

A bullet whirred overhead from the picket line. Horses crossed the river—at least a dozen with a blue roan in the lead. The stubble-faced corporal whirled the buckskin around, and shot off at a gallop, traveling in the dust of the other scout.

The roan halted beside Red, but the remaining Confederates continued their pursuit of the Yankees.

"Amanda, are you all right?"

Still shaking, she glanced over at Wil. "I botched up."

"As a matter of fact, you handled yourself quite well, but..." He reached for the pistol. "...you can let go now."

Amanda loosened her stranglehold grip and surrendered the revolver. "It's not loaded."

Wil settled back in the saddle and checked the empty chamber. "A foolish bluff, Amanda. If you take a gun out, you had best be ready to use it."

Gunfire sounded behind her. Amanda looked around in search of the Yankee scouts. "They mustn't be harmed."

"They won't be unless they resist."

"I refuse to be the cause of anyone being hurt. Please Wil—call off your men."

"Very well. Return to camp." With the order, he spurred the roan on.

Shifting around in the saddle, Amanda guided Red into the dark waters of the Potomac. With her attention focused on reaching the Confederate side of the river, the swift current caught her unaware. Red hit a deep spot and began swimming. Cold waves lapped near the top of the saddle, sending a chill through her bones.

The current grew stronger. Red compensated with powerful strokes of his legs. His feet finally touched bottom. She clucked her tongue, urging him forward. He climbed the bank, and she brought him to a halt at the picket line.

"Much obliged for your help," she said to the guard.

Dressed in tattered gray, he coughed—a deep hacking cough. So many were sick. No wonder Wil needed medical supplies.

"Glad we could be of service, ma'am," he said.

Amanda glanced back. The Confederate group was near the tree line with the Yankee corporal as prisoner.

Chapter Two

THE PRIVATE ON THE PICKET LINE saluted. Wil returned his salute and cued the blue roan toward the encampment. He entered the rows of tents. Several men hooted. More joined in, throwing fists to the sky. Whether the reason was the prisoner or Amanda, he wasn't certain. Amanda, most likely. Except for a few officers' wives, some of the boys hadn't seen a woman in months. And Amanda was a beautiful one.

He dismounted, and a black servant led the gelding away.

Outside his tent, he helped Amanda from the red stallion's back. Her feet touched the ground, and Wil found himself staring into her eyes. His hands lingered on her waist. She felt good in his arms. His body reacted. But Amanda was a lady—recently widowed, no less.

In frustration, he grabbed a canvas bag from the stallion's withers before showing her inside.

"Wil," Amanda asked, "what shall happen to the Yankee corporal?"

He motioned for her to have a seat on a camp stool. "He'll be exchanged for one of our own. No harm will come to him. You have my word."

Apparently satisfied with his answer, she spread the folds of her black mourning dress and sat on the camp stool.

He inspected the contents of the bag. Medicine for coughs, fevers, and measles. Worth its weight in gold—as it had been the time before. *Forget the past.* "Good. This will help our sick boys." He looked over at Amanda. "Can I get you something to freshen up?"

"Some tea would be lovely."

After calling his servant, Wil pulled up a camp stool and sat across from her. "A reminder, Amanda." He held up his right index finger. "One warning—and I don't expect to ever repeat myself. I don't want you risking yourself again. If you so much as spot a Yankee, you drop the supplies. They only slow you down. Understood?"

She nodded.

He reached into his pocket and withdrew a ten-dollar gold piece. He placed it in Amanda's palm, and her slender fingers curled around the coin. Too proud to admit that John's death had made life a struggle, she would accept his aid only through supply running. He wished for a less dangerous way.

"Mr. James wanted me to relay a message. He said the Washington contact has grown tired of nursemaiding sick soldiers. The next shipment will cost more."

The demand came as no surprise. "How much?"

"He didn't say." Amanda placed a reassuring hand on his arm. "Is it a problem?"

"Only that she's attempting to make a profit from the sick. I'll deal with her." Amused by Amanda's touch, he glanced at her hand resting on his arm.

With a shy smile, she dropped it to her lap.

"Now that business has been taken care of, how have you been?" Wil asked.

"We managed a harvest of corn—a small one, but it will see us through the winter."

He detected an attempt to downplay hardship. A Negro servant stepped into the tent, and Wil motioned for him to approach. The servant handed Amanda a tin cup.

"Thank you," she said.

The servant nodded and hurried from the tent.

After blowing on the steaming tea, Amanda took a sip and wrinkled her nose.

Aware the tea was watered down, he said, "My apologies for the tea, but it's the best I can do. If the Yankee blockade becomes effective, it's going to become a scarce item altogether. Never mind my troubles, tell me more."

She stared at the tin cup.

"What's wrong?" Wil asked.

Amanda blinked. "Soldiers requisitioned one of my mares. Fortunately, I had weaned her foal."

"Did they pay you?"

"As much as they could."

Politicians. He'd like to strangle them for making the country believe the war would be short. Long and bloody was the way he saw it taking shape. If they had bothered asking the seasoned officers, they would have known as much before the first shot had been fired. "I shall see that you get the rest."

"It's not your problem, Wil."

Although their association had often been tumultuous, John Graham had been a friend going back to West Point. As such, it was his responsibility to see that Amanda was cared for. "But it is, Amanda."

Her green eyes met his, and he spotted loneliness—an all-too-familiar feeling. Without thinking, he leaned across and kissed her.

Caught off guard, Amanda poised a hand, ready to reprimand him for the reproach.

"I beg forgiveness," he said with a slight bow. "That was forward of me."

She lowered her hand. "It's too soon."

Wil smiled in sad comprehension. "I understand. Long ago . . . " With a shake of his head, he waved to say that it wasn't important. Only the past, trying to creep through yet again.

"I thought you were courting—"

"Courting? I'm not courting anyone."

"But you said . . . Never mind, I don't care to hear about your dalliances." She waggled a finger at him. "And Wil Jackson, how dare you think I'm that kind of woman."

Definitely not that sort of woman. "Amanda, I'm aware that you're a lady—one to be respected. Now in spite of my bad manners, are you certain you wish to continue carrying supplies? This was a trial run. I think you have a fair idea of the danger involved."

She straightened her shoulders and set the empty tin cup on the field desk. "I'm aware of the danger, and I shall continue doing the job for as long as necessary."

He almost wished she hadn't agreed. Honor demanded that he shelter her from the harmful effects of war. "Then I will let you know the details of the next run as soon as I make the arrangements. My servant will bring your horse."

She stood, and Wil got to his feet. He lifted her hand to his lips. It trembled beneath his fingertips.

Amanda withdrew her hand and turned to leave. By the opening of the tent, she glanced back at him in confusion. It was too soon after John's death for her to think romantically, he reminded himself. Not to mention that his reputation would cause her to doubt his sincerity. She sent him a parting smile and stepped outside.

Only he could prove his intentions were honorable.

In a cloud of red Virginia dust, Wil's scout was returning. Astride the roan gelding, he lowered the field glasses.

The lieutenant brought a lathered horse to a halt beside him. Out of breath, he reported with a salute, "Yankee scouts up ahead—one, maybe two miles—at least a dozen or so, sir."

Earlier reports were verified. Amanda was scheduled to contact James outside Alexandria for supplies. He'd send a courier with the message for her to head straight south toward home. She was friendly with a number of the residents if she needed to seek shelter.

Wil jotted down a note and handed it to the exhausted scout. "See that Mrs. Graham receives this."

The lieutenant spurred his tired mount and galloped off.

Two men cantered their horses ahead to determine the Yanks' exact location. Wil shouted orders for the rest to fall in line. After riding a mile, he got a feeling deep in his gut that the Yanks were near. The forest edging the road had grown mighty quiet. Not even a bird sang.

Wil raised a hand, and the handful of soldiers halted behind him. All but one were inexperienced and eager for a fight. Always eager—until the first blood was drawn.

The men and horses lined themselves behind the trees. A meadow with yellow grass gently sloped to another forest edge. One of the boys raised his shotgun. Wil reminded him to wait for his order.

A scout returned. "They're in the woods, sir."

Confirming what Wil had suspected, he checked through his field glasses and spied the enemy.

Oblivious to the men in gray, the soldiers in blue had stopped to rest their horses. The Yanks chatted and sang, giving the impression they had gathered for a picnic rather than reconnaissance. Few took the war seriously in the months since Manassas—raw recruits even less so.

Wil packed the field glasses away. Like himself, the Yanks likely had scouts patrolling the woods. Ready to remind them which side of the river they belonged on, he drew his pistol.

The boys snapped to attention and readied their weapons.

Clearing his mind of anything but the job of driving the Yanks north, Wil focused on the men in blue. Numbers were almost even. They'd find out soon enough whether the Yanks had any belly for fighting.

Wil called the advance.

The boys whooped a war cry only possible in the face of death. Bullets flew. The Yanks scrambled for their horses. Only as an afterthought did they reach for their weapons. Two Yanks fell, then one of his own men.

A sharp sting hit Wil in the lower right arm. Somehow he managed to keep a grip on the pistol. Determined to get the Yank who had shot him, he fired.

Shock. Disbelief. The soldier clawed at his chest and collapsed with a scream.

Pain spread through Wil's arm, and his pistol clattered to the ground.

The rest of the Yanks fled. Some of his boys hightailed after them.

A blond private checked the men who had fallen. Tears filled the private's eyes over a prone gray-clad body. He sniffled and said, "Two Yanks are alive, sir. What should we do with 'em?"

One of the wounded Yanks whimpered, and huddled in a ball, trying to make himself look smaller. Wil's gaze came to rest on him. "Bring them along." He wrapped a handkerchief around his bleeding forearm.

The private pointed to Wil's arm. "Sir—are *you* all right?"

"It's a graze."

Tears gave way to a grin. "Least you got the bluebelly bastard."

Wil lacked the boy's enthusiasm. In the center of the Yank's blue jacket, a bright red stain spread. His face had a peach-fuzz stubble. He had been fifteen or sixteen at best. A boys' war. So eager to be a man, he had died before ever having the chance to grow up.

Late in the afternoon, Amanda guided the buggy up the tree-lined lane to home. Red's hooves clip-clopped against the hardened red dirt. She entered the farmyard and spotted a strapping roan gelding tied to the rail out front.

A gray-haired Negro man came running from the barn with his face wrinkled in concern. "Miss Amanda, we was gettin' worried," Ezra said, holding Red steady. "Colonel Jackson is waitin' inside."

She adjusted her black skirt and climbed from the carriage. "Thank you, Ezra." She pulled a tapestry bag from the back of the buggy. "If you could bring the rest of the supplies to the house..."

"Yes'm." Ezra led the lathered stallion in the direction of the barn.

Before she reached the house, the door opened, and Wil stepped onto the porch.

"Wil, I didn't think you would be here until tomorrow."

"We encountered a Yankee reconnaissance that had crossed the river, and I don't mean a couple of scouts. I sent one of my men to give you a message."

"I got it. I'm fine. I didn't meet any Yankees."

Worry lines faded from his face.

Pleased that she had made the supply run without a hitch, she held out the tapestry bag full of medicine.

Wil reached for it and was unable to maintain his grip. The bag thumped to the porch. He cradled his forearm swathed in a bloody handkerchief.

"You were hurt," she said.

"It's only a graze."

"It's more than a graze. Here, let me take a look. What happened?"

His brow furrowed. "I should have never involved you."

Had she heard remorse? Amanda gathered up the bag and set it on the bench inside the door. "Why?"

"Because if they had come across you instead of us..."

She detected something in his eyes—something very haunting. "I need to have a look at your arm. Let's go into the kitchen where I can see what I'm doing." Relieved that he offered no resistance, she led the way across the red brick floor, motioning for him to take a seat at the table. After collecting a porcelain basin, water, clean cloth, and her sewing kit, she sat beside him. "You didn't finish answering my question."

"John and I were young when we fought the Mexicans, but not that young." He held up his hands. "Even in the name of war, I can never completely wash the blood from them."

Uncertain what he meant, she unwrapped the bloody handkerchief.

"One of the Yankees..." His voice wavered. "He couldn't have been more than fifteen. Amanda, why do they send boys to do a man's job?"

And women. The words formed on his lips, but he didn't say them. He didn't need to. He was a man of unflinching stoic pride, and she had never seen him shaken before. She grieved with the boy's mama, wherever she might live. How many more lives would the war claim before the foolish nonsense was over?

Amanda couldn't think about that now—not with her own grief so near the surface. With her shears, she cut Wil's embroidered sleeve for a closer look at his wound. She peeled away the layers to a neat but bloody hole. The bullet had gone clean through his arm.

She set about to cleaning the wound. "You're mighty lucky you have an arm left." He flinched when she dabbed his arm with a cloth. "I know it hurts. I will forgive you this one time if you wish to swear."

His eyes crinkled in amusement. "My dear Mrs. Graham, I know how much you abhor swearing. Do you think I would bow to a minor inconvenience such as this?"

Fancy words—the raw, red wound had to hurt something fierce. "I think you would bow to whatever suits your needs best, Colonel Jackson. I'll fetch some laudanum from the supplies. It's going to hurt worse before it gets to feeling better. I also insist that you stay the night."

His smile broadened to a roguish grin.

"I have already told you that I'm not that kind of woman. Get those wicked thoughts out of your head, right now."

Wil wiped the smirk from his face. "Amanda, I know what John was like. While he was honorable, he was ignorant when it came to keeping a wife content."

Suddenly furious, she stood. "One more remark like that, and I shall see you to the door."

"So be it. From now on, I'll keep the truth to myself."

Truth? Thoroughly embarrassed by what John might have told him about their private life, Amanda reseated herself and finished bandaging Wil's arm. "I'll fetch the laudanum now."

"Save it for someone who needs it."

"You're not serious?"

"I am."

"Then I shall fix up the spare room after I pay my respects to the Colonel."

As Amanda headed for the door, she glanced over her shoulder. Wil's eyes were half-closed, and he hugged his arm next to his body. *All an act.* She resisted the urge to fetch the laudanum.

At the family graveyard on the hill, the last filaments of the day slipped beyond the horizon. In the growing twilight, she was barely able to read the Colonel's name etched on the wood headboard.

Colonel John Graham

Loving husband

"John, I keep questioning why you had to die, but I understand now—so someone else could live. I should have expected nothing less from you. Your men always came first."

Crickets chirped an evening echo. Had that been thunder in the distance? A chilling breeze swooped up the hill. With it, she felt John's presence. To better hear his whispers, she knelt on the mound of dirt, but as the breeze faded, so did his voice. Tears fought their way to the surface, and a finger stroked her on the cheek.

She grasped his hand. "John?"

"I apologize for intruding, Amanda."

Amanda blinked back the Colonel's image to Wil's lean, tall frame.

He offered her a clean handkerchief. "When you didn't return, I became concerned."

She thanked him and dabbed her eyes. "He knew exactly what he was doing, Wil."

"Who?"

"John. He told me that he knew he was going to die."

"Amanda..."

The temptation to take his hand and revel in his quiet strength was overpowering. She resisted. With John gone, she ached so much to hold someone—anyone, but he would misinterpret her actions. "I don't expect you to believe me, but I spoke with him. I felt his presence just as we're standing here now."

Wil moved closer. "I believe that you believe. You have been through a difficult time."

"He also told me how you felt."

"About what?"

"Me. Even though you hid it, he knew."

"Amanda, I regret that John died. If I could have taken the bullet for him a second time, I would have."

"I'm sorry, Wil." She dabbed the corners of her eyes with his handkerchief. "I'm so confused. John's death wasn't your fault, and neither was the Yankee boy's."

"I had best be leaving." With an abrupt about turn, he hurried down the hill.

The boy's death had shaken him more than he was willing to admit. Worried he might do something foolish, Amanda followed him.

He reached the porch and climbed the stairs two at a time. Once inside, he picked up the tapestry bag from the bench in the foyer.

"I hope you will allow me to continue running supplies," Amanda said. "I need to feel like I'm doing something useful." Ashamed to admit the truth, she added, "And I need the money. My offer to stay the night stands."

Wil's eyes raked the length of her body. "I thought you weren't that kind of woman, Amanda."

Such brashness deserved a slap. She poised to strike.

He caught her hand. "You have nothing to fear. I must return to camp. Now if you let me know where the rest of the supplies are, I'll see that you're paid and be on my way."

Blood seeped through the bandage on his arm. She lowered her hand. "That's a long ride. If you don't take care of yourself by getting a hot meal and a few hours rest, you may not make it back to camp at all, you stubborn fool. Friends admit to one another when they're in pain."

He let out a weary breath. "Amanda—"

"Wil, I saw the wound. No matter how much you pretend otherwise, I know you're hurting." She grasped the supply bag from him and searched through it for some laudanum. She held up a packet. "If I mix it, will you take it?"

He stared at her for a minute before finally agreeing.

Relieved that he no longer resisted, she convinced Wil to eat a small meal and drink the pain-relieving medicine. Afterward, she showed him to the spare room. When she returned to the kitchen, Frieda puttered about.

The old woman placed a cloth over an apple pie baked earlier in the day. The heavenly scent reminded Amanda that she should have eaten something as well.

Frieda looked up, and her sightless eyes seemed to see straight through her. "Ezra take care of da colonel's horse, since he be stayin' da night."

"Frieda," Amanda hissed.

"What child?" Frieda put her hands on her hips. "I only tellin' you what Ezra's done gone."

Amanda sank into a pole-backed chair at the table. "Colonel Jackson is a guest. He was wounded, trying to keep the Yankees from me."

Frieda shuffled over to the end of the table with her walking stick guiding the way. "Miss Amanda, I afeard you begin to think of him as more dan a fam'ly friend."

Amanda gazed into the sightless eyes. "Are you saying he doesn't care?"

"He cares—as much as da likes of him can. Miss Amanda, you a kind person. You ain't goin' to be alone."

The old woman waved her stick over to the cookstove and ladled out a steamy liquid from the Dutch oven. When Frieda returned to the table, she set a bowl of hearty beef broth in front of Amanda. "You eat dat all up. You done eat so little since da Colonel's passin' dat it worry me."

Amanda picked up a spoon. "Frieda, does the hurt ever go away?"

The Negro woman sat across from her, something Wil would never allow in his household, and it helped put her thoughts in perspective. Frieda was more like a mama than a servant.

"Da hurt get less with time." A grin appeared to crack the wrinkles in the ancient face. "You won't ask so many questions when da time right."

"I reckon you're right." Amanda sipped the broth. The tangy blend of Frieda's herbs and spices tasted good, and she spooned more hungrily to her mouth.

"At dis time more dan any other, you need to be careful. Be sure about yourself."

Already finished with the broth, Amanda hadn't realized how famished she had been. "Thank you, Frieda."

She shoved the chair from the table and went up to her room. Ever since receiving that fateful letter notifying her of the Colonel's death, she had made the upstairs storage room her sanctuary. Unable to sleep in the same room she had shared with John, she had removed her personal effects, leaving all of his belongings untouched.

Only a daguerreotype reminded her of their life together. She picked it up from the dresser. He had promised to return alive, but the honor of serving his country had intruded. What good were promises during wartime? John had fought for honor and died. She hurled the photograph to the floor and heard the tinkle of breaking glass.

"Darn you, John! How could you leave me alone like this?"

Alone? Was she really alone? Sam Prescott's daughter slumbered in the crib beside the bed. Amanda pressed two fingers to her lips, then to Rebecca's cheek. What had Sam's involvement been in John's death?

No matter the circumstances, blood didn't spill onto Rebecca's hands.

Amanda changed into a plain cotton nightdress and slid between the sheets. She clenched her teeth against the chill and laid her head to the feather pillow. No tears flowed for John. None were left.

With the nights growing increasingly brisk, she should have lit a fire. Seasons had changed, but she must continue to live. Propriety dictated that a widow remain in mourning for a full year. Hadn't her supply runs already shattered the illusion of propriety?

Almost overnight, the nation had changed. Tongues might wag, but along with the transformation of the country, she would no longer wear black.

Chapter Three

Near Washington, D.C.
October 1861

SAM PRESCOTT SIPPED FROM A TIN CUP and watched the camp come to life. Sleepy soldiers crawled from tents. Some huddled in blankets, but all hurried to get water boiling on campfires. In the chilly morning air, a steaming cup of coffee was one of the few luxuries.

Sam tossed his last drops on the fire. Smoke sputtered.

Luck of the draw for reconnaissance beat drilling green soldiers. At the same time, he wondered why anyone bothered. Except for an occasional skirmish across the Potomac, neither side had moved much since Bull Run.

He checked his pocket watch. Half past the hour. Corporal Tucker was ten minutes late. Sam collected his saddle and went down the rows of canvas tents. Outside the corporal's tent, a throaty moan from inside suggested that his timing could have been better. Tucker must have found a camp follower. The rustling of bodies made him think of Kate.

While stationed in the New Mexico territory before the war, he had begun to court again. Vastly different from the ladies in the East, western women were either Indian or hardy pioneering stock. One frontier widow, named Lucy, had accommodated his physical need.

Although he had overcome the fear of making comparisons to his dead wife, the encounters were less than fulfilling. Whether due to lack of love or being too soon after Kate's passing, he didn't know, but the acts often came up empty. Then, on their final meeting, with Lucy never suspecting anything amiss, right at the peak, he imagined none other than Amanda Graham.

Troubled by the vision, he swallowed hard and cleared his throat. "Corporal?"

Bodies hustled, and a red face peeked from under the tent flap. It wasn't Corporal Tucker.

"Garvey? I was looking for Tucker."

"Sir... uh..."

Sam tapped his foot. "I don't want to hear about your transgression. Where's Tucker?"

"Uhhh..." Garvey disappeared into the tent. More shuffling came from inside.

His patience wore thin. "Tucker!"

The flap went up. Tucker and Garvey stepped out at full attention. Now he understood why Garvey had been so embarrassed. The camp follower had only been part of the reason. But no girl appeared.

Sam checked inside the tent. Empty. "Where is she?"

"Sir," Tucker's voice squeaked, "you won't report us...?"

Sam shot a glare at the pint-sized corporal. The high-pitched voice and smooth face. Realization hit him, and he dropped his saddle. He had assumed the corporal was one of the many underage boys, attempting to pass as a grown man. Except for Garvey, *she* had fooled everyone.

He withdrew a cigar from his jacket. *A girl.* He broke into side-splitting laughter. Tears rolled down his cheeks. He barely managed to retrieve his saddle from the ground and dust the dirt from the pommel. Unable to stop laughing, he shook his head.

"Sir... Lieutenant, let me explain."

He struggled to keep any further laughter from erupting. "I think I can figure that out."

In a hollow away from the tents, the leaves of oak and sycamore trees were changing from green to muted autumn reds. Beneath leaves that rustled in the breeze, the horses stood tied to a long rope. Near the middle of the line, Sam located a bay gelding with legs so crooked it could barely be regarded as a horse. He threw the saddle on its back.

"Lieutenant Prescott, I aim to go with you," the corporal said.

"I don't think so. The last time I read regulations, they didn't allow—ladies, and I use the term loosely."

"That ain't fair."

Sam cinched the girth, and the gelding bobbed his head in protest.

"Sir, should you be riskin' your neck if I ain't willin' to do the same? It's my cause too."

Uncertain he understood her logic, he lit his cigar and inhaled deeply. "You expect to accompany me as if nothing has changed?"

"If you hadn't found us... uh..." Her face reddened. "You wouldn't never known the difference. Sir, I can still cover your backside. Fact is, I'd be willin' to bet I can outshoot you."

"That may be, but—"

"And outride you."

"I will think on it." He tossed the cigar to the ground and stamped out the embers.

Tucker ducked under the rope and saddled a mangy sorrel.

"I didn't agree to bring you along," Sam said.

She straightened her shoulders. "If you let me state my case, I won't make no more arguments."

Her plea hit a nerve. In spite of the bobbed hair, he was coming to the full realization of her sex. "I'm not certain you're in a position to protest, but I did say I would think on it. That means I shall."

Sam bridled the plug and mounted. When the gelding groaned under his weight, he couldn't fathom how the Union had a chance in hell of winning the war. Horseflesh as sorry as the bay's should have been heading for the glue factory instead of a scouting mission. "What is your real name?" he asked.

Tucker pulled the sorrel even. "Joanna is my given. My pa started callin' me Jo while I was still a babe."

Joanna, not Joe. He cued the bay forward. A dirt path wound beyond the tents and picket line out of the hollow. "How you have managed to keep your, uh, sex a secret this long is beyond me."

"That should tell you somethin'."

"Maybe." Sam brought the bay to a halt at the top of the ridge. "Or that you're crazy as a loon."

She reined the sorrel alongside him. "I suppose. And why are you here?"

"I have my duty."

"Duty." She spat on the ground.

Only in the West had Sam witnessed a woman spitting before.

"And leave the womenfolk at home. Never mind if we can't make ends meet. But then, if there's enough menfolk, it don't make no difference."

"My wife is dead."

"Ain't no kids?"

Sam's jaw tensed. With the erratic mail service, the money he had sent for his daughter's care might never have reached Amanda. "Whether I have children or not has no bearing on why you're here."

"Depends. If you got a daughter, she best have a brother, in case you go down. My pa up and died some years back, leavin' Ma a widow. She ain't got no one 'sides me. Society don't want us doin' much but have babes."

"At the rate you're going . . ."

Her gaze grew fixed, daring him to finish. "The Rebs gave us a pretty good lickin' at Bull Run."

Unsure how kids related to Bull Run, Sam grew annoyed. "What's your point?"

"As I recollect, you barely made it out of there."

After the blow to the head, he had drawn a blank. Waving summer grass on a hot July day. Out of the smoke dashed Colonel Graham. But there was something more. *Images.* Blurred, he couldn't quite make them out.

Sam kicked the bay in the side. Reacting to the spur as if waking from a nap, the animal cantered down the hill faster than he intended. Ducking to miss a low-lying branch, Sam reined in and brought the gelding to a walk. The path leveled several yards before climbing again, steeper and rockier than before. He leaned forward to allow the bay to move easier. The worthless horse groaned. He might as well get off and walk before the nag dropped from exhaustion.

At the top of the ridge, the bay drooped his head with a snort. Sam dismounted and withdrew a pair of field glasses from their case. He scanned the river's edge along the tree line. Two soldiers in gray were stationed downstream—in the same place they had been posted for weeks now.

When the corporal joined him, he held out the field glasses for her to take a look. Instead, she started to undress.

He cleared his throat. "What are you doing?"

"Ain't that why you brought me here—for your silence? Let's be done with it."

Sam caught a glimpse of a tiny, but rounded breast. Swallowing hard, he thought of Kate and how long she had been gone. Tucker certainly wasn't Kate, but... "Corporal...."

She finished unbuttoning her shirt and reached for her belt buckle.

"Jo," he said, a little louder. He grabbed her wrist.

Irritated, she looked from the hand clamped around her wrist over to him. "Ain't it what you want?"

The sight of her breast grew more tempting, and he tugged with indecision.

Jo unbuckled her belt.

"Yes. I mean no." Sam concentrated on the boyish face to keep his eyes from drifting to her open shirt. "No offense intended, but not with you."

With a grunt, Jo doubled over, laughing. "Sorry, sir. I presumed..." She clutched her sides and caught her breath.

"I know what you presumed." The incident with Garvey suddenly made sense. "That's why you and Garvey...?"

She rebuttoned her shirt, and the girlish-sized breast vanished from his view. "I ain't no camp follower and don't like it none. But you bein' a man and all, you wouldn't understand my reasonin'."

Aware of what lay concealed beneath the uniform, Sam shifted his gaze to the ground. "Try me."

"Army pays better than most. Ma's got two kids at home. Always been able to pass as a boy. Never gave a notion to sharin' a tent before signin' up. Garvey said he'd turn me in 'less I shared his bed. Didn't even know what he was talkin' about the first time. After that, didn't matter none—as long as Ma gets my pay."

"His silence means that much to you? I could have him brought up on charges."

"If you do that, I get ousted and don't get paid."

Simple as that. She fidgeted with her cap. While she was unafraid of death, the army discovering the truth of her identity was another matter. "If you should change your mind...," he said.

"Much obliged, sir."

Collected again, he realized there had been a point to her mentioning Bull Run. "Tell me something, at Bull Run—"

"I pulled several of the boys out—includin' you."

The gap in his memory refused to lift. After Colonel Graham went down, someone helped him from the battlefield—a pint-sized corporal—*Jo*. "You've earned my silence."

They had a job to do. He stored the field glasses away and put his foot in the stirrup, but hesitated.

"Somethin' wrong, sir?"

With the urgent need to urinate, he passed her the gelding's reins and motioned for her to turn around. The edges of her mouth tipped slightly, but she contained her grin.

"No need to be shy, sir. Since joinin' the army, I've seen my share of trouser snakes. Ain't no big deal—'less I get bit."

"Enough! Or I'll forget my promise."

"Yes, sir."

Jo turned, and he overheard a soft snicker. Warmth filled his face, and he sought the cover of the nearest bush. "Women in the army. Whoever gave you a physical must have been blind."

"Weren't given one. They wanted boys to sign up. Never asked if I was one."

Finished relieving himself, Sam snatched the reins from her hands and mounted.

"Didn't mean to rile you, sir. Afore long, you'll see me as one of the boys."

The short cropped hair and small frame did make her look like an adolescent boy. The baggy uniform hid her secret well. "For your sake, I hope so."

"I'll make certain."

Sam kicked the worthless nag and muttered under his breath that women had no business in the army. But a promise was a promise. He'd give her the opportunity to prove herself. At Bull Run when other soldiers had turned and run, the corporal held her ground. That kind of grit deserved respect, but if he spotted any inability in the performance of her duties, he would personally see that she was dismissed.

They patrolled the north side of the Potomac, where the Rebels stationed pickets in the same predictable places as on the day before . . . and the day before that. At a ford, the guard in butternut waved, thumbing at them in a dare.

Sam drew his Colt and aimed.

"We're out of range, sir."

Feeling like a fool, he holstered the pistol with a curse, and the Reb guffawed.

Dirty and exhausted by the time they returned to camp, Sam unsaddled the plug. He staggered to his tent. A woman—a pretty one at that—waited outside in a drab green dress. The plainness of the dress only accented her sun-browned hands and blonde hair. Unlike Tucker, this woman was a lady. Expecting her to be attired in mourning black, he rubbed his eyes to be sure he wasn't seeing things. "Mrs. Graham?"

"Sam, since when have you been so formal?"

"Amanda, if this is about money for Rebecca's care—"

"It's not."

He dropped the saddle and pulled up a camp stool for Amanda. "What can I do for you?"

Her hands went to her hips, and she remained standing. "Your brother informed me where you were stationed." Her green eyes narrowed. "Sam, I need to know. Did you shoot the Colonel?"

"The Colonel?" As he feared—she had found out about Bull Run. "Amanda, if you seriously think I killed the Colonel . . . " He held out his pistol. "Shoot me. I would deserve it."

"But Colonel Jackson said you were with John when he died."

Jackson? While Jackson had driven him mercilessly when stationed in the New Mexico territory, the experience had prepared him more than anything for the war. Without Jackson's relentless training, he wouldn't have survived Bull Run. "I didn't see Jackson."

"Sam, put the gun away. I believe you."

He reholstered the pistol. Her eyes came to rest on him, and he detected sadness. Of course—her husband was dead.

"Wil only said that John met you. He didn't know anything else."

The battlefield was a mighty big, confusing place. Sam wondered how Jackson had discovered that much about Colonel Graham. Then again, Jackson had been a career officer long before him, and his sources were probably more numerous as well. He rubbed his forehead. "I don't recall much. A Reb—Confederate—hit me in the head with a musket. Your husband helped me before going down, but the next thing I recall, I was waking in the hospital. I tried learning his fate, but Southern casualty reports aren't readily available. When I returned to duty I found out he had died at our own field hospital."

Amanda wobbled on her feet.

He grasped her elbow to help steady her. "I'm sorry, Amanda."

She sank to the camp stool. "I am too. Thank you for telling me. If you took a blow to the head . . . "

"I still get an occasional headache, but I'm fine. Is the Colonel the reason why you're in Washington?"

Her voice reduced to a whisper. "I was lonely on the farm. You know how it is."

He did know—all too well. Amanda had held him in her arms while he cried like a baby when Kate had died. "Each day will get a little easier. Is there anything I—"

"No." She straightened her plain green dress, brushed a speck of dust from it, and stood. "Rebecca's doing fine—growing big. She'll be walking soon. Sam, if it's possible, I would like to talk to you at length, but not here. I don't feel right here. I'd like to share a few stories about Rebecca. You'd be proud of her."

"I can get a pass," he suggested. "After I see to my duties."

"Set the time. Your brother insisted that I stay with him."

"Tomorrow—around two."

"Until then. Take care, Sam."

"You too, Amanda." He watched her as she hurried through the rows of tents.

"You got a soft spot for the womenfolk."

Tucker again. Irritated that the girl soldier failed to take him at his word, he grumbled, "I gave you a vow of silence. Unless you fail to perform your duties, I will honor it, but right now, you're on the edge of insubordination, Corporal."

She snapped to attention. "Yes, sir."

"Was there something else you wished to report?"

"No, sir."

"Then you're dismissed."

Tucker saluted and about-faced.

The fog lifted. "Jo—wait. At Bull Run..." A sharp pain stabbed his temple. "I recall now. *You* shot Colonel Graham."

The carriage rounded the corner, and Sam caught a glimpse of the brownstone with green shutters and a wrought-iron balcony. The driver brought the carriage to a halt out front. He paid the cabby and went through the iron gate at the end of the walk. The brass knocker barely left his hand before his brother pulled him into the slate foyer.

Charles thumped him on the back and gave him a hearty handshake. "We weren't certain you were coming, little brother."

Sam lowered his hat. "I promised Amanda that I would meet her here."

"Right." A twinkle entered Charles's eyes. "I should have known it would take a pretty lady to get you to visit Washington. We haven't heard from you since you returned to duty. Do you realize that's been over a month?" He pointed a finger. "You could have written to say you were in good health. Mother frets something fierce."

The last thing he needed was a lecture. "I came to see Amanda."

"Charles," came a feminine voice. A woman, wearing a gaudy floral dress with massive hoops and tightly coiled ringlets in her black hair, descended the stairway.

Sam gritted his teeth. "Holly."

"Sam, I thought that might be you." Though her gaze was cold, Holly reached the bottom step with a welcoming grin. "Charles, what kind of host are you? Invite your brother in. Mrs. Graham has been waiting for nearly an hour." Her grin turned sly. "I'm surprised she would meet you at all after learning the truth about Bull Run. Charles, why don't you get Sam a drink?"

Her smirk vanished, and she hooked an arm through Sam's, showing him to the drawing room.

Amanda sat near the fire in a leather wing chair. Flames flickered shadows against her hair, giving it the appearance of fibers spun from the finest gold. She held up a hand.

"Amanda," Sam said, taking her hand in his. He bowed slightly and lifted her fingers to his lips. Her eyes resembled emeralds, and her skin was soft. He never wanted to let go.

Holly intruded on his reverie. "Do tell Sam why you didn't bring his daughter along."

He let go of Amanda's hand and straightened.

"I couldn't get her a pass," Amanda said with a frown.

Holly clicked her tongue. "If it wasn't for that Negro wench of yours, but I keep forgetting, Virginia is fighting to keep darkies in their proper place."

Past experience taught him to ignore Holly's ranting. "Amanda, perhaps you would like to go elsewhere so that we might speak undisturbed."

"A splendid idea."

Sam held out his arm, and Amanda rose to her feet. She slid her arm through his.

Holly shot him a glare but stepped aside.

Charles appeared in the doorway with brandy snifters in hand. "Leaving already? You just got here."

Sam resisted the urge to speak his mind. For Amanda's sake, he remained polite. He glanced at Holly. "Amanda and I have personal matters to discuss."

With a disappointed shrug, Charles sipped from a snifter.

Sam escorted Amanda to the foyer. After collecting her burgundy cloak, they went down the steps of the brownstone.

"Autumn has finally arrived," she said with a shiver.

"I hadn't noticed. It seems warm to me—for October."

"Of course—it probably would. I've never been north of Maryland."

He lifted the latch to the iron gate.

She stepped through, and her eyes sparkled. "Thank you, kind sir."

"Amanda . . . " What should he say? He had looked forward to this moment. Now that it had arrived, he was speechless.

She touched him on the arm. "Relax, Sam."

Her reassurance reminded him of their first meeting at General Evans's reception. Colonel Graham, at the time a captain, had introduced them. They danced and talked late into the night about her blood stock. He knew then that he shouldn't feel the way he did. Not that he would have betrayed Kate, but when she died, he put over a thousand miles between them to keep Amanda from finding out.

"The fact that you were at Manassas–Bull Run," she corrected, "was coincidence, nothing more."

"I'm not so sure."

A block from the brownstone, Sam turned onto a dirt path that cut through a park. Before the transfer to the New Mexico territory, he had visited often with Kate, and strolling along with Amanda helped him forget the war for a little while.

In Maine, the trees would have already dropped their leaves, but in Virginia life poked around in places where he least expected. Pale blue flowers lined the path. Though they weren't native to Maine, Kate would have known the variety. He had to stop fooling himself. He hadn't been thinking of Kate. It was Amanda he wanted to hold. "I didn't think I was going to survive Bull Run," he said.

Amanda gripped her cloak about her, but continued walking. "Not surprising. It was your first battle experience. The Colonel used to say . . . "

Sam grasped her arm and halted. "Amanda, I recall what happened. He came toward me. I threw my gun down and I was ready to die."

She faced him but failed to make eye contact. "Sam, you needn't tell me this."

Her voice had gone soft. He didn't wish to add to her grief, but she needed to know the truth. "You would always wonder what role I played if I didn't."

"Then tell me."

"When he recognized me, he disappeared in the smoke. I went down, and the next thing I knew, a Confederate officer was helping me."

"John?"

"He tried to help me to safety behind the lines, but my corporal . . . " His throat went dry, and Amanda's eyelashes fluttered. He thought she might cry, but her eyes remained dry.

"Sam, it's over. I've dried all of my tears. To be frank, I have none left to cry. The Colonel knew what he was doing, just as you do. Frieda warned him that he wouldn't be coming back, but he felt it was his duty."

"Frieda?"

"One of my servants."

When he had been stationed in Washington, he was aware the Grahams owned several slaves.

"Don't give me that look. Two able-bodied servants ran off after the Colonel left to fight the war. Ezra and Frieda are free, which only leaves Dulcie. Oakcrest would only lease her for Rebecca's care, and I was hoping that you might be able to help her when the lease is up."

He pointed to himself. "Me?"

"I need someone I can trust who will help her come north."

"I'm not certain how, but I'll help if there's a way."

"Good." Amanda strolled again. "You haven't asked about Rebecca."

Until war broke out, he had sent Rebecca Indian trinkets from the West. Now that she was no longer a baby, he couldn't imagine what she even looked like. "I thought you would tell me what I need to know."

Amanda halted, touching him on the forearm. "Don't shut her out, Sam. With her mama gone, she needs her papa more than ever."

"That may be difficult with her in Virginia and me here." He raised his voice. "I can't even get a letter across the lines with any certainty."

She gave his arm a gentle squeeze. "I shall find a way for you to see her. I promise."

As usual, Amanda was being polite. "I will escort you to my brother's," he said.

"Of course. I'm certain you want time to visit with your family."

"Holly?"

Amanda chuckled. "She is a bit—overbearing. Not the sort I would have expected your brother to marry." A devilish twinkle entered her green eyes. "Tell me then, why did you court her before marrying Kate?"

He blinked in disbelief. "Where did you hear that?"

"Kate," Amanda answered with an impish grin.

"I'm afraid to ask, but what else did she tell you?"

Amanda's eyes sparkled, teasing him playfully. He held up a hand. "Never mind, I don't want to know. I courted Holly because I was too young to know that pretty faces can deceive."

"And now?"

Sam glanced at her hand, still resting on his arm, then at her. "Amanda, I would be honored if you'd accompany me to dinner this evening." The request was out of his mouth before he gave any thought to propriety.

"I'd like that," she said.

"You would?" Self-conscious, he brushed his uniform. Dust flew. He should have remembered to shave. Two days of beard growth was no way to meet a lady. He had been in the army too long. "Forgive me, I must be a sight."

"Why Sam, you're blushing. If I didn't know better, I'd say your intentions were less than honorable."

He cleared his throat. "With a woman as lovely as yourself I admit my thoughts stray, but I assure you my intentions are honorable." He straightened and changed the subject. "Amanda, how long are you going to be here—in Washington?"

"Another day or two. I can't be away from the farm too long."

The feeling that had seized him so suddenly evaporated. "I understand."

"If you like, we can spend tomorrow together."

"I'd like that." If a day or two was all they had together, he would gladly accept it.

Chapter Four

AMANDA COULDN'T RECALL THE LAST TIME SHE HAD LAUGHED—REALLY laughed. Certainly not since the war had begun. She shouldn't have felt her heart fluttering, especially so soon after the Colonel's passing, but as Sam stared over the brandy snifter rim, she shivered. Clean shaven and attired in a fresh blue uniform, he looked particularly handsome. "It's been a lovely evening, Sam. I want to thank you for it."

He set the snifter on the red and white checkered tablecloth. Only then, against the flickering candlelight, did she realize Sam's blue eyes were the same shade as John's. But that wasn't what charmed her, and she was wrong to take notice.

"I have enjoyed it too, Amanda."

His voice was nearly a whisper, and the way he said her name, she could almost forget the war. *Almost.* Reminders lingered—from Sam's dark blue uniform to guards with guns lining the city. And where was her contact? She had been in Washington for two days, and she had yet to meet him.

Sam swirled the amber liquid in the snifter. "Amanda, are you all right?"

She breathed in the aromatic contents. If she had partaken such a fiery drink, she would have lost all sense of good reason. He kept smiling at her. Certainly he would stop if he discovered the truth about her Confederate dealings. "Sometimes the moods creep up due to the Colonel's passing when I least expect them."

Sam sipped from the snifter. "I suspected as much."

She had resorted to an outright lie, and that fact wasn't something she liked discovering about herself. "Sam, how did you feel about the Colonel?"

"He was my friend and mentor. I respected him."

"But he fought for the Confederacy."

"Just because the politicians have decided we're supposed to be enemies, doesn't change the way a person feels."

His gaze met hers, and she wondered if he would extend her the same benefit of the doubt for aiding the South. And what would John say if he could see her now—sharing dinner with another man, alone and so soon after his death? Suddenly ashamed, she said, "I think we should be leaving."

"Whatever you say, Amanda."

There it was again. With the gentle whisper of her name, he made her forget the isolation of the past few months. At the general's reception when they first met, she had been fond of him but couldn't admit it, even to herself—until now. Not even now. It was too soon for such thoughts. Amanda got to her feet. "We must leave."

"Of course." Sam escorted her from the dining room.

Amanda collected her cloak, and once outside, she breathed in the fresh evening air. A drum beat in the distance. There was no escape from the war. What if Sam or Wil were among the fallen? If fate stepped in, they could meet on the battlefield as Sam and the Colonel had. While Wil was the seasoned soldier, Sam had youth on his side. The odds of both surviving were next to none.

Sam hailed a cab.

"I'm sorry for spoiling a delightful evening," she said.

"There's no need for an apology. I remember my own state of mind after Kate passed on."

Soon after Kate's death, he had exiled himself to the West. Certain she had been the reason, she regretted the Colonel's aid in securing him a position under Wil's command in New Mexico. The self-imposed banishment had kept him a stranger to his daughter, and now with the war, there might not be a chance to make up for lost time.

A cab halted before them. Sam helped her into the carriage. He sat next to her, and she breathed in the scent of his cologne. The carriage lurched forward, throwing her with it. Sam caught her in his arms. In the light from passing gas lampposts, she spotted a glow in his eyes.

She thanked him and straightened the folds of her dress. "Sam, why did you ask me to dinner this evening?"

"I thought you had probably guessed. To share the company of a lovely lady."

The carriage horse's hooves pounding against the dirt pavement matched the nervous rhythm of her heart. So lonely for company, she had forgotten men would read her actions the wrong way. Although Sam was a gentleman, she didn't wish to encourage him anymore than Wil.

"Some lady I am—a recent widow carrying on in public. Though I've already bent the rules of propriety, I think it's best if we don't see one another tomorrow."

"As you wish." Disappointment registered in his voice.

"It's only been three months since John passed on."

"I understand."

"Circumstances may have changed since we first met, but with the war, it's wise to proceed with caution."

He laughed slightly. "Sometimes I find it difficult to think with caution when I don't know whether I'll return to Maine in a pine box or not."

"Don't ever joke about dying."

"Amanda . . . " He gave her hand a sympathetic squeeze. "I only find it amusing because the reason why you hesitate makes me want to rush foolishly out of control. Besides, the war can't last forever."

"Colonel Jackson says at least three years."

"He said the same thing before we left New Mexico."

Hopeful that Wil might be wrong, she leaned forward. "Then you don't believe him?"

"Wish I didn't, but it's going to be a mighty long war."

Amanda pressed a hand to her chest. Both must be wrong. They had to be. "Three years— "

"Maybe longer."

"Longer?" She caught her breath, and the cab turned from the main road and rounded the corner. They passed a row of houses. The driver brought the carriage to a halt out front of the brownstone. Sam swung the door open. He jumped down and extended a hand to help her.

Amanda stepped from the carriage. They reached the flagstone walk, and a drape fluttered in the front window. Holly must have been keeping tabs on them.

At the bottom of the steps, Sam kissed Amanda's hand. "Since you have changed your mind about tomorrow, allow me the honor to escort you to the lines on your return journey?"

"I'd like that."

"Then I'll meet you the day after tomorrow." He fidgeted with his hat as if not knowing what else to say. "Goodbye, Amanda," he finally said.

The Colonel's last word when leaving for the war had been goodbye. Until then, he had never left with such a definitive parting. "Don't *ever* say goodbye. It means forever."

"Then, until we meet again." With a farewell bow, Sam retraced his steps. The iron gate creaked, and he disappeared into the cab.

Amanda waved as the carriage horse trotted away. A silly gesture. It was unlikely that he had seen her in the dark. Had she been right to cancel their plans? Feeling a tad foolish for standing in the evening chill, second guessing herself, she lifted her skirts and went up the steps.

In the foyer, a shadowy shape lurked beside the table. Holly sidled into the flickering hall light. "Sam is leaving so soon?"

Her suspicion was confirmed. Amanda wondered how long Holly had been standing there—listening. "Holly," she said in an even voice.

"Ah declare, whar's that faahhn Southern hospitality?" Holly asked in a mocking Virginian accent. "The least you could have done was invite Sam in for a nightcap." Her tone turned biting. "But then I suppose even with the prospect of a change in bed partners, the room upstairs reminds him too much of Kate. As you know, she died there."

Furious that Holly would even hint at such a preposterous indiscretion, Amanda balled her hands. "I will kindly remind you that nothing improper has happened."

"Actually, the fact that Sam will be escorting you to the lines makes things work out rather nicely. They're less likely to search you."

"Search me for what?"

"Medicine." The ringlets in Holly's hair danced when she shook her head. "Do you think Colonel Jackson went to the trouble of forging you a pass so you could do nothing more than dally with my brother-in-law? So soon after your husband's death, no less."

"You know Colonel Jackson?" Hadn't Wil said his informant was married to a Yankee captain? Charles was a Yankee captain. Amanda swallowed. "You're my contact."

Holly sneered in confirmation.

"Wil said I can refuse any shipment I choose. And I refuse to involve Sam."

"Think of all the sick boys who need medicine. Relax, Amanda, you're not involving Sam. He's merely escorting you to the lines." She tugged the hoops of Amanda's crinoline. "We can sew some packages into your petticoat."

Fully aware that she wouldn't refuse aid to the sick and wounded, Wil had her where he wanted. He had used their friendship for personal gain. Maybe he felt justified. In the hope for an opportunity to see Sam, she had secured the pass under false pretenses.

There was no sign of Sam. Part of Amanda hoped he didn't show. Throughout the night and following day, Holly had helped her sew packages into the folds of her petticoat. What didn't fit in her undergarments went into false bottoms of travel bags. If searched, she would certainly be arrested.

Charles finished hitching Red to the buggy. Amanda resisted telling him about Holly's dalliance with Wil. It wasn't her place, and a confession would likely put her in equal danger. "Thank you, Charles. Give my appreciation to Holly. Tell her that I hope she's feeling better soon."

Both knew better. A sick headache was an excuse for Holly not to see her off.

He helped her into the carriage. "Bye, Amanda. You're welcome any time."

After thanking Charles again, she guided Red to the main road. By the wrought-iron fence, a Yankee lieutenant waited, gripping the reins of a crooked-legged bay gelding. With a broad grin, Sam tipped his hat.

"I thought you might have changed your mind," Amanda said.

"Not likely."

She recalled their candlelit dinner. Along with the pleasant memory, her confusion returned. As he mounted the bay, the sword at his side clanked, shattering her tranquil image. "Sam . . ."

He gathered the reins in his left hand before looking over at her.

"I wish we had kept our plans yesterday."

He cued the gelding to a walk. "I only did as you asked."

Because she had felt guilty for laughing. Would the Colonel really never want her to laugh again? "At least I shall have something to tell Rebecca."

Sam waited for the carriage to catch up. "And that is?"

"What a fine man her papa is."

The solitude in his eyes mirrored her own. Yet it didn't seem quite as pronounced when he was near. What a fool she had been for wasting precious time—a day together—forever lost due to propriety. John's death should have served as a reminder that life could be cut short. Yet a proper widow didn't carry on the way she had. It was out of necessity, she reminded herself.

"Amanda, I must apologize for the other night."

"Why?"

"For behaving in an ungentlemanly manner."

How different he was from Wil. She suppressed a giggle. "I've done things since the Colonel's death that I wish I hadn't."

"Like accompanying me to dinner?"

The lie the other night stung. If she had an ounce of integrity, she would tell him the truth about the supplies. An absent-minded jerk on the reins brought Red to a halt. "No."

Sam trotted the bay back to meet her.

"This whole war is wrong. Three years—of living like this. I already know the Colonel isn't coming back. How many more?"

He shook his head. "I can't answer that."

Still melancholy, Amanda urged Red forward. After a few steps, the stallion stumbled in the dirt and limped on his right forefoot. "I think Red has picked up a stone."

Sam held Red steady while she climbed from the buggy. She lifted the horse's leg, and a medicine packet brushed against her thigh. A seam in her petticoat must have worked its way loose.

Sam grasped Red's hoof and scraped it out with a pocket knife. A stone popped out of the cleft in the stallion's hoof. "He should be good as new."

"After the Colonel passed on, I kept thinking what he would want me to do with my life. He would want me to do what was right—for me."

Sam glanced in the direction of Long Bridge spanning the Potomac. "Federal lines extend beyond Alexandria."

Did he suspect her involvement in Confederate activities? "I'm aware of that. I have a valid pass."

"Is there anyone to meet you on the other side?" Sam bent down and etched a wavy line in the dirt with the pocket knife, creating a crude map. "Here are the pickets." He pointed to the Federal line. "Over here are the Confederates. After you've crossed the Rebs' lines, I will meet you here." He indicated to a spot in northern Virginia.

"No."

"I've been patrolling the area for quite some time. I know where to cross the river."

"I won't have you risking your life on my account."

"Amanda—"

"I said 'No.' I meant it. Besides—I'm meeting Colonel Jackson for dinner."

He swiped a boot through the dirt and the map vanished. "I see."

"Sam—"

"You don't owe me an explanation."

Now she resorted to half-truths. While she had intended to meet Wil and deliver the supplies, dinner was at a friend's house of mutual acquaintance. Rather than inform Sam of the real reason, she had best let him jump to his own conclusions. Careful not to knock the loose package from the pocket in her petticoat, Amanda returned to the buggy. Fortunately, it remained tucked where it belonged.

They continued through the city. Like flowing water in a stream, waves of blue marched beside them. There must have been hundreds of Federal soldiers—many with smooth faces that had never known the sharp edge of a razor. Reminded of the dead boy Wil had encountered, Amanda felt a lump in her throat. Even the usually stoic colonel had been affected by a boys' war.

Near Long Bridge, garrisons stood ready for attack. Sandbags, muskets, cannon. Soldiers stared as they passed. A man in blue waved them on. Sam's presence aided her. The picket guard probably thought she was his wife. It wouldn't be so easy when she reached the actual line.

Murky water of the Potomac lapped at the wooden span. On the other side of the river lay the town of Alexandria. Like Fredericksburg, it was small, but crowded with soldiers. Beyond the town, rows upon rows of tents were pitched. Soldiers drilled, trampling fields—mostly of loyal Virginia farmers. More soldiers rooted through yet-to-be-harvested fields, stealing crops. Wagons rolled, carrying supplies and artillery. More weapons to kill. Drums. Bugles. Guns firing. And the cursing . . . This was no way for decent, God-fearing people to live. Why didn't menfolk realize what they were doing?

After all she had witnessed, Amanda believed the stories of soldiers showing no remorse and searching women right alongside men. Her hands were moist with sweat, and the reins kept slipping through her fingers. A scraggly whiskered man clad in blue raised a hand for her to stop. *Remain calm. Or he will suspect something amiss.*

Sam motioned for her to go ahead. Would he have accompanied her if he had known she was smuggling medical supplies?

Amanda withdrew a piece of paper from her bag. "I have a pass."

The guard examined the paper, and she tightened her grip on the reins. Why hadn't Wil warned her the pass was a forgery? She may have been naive in wartime ways, but he was going to get an earful.

The guard looked over at Sam. "A friend of yours, Lieutenant?"

"Yes."

To her, he asked, "Are you carrying any papers or documents, ma'am?"

Her throat tightened. She opened her mouth, but nothing came out.

"She wouldn't do anything to jeopardize her family, Private."

Sam. What would she have done without his presence?

"Yes, sir." The soldier returned the pass with a wave to continue.

Amanda let out a breath and sent Sam a thankful look with a silent goodbye—just in case. *Don't think like that.* She had made a promise. She cued Red forward.

After she crossed the picket, the sun reached its high point in the sky. The day grew warm—not uncommon for Virginia autumn. Amanda stuffed her cloak into her bag. The line of soldiers disappeared, and she continued along the narrow dirt road. Some trees had lost their foliage, but dull red and gold leaves clung to many branches.

Anxious to meet Wil and be rid of the supplies, Amanda urged Red to a trot. Several miles later, the stallion missed a beat. He took another misstep. The same foot that had picked up the stone bothered him. She reined him to a halt and climbed from the buggy to check his leg. No heat or swelling. She lifted his leg and inspected his hoof. No more stones.

Red was too valuable of an animal to take any chances. She decided to lead him. As they walked along, she spotted a subtle but definite limp in his right foreleg. The stone must have bruised his foot. Wil would come searching for her, but she didn't care for the prospect of being caught by nightfall in unfamiliar surroundings, especially with rain clouds gathering.

Amanda pressed onward, passing several farms. One farmer waved with an invitation to join his family for supper. In a hurry to meet Wil, she declined the offer and kept walking. Weary and footsore, she gained little relief from infrequent breaks.

By early evening, the clouds unleashed a downpour. She sought shelter in the carriage. Although the storm was short-lived, biting wind eliminated any protection the buggy afforded. In the fading daylight, trees looked more like skeletons raising bony fingers. Soaked to the skin, Amanda wrapped her cloak around her and led Red once more.

A horse nickered on the road ahead. Thank goodness the guards hadn't searched her. She slipped the pistol from her bag. "Who's there?"

No response. Maybe her imagination was playing tricks. She couldn't take the chance. "I said—who's there? I'm armed."

"It's me, Amanda," came Wil's voice. "I didn't mean to frighten you."

Grateful that she wouldn't be tested on whether she could actually pull the trigger, she lowered the pistol and tucked it in her bag. "Wil, you don't know how glad I am that you're here."

Hoofbeats trotted closer. She could finally make out the blue roan. Wil brought the gelding to a halt and dismounted. "I grew concerned when you were late." He lowered his hat and bowed. "Your servant, Mrs. Graham."

"I think Red bruised his foot when he picked up a stone."

"We'll store the supplies, and I'll retrieve them later."

"There's an abandoned shack about a quarter of a mile back," she suggested.

"That shall do."

Amusement lingered in his tone, and she longed to see his expression. Under the faint glow of moonlight, only the outline of his face was visible.

"You may ride my horse," he said.

"After we drop off the supplies. I'm carrying many of them on me. *Mrs.* Prescott can be a superb seamstress." She guided Red in the direction of the shack. "She's also married to a Yankee captain."

Wil joined her, leading his horse alongside him. He laughed softly. "Mrs. Prescott is an asset to me—nothing more. She visits the hospitals and confiscates medical supplies—for a price. Greed is her motivating factor."

"And what motivates you, Colonel? Why are you involved in smuggling supplies? The weakness of a pretty face?"

"I'll pretend I didn't hear that."

His tone had been unusually gruff. "Afraid of the truth?"

"I will forgive your naiveté." He was silent for a long while. When he spoke again, his voice was distant but calm. "My motivation comes from a time when there was no medicine available."

For someone close. Wil continued to surprise her. He was more complex than she had originally thought. "It wasn't my place to pry. I hope you'll accept my apology. She must have been very dear to you."

He lit a cigar. Embers glowed bright red when he took a draft. "Why do you presume it was a she?"

"A hunch. I meant nothing by it."

They continued along the road, and she breathed in the scent of his cigar. Several minutes passed before he spoke again. "When I was stationed in the Northwest, measles hit camp one winter. Most of us recovered, but the Indians . . . You're fortunate you've never witnessed what it does to them."

"I've read about it."

"Not the same. Measles can decimate a village in a matter of weeks."
He took another drag, before casting the cigar to the ground and crushing it like someone squashing a June bug. "When the doctors refused to treat them, I wondered who the real savages were."

Tolerance of Indians wasn't something she had expected from Wil. "Didn't you go west to fight Indians?"

"Very little fighting, and there were peaceable tribes."

His voice had grown reminiscent—no doubt about a lady. An Indian woman was her suspicion.

"Amanda, you're an intelligent woman. I'm surprised you haven't guessed the truth."

"Truth?"

"My maternal grandmother was Cherokee."

Cherokee? Wil Jackson—part Indian? His prominent cheekbones and black hair suddenly made sense. The revelation of such a family secret was a great personal risk—one revealing his level of trust in her. "Your secret is safe with me."

"Which is most appreciated. I don't fear for myself, but there are others."

His family in Charleston. She nodded in understanding.

"You care about everyone and everything. That's honorable. Your kindness is not something that will easily be forgotten, dear lady."

They reached the empty cabin with a sagging porch. Amanda transferred her personal belongings to her bag. Wil carried a canvas bag inside. While he was gone, she hoisted her skirts and fumbled with the hook of the crinoline. She struggled and groaned with a sudden sense that someone watched her. She glanced over her shoulder and lowered her dress.

Behind her, Wil stood with his arms crossed and a sly grin spreading across his face. "Don't let me stop you. I rather enjoyed the view."

"Wil..." She gritted her teeth. What was the use? Though his lineage was a prominent Carolinian family, he often acted like a rascal of dubious breeding. "I could use some help."

"Are you saying you trust me?"

"As a matter of fact, I do. And if you know what's good for you, you will not stray from the task at hand." Certain her message was clear, she lifted her skirts.

His hands went to her waist without his fingers roaming. The grin vanished from his face, and he unfastened the crinoline with dexterity. It collapsed in a heap about her ankles.

She refused to contemplate how he'd gained his knowledge of women's undergarments and stepped out of the crinoline. After gathering it together, she packed it away in the buggy. "Thank you, Wil."

"You're welcome." He grasped a supply bag with his right hand, but switched to his left.

"Your arm must still bother you."

"It's not so bad."

"There's laudanum in the bag."

"I appreciate your concern, but laudanum fogs my head. I need to remain alert. Yanks might appear when least expected."

The war—she could easily forget, even if for a little while. As a Confederate officer, he had no such luxury.

"There's a blanket on my horse," he said, "if you wish to rest. I'll keep watch out here."

Amanda thanked him once more. When he carried the bag inside, she untied the wool blanket from his saddle. Tired, wet, and cold, she waited for him to return before entering the shack. She spread the blanket on the dirt floor and curled on it.

Outside, she could see Wil's silhouette move in the direction of the horses. When he struck a match to another cigar, embers glowed in the darkness. She closed her eyes and breathed in the sweet scent. Tendrils of sleep captured her mind, and she envisioned a lonely battlefield with the stench of rotting corpses. Flies buzzed among living and dead alike. Covered in a pool of blood, John whispered her name in a dying breath.

A horse nickered, and she sat up. "John?" Her hand went to her throat. "John, where are you?"

"John's dead, Amanda." Wil tossed the cigar to the ground and stamped out the embers. Soon beside her, he kneeled and lightly touched her cheek.

"I had a dream about John. He was dying."

Wil drew her into his arms, and she sobbed on his shoulder. He withdrew a handkerchief from the pocket of his frock coat. She dabbed her eyes, and he said, "One of these days, you'll learn to carry a hand-kerchief."

His calm strength was exactly what she needed. "I must be expecting too much too soon. I thought I had no more tears left to cry."

"It's only been three months."

"You say that as if you understand."

"How could I? I've never been married." Wil's boots pounded against the wood as he stormed from the shack.

Confused by his moods, Amanda decided to leave him be. She would probably never fully understand what lurked underneath. John had also suffered from the mood swings—as well as dreams. So why did men wage war if it was so frightfully terrible?

Chapter Five

BEFORE DAWN, WIL ENTERED THE SHACK. DURING THE NIGHT, he had heard Amanda crying and relived memories that he thought were long forgotten. Unable to take her in his arms when she needed comfort the most, he hid behind the mask of duty. He slipped into a dark abyss where, in the insanity of the battlefield, he could channel it to a calculated fearlessness.

First light trickled through a broken window pane. Almost angelic, Amanda slept peacefully. He hated to wake her. Bending down, he stroked her soft cheek. "We need to be moving. Your horse should be rested."

Through partly closed eyes, she failed to budge from beneath the blanket's warmth.

His stomach rumbled. Wil returned to his horse and searched through his saddlebag. He located some hardtack, but his hand squished against something soft. A grub wiggled beneath his fingertips. Hard bread and fresh meat. Too early in the morning to see the humor, he decided he wasn't that hungry. Not yet.

Instead, Wil pulled a cigar from his jacket. He chewed on it while saddling his horse, recalling a muggy summer morning in Virginia—the opening battle of civil war. Through the artillery fire, he had heard the screams. Before the charge, a yellow-haired private had wanted nothing more than to go home. He had quoted the private the required speech of duty. In reality, the boy could have never imagined what to expect. Many officers had no battle experience either. As a veteran, he'd known what lay before them. After the guns had opened fire, the boys looked to him for guidance. He had led the men and fought with a fury that had even taken him by surprise. Still, the private had died.

A cry came from inside the shack. Wil turned toward it. He focused on the sound and realized it wasn't a cry, but Amanda moving about in the growing morning light. He blinked back the image from Manassas.

The blanket was in Amanda's arms, and she stepped from the shack into the morning chill. "Good morning, Wil." She sent him a cheery smile. "Wil?"

"Amanda . . ."

Her smile faded. "I had hoped you'd be in a better mood this morning."

"I kept watch while you slept," he grumbled.

"I don't need a man to protect me."

She shoved the blanket into his arms and hit his wound. His cigar fell, and he gritted his teeth to keep from crying out.

"I didn't mean to be sharp," she said, "but sometimes you can be very annoying."

Relieved that she hadn't noticed his distress, Wil tied the blanket to his saddle before reclaiming the cigar from the ground. His last one. He rubbed his eyes, butted the cigar on the heel of his boot, and stuffed it in a pocket for later. "I tend to have that effect on everyone. I beg forgiveness."

Her brows knitted together. With her blonde locks straying and a wrinkled dress, she had a delightful rumpled look—like after sharing a night together in bed. He had to be careful. Amanda was a lady, and he hadn't been with such a woman in a long time—too long.

The sparkle returned to Amanda's green eyes. "With all you've done for me, I can't stay mad. Besides, you look like you could use some sleep."

Wil bit his tongue to withhold his real need. She touched his arm, and he resisted the temptation of sweeping her off her feet. In the shack, he'd be able to taste her mouth, feel the tightness between her thighs, while teasing her nipples to rigid peaks.

"Wil?"

"Amanda—if you wish me to behave in a gentlemanly manner, I suggest you remove your hand, or I will carry you inside. Sleep is not what I have in mind."

In disgust, she threw her hands in the air. "There is no hope for you, Colonel Jackson." With a swift turn, she headed down the hill to the pond at the bottom. "I'm going to wash the sleep from my face. If you care to join me, I shall expect you to mind your manners. Perhaps the cold water would be of some benefit to your current state."

She disappeared through the yellow grass, and he couldn't help but laugh. He tightened the roan's girth, before checking Amanda's stallion for soreness. No heat or swelling.

"Wil . . ."

Uncertain whether Amanda had called him, he raised his head. The call came again.

Wil detected urgency and drew his pistol. Barely able to grip the gun, he ignored the pain in his arm and cursed. If anything happened to Amanda . . . He reached the top of the hill.

Near the pond, a scraggly-haired boy aimed a shotgun at a Yank. On bent knee, the bluecoat had tears streaming down his face. Wil navigated through the tall grass and overheard the Yank begging for his life. *Where was Amanda?*

He finally caught sight of her standing to the side, pleading with the boy not to shoot. Wil restrained himself. This wasn't the battlefield. The Yank had most likely been scouting the area and happened on a loyal Confederate household. Too young for military service, the boy had captured the Yank and brought the battlefield home. If he guessed right, he could use the fierce loyalty to his advantage without bloodshed. If he were wrong—well, there were worse places to be buried than Virginia.

Wil lowered his pistol and stepped from the underbrush into the open. "I'd like to thank you for capturing my prisoner."

The boy sent him an appraising glance. "Your prisoner?"

"Lieutenant Colonel William Jackson," Wil said. "You will, of course, be rewarded for your efforts."

Suspicion changed to a bucktooth grin. Wil guessed the boy was only twelve or thirteen, but he carried a gun like he knew how to use it. In spite of the boy's youth, Wil realized he mustn't underestimate him.

"I ain't heard tell of no Lieutenant Colonel Jackson. Any kin to Stonewall?" the boy asked.

If Wil had a romp beneath the sheets with a pretty lady for every time he was asked that question, he would certainly be a most satisfied man. "Afraid not, but I made the general's acquaintance at West Point."

The bucktooth grin widened in idol worship, and the shotgun sank a little lower.

He had best not tell the boy his true thoughts about Tom Jackson. While a brave soldier, Stonewall was one of the oddest men he had ever met. "Do you intend on releasing my prisoner to me?"

The boy flipped a silver coin in the palm of his hand. "Do I get to keep the Yankee money?"

Still on bent knee, the Yankee sergeant broke into a sweat. Wil smelled urine in the mix. He reached into his vest pocket and withdrew another coin and tossed it. "I don't think he's in a position to argue."

The boy caught the silver. "Thanks, Colonel. I felt like I was missin' the fun. All the fightin' will be over afore I'm old enough."

If only that were true . . . Most likely if they met again, he would be ordering the boy to his death.

Wil holstered his pistol, and the boy vanished in the waving grass. Amanda rushed over to help the Yank to his feet.

The sergeant's nostrils flared, and he doubled over, looking as if he might retch. "Why'd you do it, Reb?"

"I don't take kindly to being called *Reb*."

The Yank gulped for air. "Colonel." He cleared his throat, sounding like his stomach hadn't settled. The sergeant swayed on his feet. "Sir . . ."

"I don't condone executions."

Still pale, the sergeant said, "So you're the enemy."

"Because of power-hungry politicians."

"Never met a Reb—Confederate—up close before." Tears appeared in his eyes, and he finally met Wil's gaze. He thrust out a trembling hand. "I owe you my life, Colonel. I'll take my place as your prisoner."

Wil disregarded the pain in his arm and shook the Yank's hand. "That won't be necessary. We didn't meet in battle—but if we do . . ."

The sergeant nodded—kill or be killed. Politicians made the war. Politicians would decide when to end it. Until then, blue and gray would fight and die for the likes of bureaucrats. In disgust, Wil headed up the hill to the shack.

"Wil," Amanda said, joining him. "I want to add my thanks for what you did. You constantly surprise me."

"For showing mercy to the enemy? The war is young, Amanda. There will be much bloodshed ahead. There's no sense in spilling it unnecessarily."

With a shiver she folded her arms over her breasts, obviously hoping the worst was behind them.

"As it is, I'm taking a chance he isn't concealing a gun the boy missed."

"Even if he is, he wouldn't shoot you in the back—not after the way you helped him."

"That kind of thinking got your husband killed."

Amanda cast a glance over her shoulder. "He's gone."

Wil snorted a belly laugh. "Probably halfway to Yankee lines already."

"You knew he'd run."

"I didn't." Nearly at the top of the hill, he stopped. "He's young and inexperienced—the first time he's faced death. A man will either fight or flee. Sometimes men who run are more dangerous than the ones who stand their ground."

Confusion entered her eyes.

"Something you needn't worry your pretty little head—"

"Wil, I have troops passing through my property from time to time. If it's going to get worse, I need to know what you mean."

Women shouldn't carry the burden. Men should be present to protect them from the inevitable looting—and rape. Regrettably, he couldn't shield Amanda from wartime reality. If he armed her with the truth, she could at least protect herself. "You know exactly where you stand with a man who will hold his ground—whether good or bad. But the one who runs is fear driven. If there's anger mixed with the fear, then he's just as likely to strike a weaker victim."

She pressed an open hand to her chest. "Such as a woman or child. I could have been . . . " Her green eyes turned seething. "And you risked being shot in the back on a hunch that he would run for dear life?"

"All of life is a gamble, Amanda."

"One which you shall eventually lose, Colonel. Sometimes I wonder if you have the good sense to realize there are times when you should be afraid." Amanda gathered her skirts together and hurried up the hill.

By the time Wil reached the top, she was checking the red stallion's foot. "We'll ride my horse. Your servant can fetch the buggy later."

Her shoulders stiffened. Even though she had been married to a military man, she was not a woman used to being ordered about. He exhaled a weary breath. "My requests often come out as commands."

She faced him. "Tell me, Wil, what happens if it's not battles or dying that a man fears?"

Suddenly intrigued, he crossed his arms. "Such as?"

"Aren't some men afraid of showing weakness?"

Fear? He had never thought of showing weakness as fear. Offering no response, he untied his horse from the rail and mounted. He extended a hand to help her aboard.

Her hands went to her hips. "I'm waiting for an answer."

"I've already warned you that fear mixed with anger is a deadly combination."

"Then you admit . . . ?"

"I admit nothing." He offered his hand once more. Amanda's fingers curled around his hand, and he lifted her on the gelding behind him. Close again. And she was afraid to touch him. "I don't bite, Amanda."

She blushed, and her arms went loosely about his waist. "Your horse is lovely. What's his name?"

Leading Amanda's stallion behind them, he cued the roan to a walk. Resorting to small talk confirmed her intelligence. "Poker Chip."

"More of your distinct sense of humor, Colonel? Did you win him in a high stakes card game?"

"He's out of a spotted mare I brought back from the Northwest. The Nez Perce call their spotted ponies Appaloosa. When bred with a thoroughbred, Poker was the result."

She twisted slightly in the saddle, and her face wrinkled.

Amused, Wil continued, "He has a spot the size of a poker chip on his . . . " He caught himself. " . . . rump."

Amanda shoved her skirt aside and checked the gelding's spot. "I'll trust your word that it's the size of a poker chip." A gentle pink flushed her cheeks. "Wil, you are no gentleman."

"I have warned you." Her gaze met his, but she looked shyly away. Still vulnerable—yet she was becoming more comfortable in his presence. Wil diverted his attention to the countryside. Because of his military career, he had traveled extensively. Although he hailed from South Carolina, home was wherever he was stationed. At the same time, he could never renounce his heritage.

Deciduous forests and gently rolling hills reminded him of Manassas. Much to the Northerners' surprise, Southerners had every intention of defending their homes. The Virginia battlefield was only a bloody beginning.

By evening they turned onto a lane toward Amanda's white-frame farmhouse. Her free servant waved from the barn. Wil slid from Poker's back before reaching up to help Amanda. He hoped she hadn't noticed that he resorted to the use of his left hand. *Afraid to admit weakness?*

Ezra joined them. "We was gettin' worried, Miss Amanda."

"Red stepped on a stone and bruised his foot," she said. "Colonel Jackson was kind enough to escort me home."

"Ezra," Wil said. The Negro averted his gaze to the ground. "See to the horses."

"Yessir."

"Wil..." As Ezra led the horses to the barn, he felt Amanda's gentle touch on his arm. "I would appreciate it if you didn't order my servants about."

He was doing it again. "I'm a military man, but I will try."

Amanda led the way through the gate of the white picket fence to the house. Once inside, she hung his hat and jacket on a peg by the door. They went into the parlor. A colored girl sat on the floor playing with a young child—Sam Prescott's daughter.

The child toddled across a braided rug. The servant, Dulcie, plucked the toddler from the floor and brought her to Amanda. When the child babbled, Amanda scooped her lovingly into her arms. The child had dark hair—almost black—the same as Benjamin's, Wil noted. Come spring, his son would have been eleven. He passed each birthday in silence.

"Wil?"

He blinked and extended a forefinger. The girl latched onto it with a gurgle.

"Would you like to hold Rebecca?" Amanda asked.

He withdrew his finger from the toddler's grasp. "What would I know about children?"

"Just the way you looked at her. I thought... Never mind."

Propriety would keep her from asking what was really on her mind. "I haven't sired any bastards."

She closed her eyes. "That's a terrible way to refer to a child."

"You wanted to know. I supplied the answer." He turned to leave.

"Wil..."

Before his mind sank through the dark abyss, he felt the touch of her hand on his arm, drawing him back.

"No matter what, a child should be loved. I wouldn't have thought less of you if you had admitted you had a child as long as he was loved." With a mother's adoration, she straightened a stray wisp in Rebecca's hair. Unembarrassed about propriety, she continued, "I know John was disappointed that I never gave him a son. Then when Kate died—I love Rebecca as if she were my own. When Virginia seceded, I worried Sam would send her to his family in Maine—or to his brother and..."

She stopped short of saying Holly Prescott's name. "Amanda, I'm aware of Mrs. Prescott's virtues—or lack thereof. If Lieutenant Prescott ever considered her as a mother for his daughter, then he is a fool."

"Miss Amanda..." An old Negro woman wandered into the parlor, waving a walking stick in front of her. "I got a hot meal waitin'."

He seriously doubted Negroes were as simple as one was led to believe, but the glaze of Frieda's eyes was a perfect defense for pretending ignorance when the occasion warranted. One to watch.

"For your company too." The old woman retreated from the room.

Amanda returned Rebecca to Dulcie and led the way to the kitchen. "Let's take advantage of Frieda's kind offer."

He withdrew a chair from the table and waited for her to be seated. "Thank you, sir."

He sat on the opposite side, and her eyes glowed. The lack of sleep must have been catching up with him, or he was getting old. At one time, if a beautiful woman sat so close, he'd be able to think of nothing else.

Frieda set plates of chicken and dumplings with generous portions of cornbread on the table. Unlike the sorry state of his rations, no grubs wiggled about.

"Eat up," Amanda said. "I'm sure you're famished, and you have a long ride ahead of you tomorrow if you're going to retrieve the supplies."

There was nothing suggestive in her statement of spending the night. He hadn't expected it. Wil savored the taste of home cooking for a change of pace. And he looked forward to sleeping in Amanda's feather bed. He'd relish the bed even more sharing it with Amanda, but alas . . . The meal must have revived him.

"I have some wine to wash it down with." Amanda brought a bottle to the table and poured two glasses of blood-red Burgundy.

Why did everything remind him of blood? The war had barely begun.

"I was saving it for when John returned," she said, reseating herself, "but that's pointless now, isn't it?"

Aware that she was reaching out, he pulled back. Always—he pulled back. If only he could take her into his arms and give her the comfort she sought. "Amanda, I wish you would take the money without smuggling supplies."

Her glass clinked against the wood as she set it on the table. "I earn my keep, Colonel. Or did you have something else in mind? I refuse to be a high-priced strumpet like—like Holly Prescott." Red-faced, she shoved the chair back and ran from the kitchen.

Even when he tried being honorable, he said the wrong thing.

Frieda jabbed a bony finger in his direction. "You hurt Miss Amanda and you answer to me."

Wil stood, but decided to let the transgression pass. The old woman was merely protecting Amanda. He couldn't damn her for that. He reached into his pocket and tossed a gold coin onto the table. "See that Amanda gets the money. I'll send word when it's time for the next run."

A grin crinkled the old woman's face. "Dere's more to you dan I thought. I feel da way you fret about her."

He didn't like the way the old woman probed his mind. As he passed, her sightless eyes seemed to follow.

In the parlor a cornhusk doll lay on the floor where Dulcie had been playing with Rebecca. The servant girl met him in the foyer and automatically lowered her dark eyes. "Miss Amanda put da baby to bed. She be right down. Is dere anythin' I can get you?"

"No."

"May I be excused?"

"I'm not your master. You don't need my permission."

Dulcie gathered her threadbare skirt around her as if she were afraid of her own shadow.

He heard humming come from upstairs and followed the sound.

Amanda stood over a crib, trilling like a thrush.

"Amanda..." Wil looked into the crib and saw Benjamin. His brown skin had been darker than his own—more like his mother's. "I meant no insult when I asked you to stop running supplies. If you're arrested, there's nothing I can do to help."

"Why, Colonel, you were being protective."

"You're a lovely lady worth protecting."

"And now you're trying to steal my heart—the dashing Mexican War hero."

"Amanda—"

"No, Wil, let me finish. Ever since John died, I've seen it in your eyes. I know you care, but I can't return what you want from me—not because it's too soon."

His hope faded.

"There's something inside you—something dark. It creeps through on occasion. At first, I thought it was the war. That may be part of it, but there's more. Something you struggle to keep hidden. Quite frankly, it frightens the heck out of me."

Wil glanced at the bed. If he took her in his arms, comforted her, and told her everything would be all right, she'd relent. With a few token gestures of affection, he'd claim victory. But Amanda wasn't like other women. She was a lady to be respected. In her presence, he could climb from the abyss that his mind so often drifted to. "I'll leave now."

"It's best," she whispered.

His spurs jingled as he went down the stairs. Frieda's stooped form stood at the bottom. She leaned on her walking stick. Unblinking, the glazed eyes seemed to watch—reading his mind again, no doubt.

"Dey took my boy away when he be ten, put him on a block and sold him like one of your prized horses."

"I don't sell prized horses."

"Don't matter none. Others do. Ain't never seen my boy again. Good as *dead*."

Emphasis on the dead revealed that she knew about Benjamin. At one time he would have been intolerant of such insubordination. *Getting soft—or old.*

After collecting his hat and jacket, Wil stepped outside to the brisk fall air. He struck a match to his last cigar. He remained unfulfilled—not only in the physical sense, but there was something else—buried deep. Not the ominous place where he usually sank, but a warmth, filled with laughter—Amanda's laughter. Something he hadn't felt since . . .

He choked back the smoke. When had it happened? It couldn't be love.

Wil flicked the ashes. Those sort of foolish feelings only weakened a man, compromising his judgment on the battlefield.

Chapter Six

THE WEATHER WAS FAIR AND WARM FOR DECEMBER. Christmas had arrived at the brownstone. Pine boughs decorated the mantels, and the heavenly scent of baking fruitcakes filled the rooms. After Amanda had made a successful supply run without incident in November, Wil had secured a pass for her return to Washington for the holiday. She frequented the same social circles as before the war, making the day without John seem less lonely.

Even Holly was caught in the spirit of the occasion. After supper, they retired to the parlor and sang carols. On this night, Amanda felt John standing beside her. His baritone voice joined them in "Silent Night."

After the hymn, Charles raised his glass in a toast. "To peace."

Amanda followed suit, but glass shattered against the fireplace, breaking the serenity of the moment.

Sam strode from the room, and Holly arched a brow. "A bit huffy, isn't he?"

The door in the foyer slammed.

Amanda collected her cloak and stepped into the winter night. The wrought-iron gate creaked. "Sam?"

A shadowy figure stood beneath the gas lamppost at the end of the walk.

"Sam."

He faced her. "How could you, Amanda?"

She went down the steps. "How could I what?"

"Raise a glass to *peace?*" He spat out the word as if it had been poison. "You of all people. Charles has a desk job, and Holly—well, she only thinks about what suits her. But you—how could you forget?"

Uncertain what she was being accused of, Amanda moved closer. "Forget what?"

"How your husband died."

The dream of John calling to her while dying on the battlefield haunted her. "I can never forget. Even in the name of war, I will never forgive your corporal."

"Then why would you toast to a false hope? Wishing for peace doesn't make it fact. It's a fanciful dream, Amanda. Come spring, there's going to be fighting like this country has never seen before."

With a shiver, Amanda joined him near the gate. On the day Virginia seceded from the Union, it was guaranteed to become the main battlefield. Sam would be in the middle, fighting against her home state. "It's Christmas. Spring is a long time away."

"To pretend it won't happen makes a mockery of the Colonel's death."

Three years of war. Both Sam and Wil had said it would last at least that long. Another two? What did they know that others didn't? When the blockade choked the South from the rest of the world, day-to-day survival would become a struggle. Hospitals were already swamped with sick and wounded, and the few medical supplies she smuggled across the lines would make little difference to the troops.

"We can't give up hope, Sam. If we do, we might as well join the Colonel."

"I've seen the elephant. I hope next Christmas you will feel the same way."

Seeing the elephant. At one time, she thought it a peculiar phrase, but she understood men's hopes that seeing a battle would be just as rare. "I will."

The iron gate creaked as he closed it. "Forgive my weakness. When you say it, I almost believe it."

Weakness? Already she saw hints of the dark, foreboding moods. A long war would change him. If Wil was any indicator, the change wouldn't be for the better.

"There's nothing to forgive," Amanda said. "Shall we return to the parlor and drink that toast?"

Sam lifted her hand to his lips. "Thank you, Amanda. I should be consoling you, not the other way around."

Through the light from the lamppost, his kind eyes showed their appreciation. Before the war's end, he would certainly discover her hypocrisy—smuggling supplies for the South, while remaining support-ive of Northern friends. Tonight—on Christmas—the season of hope, she shoved those thoughts from her mind and would live by her words.

Fair weather changed to snow when Amanda greeted 1862. The reunion in Washington had been fleeting, and with the arrival of the New Year she was reminded of the fact that she would be facing the year—along with the years to come—alone.

Mama and her sister, Alice, had dropped by from Fredericksburg to cheer her, but her spirit sank lower. Mama was all but beside herself and, more than a week later, she still had house guests.

Amanda snuggled close to the fire in the parlor, cuddling Rebecca in her arms.

The toddler rubbed her eyes and wailed.

Before Amanda could react, Dulcie scooped the child from her arms.

"Dulcie, you needn't run every time she squeals. Mama and Alice are here to help."

"I know you bin feelin' poorly."

Rebecca flailed her arms and shrieked louder.

Dulcie looked from Amanda to Alice and Mama, then back again. "It be gettin' late for a young 'un. I feed her and put her to bed."

Feeling of little use these days, Amanda settled back on the tapestry sofa. "I think Dulcie was mistreated before coming here. She's very nervous."

Alice leaned closer. "So what are you going to do about it?"

Three years separated them. Amanda had faced the rigors of farm life to keep Papa's memory alive, while Alice had followed Mama's dream and completed finishing school. She had become a proper

woman of poise and distinction in the community and was often surrounded by dashing suitors begging for her hand in marriage. Her little
sister rejected all proposals outright, adding to Mama's worry that she
might wind up a spinster.

"Rebecca's papa," Amanda replied, "says he'll help her go north
when Oakcrest demands her return."

"Shh . . ." Mama pressed a finger to her lips from the safety of the
velvet wing chair. "It's illegal."

"The house doesn't have ears, Mama. No one's going to hear us."

Frieda shuffled into the parlor. "Miss Amanda, dere's a rider
comin'."

Thankful for the interruption, Amanda heard a horse gallop up the
lane. Probably Colonel Jackson coming to collect the supplies she had
brought from Washington. Supply smuggling was illegal. Apparently
that fact had escaped Mama's notice.

Amanda parted the lace curtain. The lamp nearest the window cast
a flickering, broken light on the yard, but the roan's gray hairs stood
out. Wil halted Poker Chip opposite the picket fence. Her mood lifted,
and she went to greet him. After she pulled him out of the cold, she
took his hat and woolen overcoat. A third gold star was sewn to the
collar of his frock coat.

He blew on his hands and wiggled frozen fingers. "Amanda, I shall
never get used to northern winters."

"Northern?" She hung the overcoat on a peg, and he unbuckled
his weapons belt. "I think the Virginia legislature might argue that
assessment. Wil, it is good to see you. Come in and warm yourself
by the fire. Mama and Alice are visiting. You can tell us when you
were promoted to full colonel." She led the way to the parlor. "You
remember my mama and sister, Alice?"

"Of course." His dark eyes exchanged more than a casual glance
with Alice, and his smile widened to a grin. He bowed slightly and
took Mama's hand. "Mrs. McGuire. A pleasure to see you again."

He might not be a gentleman, but he certainly knew when to turn
on the charm.

Alice raised a hand.

Wil obliged the gesture and kissed it. "Miss McGuire."

"Alice." Alice tilted her head with a coy smile.

"Alice," he agreed. "As I recall you wore pigtails when we last met."

"Colonel . . . " Alice giggled. "You embarrass me. We have seen one another since Amanda's wedding. You were a captain on our last meeting."

"Before being shipped off to New Mexico. How could I have forgotten? My humble apologies. You have grown into a lovely woman, Alice."

Alice stole a shy glance at Wil, and Amanda detected trouble brewing. Inexperienced in the way things were between men and women, her sister could be taken advantage of by the likes of Wil. "Alice," Amanda said, "I could use your help fetching some tea."

"Of course, Amanda." Alice got to her feet and sent Wil a taunting glance.

Oh dear, it was worse than Amanda had originally thought—her sister wanted him to take notice. And Wil's roguish smile warned her he realized that fact.

Worried sick, Amanda ignored Dulcie feeding Rebecca in the kitchen. She turned to Alice. "Colonel Jackson is much too worldly for you."

Alice pressed a hand to her breast. "What on earth are you talking about?"

"Don't pretend. I saw you fluttering your eyes at Wil."

"Amanda, I do believe you're jealous."

Flustered that she must spell it out, Amanda raised a finger in protest. Jealous? Over Wil? She lowered her arm. "I'm not jealous. He's not like your other beaus. Wil's not the marrying kind, but it won't stop him from seeking your virtue."

"You needn't fret, Amanda. Colonel Jackson is delightfully handsome, but I want no part of courting a military man. Unfortunately, they're all military these days. Now scoot back to the parlor." Alice waved her from the kitchen. "I'll see to the tea."

Relieved that Alice possessed some good sense, Amanda returned to the parlor to the sound of Mama's laughter. Wil had a way of dazzling women of all ages. If only others knew him like she did. She breathed in the strong scent of wood smoke and reseated herself near the warmth of the crackling flames. "Wil, tell us when you were promoted."

His coal-black eyes broke contact with Mama's. "A month ago. The army is finally acknowledging the fact that a man doesn't need to be from Virginia to make a worthy officer in the field."

Half-suspecting that was part of the reason why John had been promoted to colonel when Wil had more field experience, Amanda was pleased he accepted the politics of military life good-naturedly. "I thought you might be in Charleston for the holidays," she said.

"I was for Christmas." He wriggled his fingers in front of the fire. "I had a homesick servant who remained behind, and the family is as antiquated as ever in their thinking. My presence wasn't needed or . . . ." He turned to warm his back.

Amanda detected family strife and inferred the missing word to be "wanted."

"Just came from Richmond. I was concerned how you had fared on your first Christmas alone. It was an excellent idea to visit friends in Washington to help you through it."

"Not to mention to your benefit."

At the hint of smuggling, Mama tugged on the glass beads around her throat.

Amanda continued, "It's kind of you to think of me, but as you can see, I'm hardly alone."

Alice glided across the floor with the grace she had learned at finishing school. She carried a silver platter and a teapot.

"Indeed you're not," Wil said with a growing smile.

Thank goodness for her little talk with Alice in the kitchen, or she'd be fretting something fierce by now. To be on the safe side, she shot Wil a mind-your-manners glare.

In a more typical terse manner, he said, "Amanda, I need to discuss a private matter."

"If it's about the supplies, you can speak freely. Mama and Alice would have wondered where I got the money if I hadn't said anything about the runs."

He watched Alice again as she poured the tea into bone china cups. "Very well. I was hoping you might make another run."

Amanda straightened. "So soon? You haven't collected the supplies I brought from Washington."

No longer distracted, he nodded his thanks when Alice handed him a teacup. "I will."

Mama twisted the beads between her fingers and got to her feet. "I think I shall retire."

After they bid her good night, Wil continued, "Amanda, the Yankees are likely to stay quiet until spring. After that, there will be some heavy fighting. If you think you're up to it, you should be able to make several runs before the spring campaign."

Intrigued, Alice joined Amanda on the sofa. "When do you want the first one?" Amanda asked.

"Within the week. No one suspects you. We must take advantage of that while we can. Depending on how things go shall determine the timing of the next one." He opened his mouth but closed it again.

"Do you expect problems?"

He set the full teacup on the silver platter and tugged on his moustache. "If everything goes according to plan, I'd like you to bring a wagon across the following time."

Amanda narrowed her eyes. "A wagon? You want me to bring more than food and medical supplies across, don't you? I won't do it. Do you understand? I simply won't take part in the killing."

Cool and calm as always, Wil grasped her hand. "Relax, Amanda. I made a promise. You can refuse anything you're uncomfortable with. To be frank, I'm relieved you said no."

She yanked her hand from his grip. "And that's it? You're relieved I said no."

"I'll do it."

Both looked in Alice's direction.

"I'll do it," Alice repeated. "I have no qualms about carrying arms. Anything to aid the Confederacy."

Alice's patriotism was blinded by naiveté. "It's too dangerous," Amanda insisted.

Wil studied her sister as if he might be considering the proposition.

Fear for Alice's life fled to the forefront. "Wil, please don't agree to this. We're friends."

"You're trying to protect her from something that all in the South will eventually experience firsthand, but I'll abide by your wishes."

Alice stood in protest. "Amanda won't decide for me. I'm not a child anymore."

A dirty little grin appeared on Wil's lips. "No, you're not."

Disgusted with their dallying, Amanda had heard enough. "I need to check on Rebecca."

Upstairs, Rebecca slept soundly in the crib beside the bed. Thankfully, Dulcie had made a fire to break the winter chill. Amanda draped a woolen blanket over the child. "I wonder how your papa is, Rebecca. Is he warm? Does he have enough to eat? Most of all, I wonder if he thinks of you."

Her spirit sank lower, and she thought of two holiday seasons before. She and John had traveled to Washington. Kate had been looking forward to Rebecca's birth. Unable to conceive in eight years of marriage, Amanda had envied her friend. Nearly dissolving into tears, she barely managed to keep her poise.

Amanda tiptoed from the bedroom. At the top of the stairs, Alice's laughter drifted her way. No doubt Wil was filling her head with all of the things she wanted to hear. Alice was right. She *was* jealous. But Wil wasn't the sort of man to devote himself to one woman. One woman indeed. Both rumors were probably true—the Carolina girl *and* Holly Prescott. Suddenly furious, she guessed whose notion it was to smuggle arms. Selling weapons meant money.

"Wil Jackson!" She stormed down the stairs. "How dare you!"

Side by side, Wil and Alice sat a few inches apart on the sofa.

Amanda reached over the mantel for John's hunting rifle, and Alice jumped to her feet. "Amanda, what has got into you?"

"Ask him who he met in Richmond." Amanda aimed the rifle in Wil's direction. "Give me one good reason why I shouldn't shoot you where you stand."

Wil held out his hands with his palms facing up. "I'm unarmed. Do you keep the rifle loaded the way you do the .44?"

Tempted to call his bluff, Amanda fingered the trigger. "In the study, Colonel. I'd like to speak with you in private."

He obeyed her demand and turned in the direction of the study.

She lowered the rifle, and a blast shook the room in a cloud of smoke. "Wil!"

He glanced at the splintered wood next to his foot. "Your aim is off, Amanda."

Calm to the end. No wonder he was steady under fire on the battlefield. She wished she could say the same for herself. Trembling, Amanda shoved the rifle into Alice's arms. "Take it. Before I do something fool-ish and mean it. Wil—in the study."

He saluted.

Annoyed with his tomfoolery, she followed him to the study.

He nestled in John's chair. "You'd make a fine officer, Amanda. Not many women can give orders the way you do."

"Stop toying with me."

His eyes widened in mock horror.

"Wil, who did you see while in Richmond?"

He propped his feet on the desk as if he owned it and leaned back in the leather chair. "The President and his lovely wife. General Hensley. Captain—"

"Holly Prescott?"

"As I recall . . ." The corners of his mouth turned up in a smile. "She may have been there."

"With a forged pass, no doubt. Fancy that—only a short time ago, she was playing the dutiful wife to a Yankee captain in Washington. I wonder what excuse she gave her husband to join you in Richmond."

He shrugged that he didn't know. "Not my concern."

Amanda wagged a finger. "I risked my life bringing supplies across the lines only to find you've been dallying."

"Business—she brought supplies to Richmond."

"And during one of your *business* discussions, the two of you just happened to cook up a scheme of smuggling arms across the lines."

"Amanda, there's no reason to get riled." He crossed his legs, and a spur scratched the desktop's finish. "You may recall, I asked to speak to you in private."

He had. She calmed slightly. "So?"

"I never expected you to smuggle arms. It's not in your nature. If Mrs. Prescott had brought it to my attention, she would have been rejected. But the request came from the general."

"Through Holly?"

"Most likely."

"You must have lost your influence if she's scheming behind your back."

His eyes danced. "Mrs. Prescott is drawn to power and money, sim-ple as that. Not much of either in smuggling medical supplies, but arms—that's another story."

"I'll never understand how you tolerate someone you can't trust."

"Trust is relative. The trick is knowing how far someone can be relied upon."

He *was* worldly. Isolated on the farm most of her life, she'd have to live over a hundred years to learn as much as he already knew. "I didn't mean to shoot at you."

"I'm aware of that."

Bold and self-confident too. That's why women flocked to him. He showed no sign of the dark moods, and she wondered if Holly had played a role in that. Men often got ornery if their needs weren't met. Amanda blushed just thinking about it and flipped his boots from the desk, nearly unseating him. "I will thank you to leave my sister alone."

He straightened in the chair and met her gaze. "I have no interest in your sister."

Her breath grew uneven, and she wished she could loosen the laces of her corset. "Then I shall appreciate it if you don't lead her on. She might think you truly care. I don't wish to see her hurt."

Spurs jingled as Wil got to his feet. "I'll honor your request." With a bow, he lifted her hand to his lips. The charm—he always knew when to turn on the charm. "Besides," he said, "I prefer my women with more experience."

She jerked her hand free of his grip. He caught it and gave her a light tug. Her body pressed against his chest. He cradled her head in his hands and kissed her with his moustache tickling her nose. She tried to resist, but her lips gave way. No man—including John—had ever kissed her so deliberately, but with tempered force. Why didn't she pull away?

His strong arms—while in them, she could pretend the war didn't exist and John's death had been an awful mistake. But it was more than safety. Wil made her feel alive again.

When their kiss ended, she remained in the comfort of his arms.

"I'll not apologize, Amanda. You're a beautiful woman who deserves more than John's indifference."

Uncertain what bothered her more—his in-depth knowledge of her married life or the fact that he had succeeded in titillating her senses—she stepped out of the embrace. "You were friends. How can you speak that way?"

"What way? The truth? Amanda, I know what John was like."

Cold. He had rarely put his arms around her. She couldn't make the admission, and Wil held her again. "I'd treat you like royalty."

Amanda twisted free of his grip. "I have more dignity than to be a kept woman. Wil, throughout the years, I ignored the rumors, but with John gone, I can't. No wonder you're fearless on the battlefield. You live for the moment. It takes more courage to love one woman and raise a family."

He clenched a hand, but relaxed it. "I've never pretended to be someone I'm not, but there are things the rumormongers don't know. You have misjudged my intentions."

Misjudged him? How? A smile crept to her lips. "Why, Wil Jackson—there was someone special, wasn't there?"

The emotionless mask fell in place. He tossed a couple of gold coins to the desk and strode for the door. "If you would be kind enough to tell me where you have stored the supplies, I shall retrieve them and be on my way."

So that was the reason—a woman from the past, and he had loved her with all the passion he lived by. "I hid them in the barn. Ezra will help you. Wil . . . ?"

In the foyer, he placed his hat on his head. The sword rattled as he strapped on his belt. "I don't care to discuss it."

"That's your prerogative, but don't expect me to understand without some sort of explanation. The way you carry on, I see a very different picture."

Alice joined them. "The talk in private must have helped."

Wrinkles crinkled around Wil's eyes, and he put on his overcoat. "A most pleasurable discussion."

Warmth entered Amanda's cheeks.

He bowed. "Good evening, Mrs. Graham. Miss McGuire."

When he opened the door, a sharp winter wind blew into the foyer. Amanda rubbed her arms, and Wil stepped outside, closing the door behind him.

"What did he mean by that?" Alice asked.

"With Wil, one never knows." Before Alice could question further, Amanda rushed up the stairs to her room.

In her sanctuary, Rebecca slumbered. Amanda parted the curtain and spotted the glow of burning cigar embers. Wil stood near the gate of the picket fence. He rubbed his hands against the cold before disappearing into the darkness.

Amanda picked up Rebecca and cradled her in her arms. Without changing into a nightdress, she climbed beneath the sheets. She tucked the quilt to Rebecca's chin to keep out the chill. She liked having Rebecca in bed with her, but kept thinking of Wil. All this time, he had wanted her love. Fancy that, Wil wanting the love of a woman.

Chapter Seven

L EAFLESS TREES CHANGED TO THE GREENS OF REBIRTH, and the Northern blockade strangled its hold on the Confederacy. With each passing day, food items and medicines grew scarcer. The entire South would soon be reduced to subsistence living. As a result, supply runs became more frequent. While the money relieved some of the financial burden, Amanda held firm and refused to smuggle a wagon shipment across the lines.

She brought Red to a halt near the hundred-year-old oak with the branch in the shape of a dipper. Full circle—the same spot where she had made her first run. As usual, James was late. She half-suspected that was the way he preferred things, and she let Red graze. Even after meeting the burly man on several occasions, she still had no idea whether James was his surname or given.

In recent weeks, the Yankees had grown restless. Scouts and reconnaissance parties patrolled both sides of the river. More cautious than during her earlier runs, Wil kept her near the Confederate line, and with the Potomac only a couple of miles away, he was almost within calling distance.

She twisted the braided leather through her fingers, feeling as jittery as a worker bee that had bear claws searching for honey in the beehive. After all of the successful runs, she thought her nerves would have developed some fortitude.

Red sensed her tension and pawed the ground.

"Easy, Red. We shall be away from here just as soon as we collect the supplies."

Beyond the glade, hoofbeats drummed in the rhythm of a gallop.

Alert and ready to move, Amanda cued the stallion behind the oak.

The pounding hooves got closer, and Red broke into a sweat. A black horse with a white blaze bounded into the open and slid to a halt almost next to her. The husky, unshaven rider was James.

She reined Red around to meet him.

"Stay where you are, Mrs. Graham."

She halted Red and remained behind the leafy brush and gnarled brambles.

Out of breath, James gulped for air. "Got Yanks on my tail. Don't say nothin'. Just listen. I'll get the supplies, but first . . . " A pudgy hand reached through the leaves with a slip of paper.

Numbers filled the page. At a casual glance, the numbers appeared random, but Amanda detected a pattern. A cipher.

"Make certain the Yanks don't get this. They're movin'. It tells our boys their strength."

"I can't—"

"Shhh . . . "

Her breath quickened, and Amanda resisted the temptation to shred the slip of paper. She hadn't agreed to deliver coded messages. Possession of a cipher would brand her as a spy. And spies were hanged.

The sound of rumbling hooves filled the air. *Yankees.* At least a dozen traveling mighty fast. Her heart felt like it had drifted to her throat. She fought the urge to run and slipped the cipher under the knot in her hair.

After she covered it over, James thrust saddlebags through the leaves. She checked the contents—morphine, quinine, and bandages—nothing out of the ordinary. She threw the bag across Red's withers.

James shoved a large canvas bag in her face, and hooves pounded closer. He clutched more saddlebags. "Two more."

Branches snapped and horses crashed into the glade.

Red tossed his head. Amanda tightened the reins, but the stallion tugged on the bit. Behind the protective curtain of leaves, she managed to keep her grip. She steadied their position.

Chestnut, bay, and gray horses carried soldiers in blue toward James. He flung the saddlebags to the ground and spurred the black horse in the side. The pair darted off at a full gallop.

Red fought to be moving, and Amanda's muscles strained. She held him in check.

A soldier shouted for James to halt.

Sitting quietly, she would wait until the danger had passed before venturing out.

The thud of hooves vanished, and the forest grew quiet. A thrush sang in a poplar tree. The trilling music made her think of home and how that was where she wanted to be right now—not in some distant forest in Maryland. The thrush fell silent, and a breeze flowed through the oak, rustling fresh spring leaves.

Determined to collect the supplies, Amanda leaned forward in the saddle and froze. Her skin crawled. She wiggled a finger. There—she was moving again.

A crow cawed, and a gun went off. Red tried to bolt. Nearly unseated, she struggled with the reins.

Another gun discharged.

In the dying echoes, peace descended upon the forest once more. The thrush began singing again. So tranquil—in perfect harmony. Amanda slid from the saddle to claim the saddlebags. Brambles ripped her sleeve and dug into her arm. She clamped her teeth against the pain and managed to grip the aged leather.

Red's eyes bulged. She jumped up and steadied his bobbing head.

A riderless horse with stirrup irons swinging streaked past. A black one with a white blaze.

To keep Red from calling out, she held his nose next to her body.

A string of soldiers rode into the glade and halted near the oak. A pock-faced private with a wispy moustache dismounted. She held her breath. If she wanted, she could reach through the brambles and touch his arm. He inspected the saddlebags and tossed them over his horse's withers. Laughing and joking among themselves, a sergeant bragged about the Copperhead he had gunned down.

James—dead? *Yankee justice.* Amanda bit her lip to keep from crying out. She would proudly deliver James's message to Wil.

The soldiers rode on. Their voices drifted, and she climbed into the saddle. Reining Red around, she cued him into the open.

A soldier pursued her.

She clicked to Red for speed, but the pock-faced private cut in front. She brought Red to a halt as the first rider, a lieutenant with sandy-brown hair, pulled even. She drew her pistol and leveled it at his chest.

The lieutenant reined his horse back. "We won't hurt you, ma'am."

"Like James?"

"James?"

"You will know the name of the *Copperhead* your sergeant so proudly killed."

"I'm sorry, ma'am." His sandy-brown hair reminded her of Sam's.

Her finger remained on the trigger, but as Amanda had feared, she couldn't shoot. She lowered the gun.

The private searched through the saddlebags. "Medicine and bandages," he reported to the lieutenant.

"Supplies for the sick and wounded. I wouldn't carry weapons or ammunition."

The lieutenant's eyes held compassion but not Sam's familiar kindness. "I can't let you have them, ma'am, and if I let you go, the captain will have my hide."

"Then take the supplies. Your captain doesn't need to know you captured me."

"I'm sorry, ma'am."

Wil's warning that he would be unable to help sank home. She surrendered the pistol. But Sam might be able to put in a good word. "Can you send a message to a friend?"

"I can't wire across the lines."

"My friend is Northern."

The lieutenant spat. "Another Copperhead?"

"He's in the Federal army—same as you."

His gaze softened. "I'll see what I can do. Who do you want to contact?"

Now that she thought about it, Sam might be difficult to locate in the field. "Captain Charles Prescott. Washington."

Shot through the head, James was dead. Wil searched through the man's belongings. The Yankees had already stolen anything of consequence.

He ordered a couple of the boys to tend to the burial and mounted Poker Chip.

Under the oak where Amanda was to have contacted James, his lieutenant reported. "No sign of a struggle, sir." The bearded man pointed to hoof prints in the mucky ground. "It appears Mrs. Graham tried to make a run for it, but the Yanks nabbed her before she had the chance."

His hand curled to a fist. Why hadn't Amanda shot the bastards? Careful—he had to keep his anger in check. But he couldn't let anything happen to her—*not like the time before*. Wil bottled his rage. "Find where they've taken her."

The lieutenant eyed him. "Sir?"

"You're my best scout. I don't believe my request was difficult to understand. Report back to me once you've discovered the location."

With a salute, the lieutenant reined his mount around and followed the tracks on the ground. If any harm came to Amanda, he would kill as many Yankees as he could.

Thank goodness for small blessings. At least the Yankees hadn't searched her. Amanda had overheard tales of the liberties some soldiers had taken, but the message James had given her remained safely hidden in her hair. Guards were posted outside the tent, but they had remained gentlemanly and allowed her privacy.

The flap of the tent went up. Familiar blue eyes made Amanda think of Sam. Eager that he was willing to help her, she sat up on the cot. But it was Charles, not Sam. "Charles? I didn't know who else to contact."

Charles removed his hat. "I understand. Amanda, I think with the general's help I can get you pardoned this time, but if you're caught smuggling again—"

"They will send me to prison."

He fidgeted with his hat. "Most likely."

His message was clear. She wouldn't be able to care for Rebecca or run the farm from prison. "How's Sam?"

"Except for a letter shortly after your visit, I haven't heard from him. None of the family has. Sam has changed and not for the better."

"War often does that to men."

"Certainly he can write and let us know that he's all right. Is that too much to ask?"

"No, Charles, it's not."

Charles traced a finger over the hat's brim. "I wired him about your arrest. Some troops have moved. I don't know whether his regiment is among them."

Ashamed by the trouble she had caused, Amanda lowered her head.

"How's my niece?" Charles asked.

More than happy to discuss Rebecca, she smiled. "She's talking. Proper food and clothing will be difficult to find with the blockade."

Charles shifted his weight on his feet. "I realize that it's not an ideal solution, but let Holly take her."

Holly—a mother? What would Charles do if he knew of his wife's Confederate involvement? "That wouldn't be proper. Kate wanted me to look after her, and not having children of my own, I do enjoy her company."

"This isn't about Kate! Kate never expected her daughter to grow up in the middle of a war. Sam should have made sure she was out of the South with the first shot. I would think your primary concern would be that Rebecca has enough to eat. Holly may be an opportunist, but *I* can provide that."

Determined that Holly would never lay a hand on Rebecca, she said, "If necessary, I shall do without, but Charles, I can't give her up. I love her as much as if I had birthed her myself."

He placed his hat on his head, and once again his eyes flickered in the way that reminded her of Sam. "I will see what I can do about getting you back home to her."

"Thank you, Charles."

"If things get too difficult, don't forget where we live."

The flap fell in place, and she had the tent to herself again. She wondered where Sam was. If his regiment had moved into Virginia, then he would likely face battle soon—near her home.

Chapter Eight

WEIGHTED DOWN WITH A SADDLE over his shoulder, Sam dragged between the rows of tents. After a long night's ride, the lightweight military saddle felt heavy. Barely able to keep his eyes open, he came close to dropping the saddle and making a bed on the ground.

Corporal Tucker stepped in front of him and waved a snappy salute.

Too exhausted to return the salute, he grumbled, but couldn't remember what he had said after uttering the words.

"Only a plum fool would volunteer for reconnaissance," she said.

"Beats drilling green soldiers."

"And when you do, you drill too hard."

Sam motioned for her to leave. He finally located his tent and staggered to a halt. "Later."

"You said the same yesterday. The boys are mighty riled and you keep puttin' off their grievances, sir. Doubt I can stop them from goin' to the captain."

"Let's see if they complain once we start moving. The captain expects orders soon, and just recall what I had to work with. Most of the boys didn't know their left foot from the right, let alone how to fire a musket." He crawled into the tent. Thankfully, he had it to himself. He usually did after a night of scouting. He dropped the saddle and collapsed, using the saddle in place of pillow.

"Permission to speak freely, sir?"

"I don't recall giving you permission to enter, Corporal." Sam pulled his hat over his face. "Oh, what the hell—granted. But remember I don't give a tinker's damn what the boys think. And if you try and use the fact that you're a girl so I'll go easy on you, I'll forget my oath and march you to the captain myself. The army's no place for a female."

"Boys say you're bitchy because it's been too long since you shared the company of a woman."

Now there was a thought. If he had been fully awake he would have responded.

"Garvey says if you'd get some horizontal diversion you'd stop yellin' at them."

Irritation gave way to anger. Sam raised his hat. "What the hell does Garvey know? I reckon he has someone in mind?"

A lopsided smile formed on Jo's boyish face.

"I see. No, thank you. You're as foul smelling as the rest of us. I at least like my ladies looking and smelling like one."

"I ain't offerin' myself, sir. Garvey knows which camp ladies prefer officers."

Suddenly wide awake, Sam sat up. "If I find it necessary to attend to such needs, you can bet it won't be with one of Garvey's whores. Now tell Garvey that he comes to me personally next time, or he will be in irons. For some reason, he's got the sick notion that you can wheedle me. Tell him that if any of the boys wish to speak to the captain, I will escort them personally. Dismissed."

The girl soldier saluted and about-faced.

"Jo . . ."

Straightening her shoulders, she returned to attention.

"Tell them, I will try not to ask so much, but the Rebs are going to be ready. We've waited too long to move, and it's given them the time they need to prepare."

Jo swallowed noticeably at the news.

"Unlike some of us," he said, "you're free to leave."

" 'Less you turn me in, you can't be rid of me that easy."

"I gave you my word."

"Thank you, sir." She slapped a hand to her forehead and withdrew an envelope from her pocket. "Almost forgot. This came."

Sam held up the envelope to the light. He rubbed his eyes—a telegram from Charles. Amanda was in custody. *Dammit, Amanda.*

"Bad news?" Jo asked.

"A friend has been captured."

"He'll be exchanged."

What should he do about Rebecca? He buried his head in his hands. "She's not a soldier. She was caught smuggling supplies for the Rebs."

"The secesh lady who came to camp. The boys wondered who she might be."

Amanda's visit had obviously been the source of tongue-wagging rumors. No wonder the boys thought he required the company of a woman. "She was a friend of my wife's."

"Where is she, sir?"

Sam checked the telegram. "Camp Brightwood."

"That's not far. I bet we can put in a word or two to help her."

"We?"

Her grin widened. "You don't expect me to let you outta my sight. Why, you might just fall head over heels for a real lady and resign. If Garvey gets promoted, he'd be even uglier."

"Thank you, Jo." When he had discovered her true identity, she hadn't been the only one to gain an ally.

For some reason, the Yankees were stalling her release. Charles had assured her the general's order would arrive within a day or two. Four days had come and gone, and Amanda remained under constant guard, only allowed to leave the tent to tend to basic necessities.

After pacing the length of the tent, then back again, she called the guard. "I demand to speak to the colonel."

The guard poked his head through the tent flap. "Sorry, ma'am."

" 'Sorry, ma'am.' " She gritted her teeth and stamped a foot. "Sorry— I bet you are. Get me Captain Prescott!"

"Captain Prescott has returned to Washington, ma'am."

Washington? Charles had returned to Washington without saying goodbye? Amanda picked up *A Tale of Two Cities* from the cot. After flipping through several pages, she tossed the book at the guard. He ducked, and the book sailed into the unfortunate soldier behind him. "Next time, I'll make certain it's breakable!"

The unlucky officer rubbed his shoulder. "I shall remember that."

Amanda blinked. Sam had sprouted a moustache since Christmas. "Sam, it really is you." Comforted that he was alive and fit, she ran into the morning air to greet him. "Sam, what are you doing here? Charles said he hadn't heard from you. I feared you had been sent to Virginia."

His eyes reflected their disappointment as he removed his hat. He handed her the book. "Amanda, you're free to go. Your horse should be here any minute."

"Just like that? You obviously know why I was arrested."

"How long have you been smuggling supplies for the Rebs?"

As she had feared, he wasn't taking the discovery well. "I wouldn't carry arms. I hope you realize that."

"How long?"

Her heart sank. If he wouldn't take that fact into account, he wasn't likely to forgive her actions. "Since John's death. Boys were getting sick, and it was a way I could help. I also needed the money."

"I have tried sending you money."

"This isn't about Rebecca—or you. I have a farm to run. I lost any chance to a pension when my husband chose to wear gray."

His gaze grew harsh. "I'm sorry, Amanda, but Rebecca will be returning to the North."

"Not Rebecca—she's like my own."

"You should have thought of that when you decided to steal supplies."

"Steal? I'll have you know, I don't *steal* supplies. If the Yankees hadn't cut off the South from the rest of the world, there would be no need for my services. I was helping the sick and wounded—nothing more. You said you respected the Colonel, but you make a mockery of his memory by not giving me the same benefit of the doubt."

"And you make a mockery of Kate's."

A horse nickered. A young soldier led three horses down the aisle between tents toward them. Red jerked on the lead, almost yanking it from the boy's hands. *A corporal.* Was he the one who had shot John? No, Sam certainly wouldn't be that cruel. Even now.

"Easy, Red," she said.

The stallion stopped tugging on the corporal's arm. Odd—but the corporal's gait was refined, almost delicate, when he walked. Amanda patted Red on the neck. The horse shook his head playfully. His coat gleamed blood red as if freshly curried. "He's been treated well. Are you escorting me?"

The corporal handed the reins of a sorrel to Sam.

"I have orders to make certain you leave Maryland," Sam replied. "This is Corporal Tucker. He will be accompanying us."

The corporal tipped his hat. "Mrs. Graham . . ."

The soldier's voice was as peculiar as his gait—high-pitched and wheezy.

Sam's hands went around Amanda's waist to help her mount up. Once in the saddle, she straightened and met Sam's gaze. "Rebecca will stay with me. I'm her mama."

"I've made up my mind, Amanda. My sister in Maine will care for her."

"At least you're not fool enough to consider Holly."

His eyes narrowed.

"Who shall I expect to cross the lines to collect her?" Amanda asked.

Sam grumbled an oath and mounted the sorrel. As the corporal climbed aboard his horse, his movement seemed fluid—maybe even graceful. Convinced she was seeing things, Amanda shook her head. Corporal Tucker was simply one of the many underage boys, but Rebecca—she had to convince Sam about Rebecca.

Sam brought the sorrel even with Red. "Ready?"

She squeezed Red forward, and Corporal Tucker joined them. They made their way past the tents and out of camp.

"You're from Virginia, Mrs. Graham?" the corporal asked.

"That's right. I'm a widow." *Regret.* Was it her imagination that she had seen regret in the corporal's eyes? "I live near Fredericksburg with my three servants and Rebecca—*my* daughter."

Sam gave no hint that he had heard her.

The corporal removed a gauntlet and stretched his hand. His build was smaller than most men's, and his hand was even tinier. He was much lighter on the rein than Sam—more like herself. "Are you also from Maine, Corporal?" she asked.

"Minnesota, actually."

"You're certainly a long way from home."

"Didn't want me in Minnesota." He chuckled and traded a sly glance with Sam. "So I joined up with the Mainers, thinkin' they would be like the boys back home. You know—loggers and trappers. Turns out they ain't nothin' but a bunch of boat makers and fishermen with a few farmers thrown in for good measure." He went on to gripe about drilling rigors and marching—on and on without really saying anything.

Relieved when it came time to rest the horses, Amanda thought she'd be spared of further chatter, but Sam grabbed a pair of field glasses and climbed a nearby ridge. At the top, he raised the field glasses to his eyes.

"Might as well rest up, ma'am," the corporal said. "Got a few miles before reachin' the river."

Amanda watched Sam on the hill. "Are you expecting company?"

"Not to my way of knowin', but the lieutenant don't like surprises neither. He gets ornery if things don't go his way."

"I bet he does."

Corporal Tucker withdrew some paper and tobacco from a pocket in the faded blue jacket. He sprinkled the tobacco on the paper for a cigarette.

Amanda regarded the corporal curiously. Boys often smoked to show their manliness, but something didn't seem quite right. Once she had caught her sister sneaking a smoke behind the barn. The corporal's fine-boned hands reminded her of Alice's.

He struck a match to the cigarette and inhaled. "Ain't my place, ma'am, but he was frettin' something fierce about you."

Amanda glanced to the ridge. Sam continued scanning the valley—almost as if looking for someone. *Confederates must be in the valley.* Her heart skipped a beat. "How do you mean?"

Smoke plumed from the corporal's nostrils. "When he found out you were arrested."

Amanda focused on the pistol strapped to the corporal's side and felt sick to her stomach. Was it the same gun that had killed John? In spite of the warm day, she shivered. John was dead, but Sam was very much alive.

She climbed the steep embankment and tripped on a rock. Nearly falling, she caught a foot in her skirt, but Sam got a grip on her arm before she tumbled down.

"Why didn't you warn me you were coming up?" He hoisted her to the top.

"After what was said..." She brushed the dirt from her skirt. "I wasn't sure you would speak with me."

"I didn't mean...Yes, I did. What you're doing is dangerous. I worry—"

"That Rebecca will lose me. She won't. Does that mean you won't be sending your sister for her?"

He lifted the field glasses to his eyes without an answer.

From her vantage point, patchwork fields were spread between the hardwood forests in the valley below. Nothing seemed out of the ordinary. "I fret too. I worry that Rebecca's papa will be among the fallen."

He lowered the field glasses. "We will be moving to Virginia soon."

The war would soon be on her doorstep, and Sam would be part of it. The cipher remained tucked in her hair. How could she deliver such a message without hurting him? "Do you intend on taking Rebecca from me?"

"If I'm a stranger to her, what would my sister be?" His sword rattled as he clambered on a boulder to a higher vantage point. Bending down, he raised the field glasses.

"Who are you looking for?"

"Rebs. Before we left camp, I received word a scouting party had crossed the river."

Careful not to stumble, Amanda lifted her skirts and stepped up on a rock. When Sam straightened, her added height put her face-to-face with him.

"The war is going to get close—too close maybe. Promise me that if you hear the guns, you won't stay to defend the farm."

"I can't make a promise like that."

"If necessary, you can rebuild. Amanda, I've witnessed firsthand what happens to civilians who resist. It's going to get worse, and many officers pretend they don't see."

She unwrapped the knot in her hair and removed the message from underneath.

"What's this?" he asked.

"Federal troop movements and strengths. I refuse to be part of the killing."

A soft quiet returned his eyes. "You constantly amaze me." A horse neighed in the distance, and Sam returned to gazing through the field glasses. "Rebs. " He seized her hand and nearly dragged her down the steep embankment toward the horses.

Her skirt tangled around her legs. Amanda lifted it higher, but gunfire echoed from a clump of trees. Sam urged her to run faster. When they were halfway down the hill, Red's reins slipped through the corporal's fingers. The stallion bolted.

A bullet whirred overhead. More shells flew in their direction—all aimed high.

Her foot twisted at an odd angle. She pitched forward and began sliding down. She lost Sam's protective grasp. Headfirst, she flailed, struggling to latch onto a handhold.

Near the bottom, Sam gripped her arm, and her downward motion halted.

"Sam, go ahead. They won't hurt me."

Sam waved the corporal on, and he helped her sit up.

Muddled and wobbly, she attempted to get to her feet. A stabbing pain shot through her ankle. "My ankle—I think it might be broken or sprained."

He gathered her in his arms and carried her. Out of breath, he put her down but left an arm around her waist for support.

"Sam, they won't harm me. Run, before it's too late."

A bullet sailed overhead, and he cast a glance to the haven of the woods. "I can't." He gave her arm a gentle squeeze and made certain she kept her balance before letting go. He paced a dozen steps away and drew his pistol.

"No!" Amanda limped toward him. Spasms shot through her ankle.

Grass and dirt flew in the air as a bullet hit the ground near Sam's feet. He didn't flinch.

"Hold your fire!" a voice called from the woods. Astride Poker Chip, Wil rode into the open. "Prescott, it's been a while."

Five soldiers clad in gray—all with their weapons trained on Sam—formed a line next to Wil.

"He was helping me," Amanda said.

"I can see that," Wil replied dryly. "I apologize for not arriving sooner, Amanda. Did they harm you?"

"No, but I twisted my ankle just now."

"I will have the doctor examine it when we return to camp." Wil holstered his pistol and motioned for his men to lower their weapons. "Put the gun down, Prescott. I won't have an old friend shot."

"Old friend? I can't say I fancy your greeting."

Wil dismounted. "How was I to know it was you?"

Sam lowered the pistol. "Captain—"

"Colonel," Wil corrected.

"Really? I thought the Rebs would have made you a brigadier."

"*Touché*—imagine my surprise that you remain a lieutenant."

Reassured that friendship could remain intact in spite of the war, Amanda hobbled toward Wil. His dark eyes came to rest on her as she limped nearer. He lent her a steadying hand, and she gratefully accepted his aid. "Thank you, Wil,"

Wil shifted his focus back to Sam. "Prescott, I saw hesitation in your eyes. In battle, you would have been dead."

Sam met Wil's gaze in a challenge. "You always were a bastard."

Wil grinned. "At last, the truth." His grin vanished, and he met Sam's threat. "Whatever it takes to keep my men alive."

Sam straightened to attention and saluted. Wil returned it.

From the cover of the woods, one of Wil's men muttered a string of oaths and dragged Corporal Tucker behind him. He tossed the corporal at Wil's feet, shaking a bloody hand. "She bit me! You heard right—*she*. A she-devil."

Wil threw his free hand to his side and laughed.

So that was the corporal's secret. But the pain. Strong arms caught Amanda as blackness drifted over her.

When Amanda came to, she was lying on a cot with her corset laces loosened and the top buttons of her dress undone to help her breathe. A dull ache lingered in her head, and a man's face hovered over her. She placed a hand to her temple and attempted to rise. "Sam?"

"Prescott's not here." Wil gently pushed her back to the cot.

Amanda blinked. His face came into focus, and he stared at her in concern.

"What happened? Where's Sam?"

He placed a tin cup to her lips. "Here, drink this."

She took a sip and nearly choked. *Whiskey.* She had no notion how men tolerated the bitter drink.

"We're reduced to folk remedies."

His words reminded her that she had lost the supplies. With difficulty, she gulped the remainder of the drink. The ache in her head faded, and she became aware of a dull throb in her ankle. Wil sat so close that warmth radiated from his body. He smelled of the sweet aroma of cigars. "Wil, what have you done with Sam?"

His jaw tensed. "Nothing. After spraining your ankle, you swooned. I brought you back to camp. I presume Prescott returned to Yankee camp, along with his *corporal*. Women in the army. What will the Yanks think of next?"

Suddenly drowsy, she closed her eyes. "How is it different from women smuggling supplies?"

"My good woman, you're not pretending to be something you're not. If I would have suggested shipping the corporal off to prison like a man, she would have probably broken down in tears."

"So all women are nothing more than teary-eyed females?" Not only had the whiskey made her sleepy, it had loosened her tongue.

"I don't believe I said that," Wil grumbled. "I will have you know I was ready to storm the Yankee camp to rescue you. The gratitude I get is taunts."

Amanda lifted an arm, pretending to carry a sword, and giggled. "Dashing to the end."

"Now you mock me. Amanda, I believe you're drunk."

"Drunk? I've never—" She hiccupped. "If I am, I have you to thank for it."

"I have been accused of many things, but deliberately getting a woman drunk is not among them. I don't need to resort to such tactics." He leaned forward to kiss her lips.

As the kiss grew more intimate, she wanted to resist. His hand went under her skirt and squeezed her posterior. She pushed away from his embrace. "Please don't. It's not right."

His gaze rested where the top buttons of her dress had been unfastened.

Amanda rebuttoned them. "You're the one who took liberties with me. You are no gentleman, Colonel Jackson."

A devilish spark entered his eyes. "I admit that I'm no gentleman, but I'd never take liberties of a lady—at least not without her consent."

"I did not tell you to unfasten my dress *or* loosen my corset."

"In the future I shall remember that. Propriety is more important than ministering aid."

"Ministering aid..." Disgusted, Amanda rose, but her ankle stabbed a painful reminder.

Wil's arms went around her waist to help steady her. He wrung a cloth in a basin and wrapped it around her ankle. The cool, gentle touch felt good—a side of him she had never witnessed before. "Where did you learn to tend like that?" she asked.

"When you've been in the army as long as I have, you learn to take care of yourself—as well as others. Sometimes it's a long wait before supplies arrive—if ever."

"I'm sorry I lost them."

"There was no hidden meaning. Your safety is more important than a few bags of laudanum. As you may recall, I've been stationed in some isolated outposts."

"Like the Northwest—when the Indians came down with measles?"

"Yes."

In a peculiar sort of way his voice had grown detached. "Did she die of measles?" Amanda asked.

"Did who die of measles?"

"The woman you refuse to discuss."

He crossed his arms and leaned back with a grin. "I thought you didn't want to hear about my kept women."

"Lord knows why sometimes, but I value our friendship. Until you let *her* go, I don't think you can truly love another."

The emotionless mask slipped into place, and he got up from the cot. "I have some matters to attend to. I will leave you to your privacy."

"Wil..."

He snatched his hat from the field desk and glanced over his shoulder.

"I do care," she said.

"Prescott was concerned about leaving you in my care. I assured him you would be safe here." He shoved his hat on his head and left the tent.

Alone again, Amanda wondered who the mysterious woman from his past had been. Something haunted him. Something he couldn't let go. He had sidetracked her reference to measles. Had she died from them?

Chapter Nine

Near Richmond, Virginia
Late June 1862

SHADED BY OAK TREES, THE SLEEPY MILL was almost idyllic. In the sweltering heat, the pond rippled. Orders were to keep marching. The Yankees were on the run. Guns clattered beyond the next hill. Wil cued Poker to a walk. On the run, indeed—the Yanks were probably dug in.

The column forded a creek. Men in gray and butternut hobbled toward them, retreating to the rear. Soon, he'd have the chance to kill a mob and be rewarded for it. If he survived. He didn't dwell on the thought. Duty came first. Hadn't Amanda equated his inability of revealing weakness to fear? Fancy notion.

The guns got closer, and the brigadier brought the command order to form the regiment to the right. "Colonel, you must break the Yankee line at all costs. Is that clear?"

All costs. The fight must not have been going well. "It is, sir," Wil replied with a salute. He called the company commanders and relayed the orders.

The brigades on both flanks were already engaged. An aide led Poker to the rear. The Yankee line must break, and he envisioned the blue line dividing in his mind. *All costs.* He raised his sword. Forward.

The sun sank behind the ridge, and they marched past the shattered ranks of wounded and dying Confederate soldiers. They reached the crest. Rows of soldiers in blue waited on the opposite hillside. Sheets of flame illuminated the growing twilight as canister tore through the ranks.

Wil lengthened his stride, waving his sword. He raced down the hill into waist-deep water. A deadly lead spray struck more men. Bayonets gleamed in the fading daylight. He slogged through the mud and charged up the hillside with a war cry—a yell that had brought sheer terror in many bluecoats' hearts.

His men hadn't fired a shot, yet the Yankees scattered from their breastworks. Finally in range, Wil gave the order to fire. More Yankees scrambled, but an officer on horseback with his hat on his sword tried to rally his men. The Union line was crumbling.

Another blue line fired. Nearly blinded by the flames, Wil could only make out layers of smoke and blazing cannon. He could barely breathe. Word traveled down their line. *Cavalry.* Men on horses leveled their swords at the Confederate line.

"Fire!" Wil ordered.

Among the screams, frenzied horses trampled wounded soldiers. Half of their regiment was dead. The Yankee line broke, but with darkness setting in, the hole had come too late to make use of it.

Early morning mist blocked Sam's view of the hillside. Wounded lay on the field where they had fallen. Their groans and wails had filled the night. After a week of heavy fighting, hundreds were dead. The captain and Private Garvey were among those killed. With Garvey gone, no one was left to blackmail the girl soldier. Or would another take his place? In spite of his initial doubts, he'd hate to lose a soldier with Jo's determination and grit simply because of her sex.

The sun slowly burned the mist away. Rebel losses must have equalled their own. On one occasion they had faced his old commander's regiment. If he ever met Jackson in battle, one of them would wind up dead. How could he kill the person who had prepared him the most?

He couldn't shoot Jackson—anymore than Colonel Graham. But Jackson fought mechanically. Former comrades or not, they were enemies. Sam covered his mouth and fought back a yawn. War wasn't supposed to be like this.

The mist cleared, and Sam shuddered. On the lower slope, gray-clad bodies covered the hillside. Losses in the hundreds? *More like thousands.* Many were dead. But the rest. He closed his eyes. Enough of the wretched souls were alive, lending the field a grisly crawling effect.

Chapter Ten

ANOTHER MONTH PASSED. Amanda's ankle had healed, but with heavy fighting in the Shenandoah Valley and around Richmond, she had made no more supply runs. Federal reserves were practically on her doorstep near Fredericksburg, yet when a letter arrived the previous day by courier, it came as no surprise. With Wil's many contacts, someone capable of getting correspondence across the lines was nothing out of the ordinary for him.

Instead of the specifics for another supply run, Amanda had unfolded the letter, not to Wil's familiar scrawl, but Holly's neatly penned signature at the bottom of the page.

Holly had given Wil up for dead. On one occasion, Charles had nearly stumbled on the cached supplies in the cellar. Meet her in Dumfries in a week's time, or she would dispose of them.

Quick and to the point. If Amanda failed to hear from Wil, she would fetch them.

In the August heat, she paused from the tedious quilting drudgery and fanned her face. Even with every window in the farmhouse opened wide, not a curtain ruffled. Ready to wilt, she'd rather think about a tall glass of lemonade rather than blankets and quilts, but Rebecca would be ready for the trundle bed come fall.

"Miss Amanda," Frieda said.

"I was thinking that the Colonel's been gone for over a year now. The daylilies are in bloom in the bottomland. After it cools some this evening, I shall pick a bouquet for his grave."

"You ain't bin thinkin' of da Colonel. You bin frettin' since dat letter come yesterday."

Amanda curled her fingers around the old woman's bony hand and gave it a gentle squeeze. "I need to make another supply run."

Sightless eyes widened. "It ain't safe."

"I'll meet my contact in Dumfries. That's well away from any fighting."

"I don't like it. Not one bit. Why, I'se half a notion to tell dat colonel friend of yours what I think."

Frieda would have liked the idea even less if she knew the letter hadn't been from Wil. "We'll talk about it later."

Frieda pointed a gnarled finger. "Won't make no difference. I ain't changin' my mind. And if you know what's good for you..." She cocked her head. "Riders comin'."

Amanda heeded Frieda's warning and scrambled for John's hunting rifle. On a couple of occasions she had shooed Yankees stealing vegetables from the garden. With a solid grip on the rifle, she peered out the front window.

Four soldiers in faded blue entered the farmyard on horseback.

She hurried outside. Near the picket fence, she aimed the rifle.

The man leading the group wore lieutenant's bars. Briefly, she thought of Sam as he brought his gray horse to a halt and tipped his hat. "Ma'am."

"We don't have any food to spare. Now ride back the way you came."

Sweat beaded on his forehead. He waved his hat to fan his face. "We mean you no harm. We've had a long, hard ride and hoped to fill our canteens."

The lieutenant could have been Sam. With a twinge of guilt, she hoped that if he were thirsty, some Southern woman would respond in kindness. Amanda lowered the rifle and motioned to the well at the side of the house. "Help yourself."

"Thank you kindly, ma'am." He barked orders to the men.

Soldiers dismounted in perfect military unison and led the horses to the well. Judging from the thick dust covering their jackets and hats, Amanda guessed they must have been in the saddle for days.

A red-haired private with freckles covering the bridge of his nose cranked the bucket from the well. They passed the bucket from man to man for the horses to drink. A light, almost delicate-striding corporal stepped next to the private. *Corporal Tucker?*

She blinked back the vision of the girl soldier. This corporal had a blackened face, hinting at whisker growth. Under the harsh glare, she had mistaken him for Tucker.

The lieutenant filled his canteen last. "Much obliged, ma'am. I'm Lieutenant Sheldon."

Amanda shoved a damp, stray lock away from her face. "Mrs. John Graham." Thunder rumbled, and she looked to the sky. Good, clouds were building. While they were in need of rain, the sound had made her fear the guns of war had finally reached her home. "I would appreciate it if you'd hurry." She waved a hand in front of her face. "It's mighty hot out here."

"My apologies. We don't mean to keep you from your chores."

At least they were polite. Amanda loosened her grip on the gun.

The lieutenant muttered to one of the men while fanning his face with his hat.

Uneasy once more, Amanda stepped back, running straight into the red-haired private. Before she could react, he snatched the rifle from her hands.

"This is an outrage, Lieutenant. How dare you repay my kindness with deceit."

His smile vanished. "I'm sorry, ma'am. The captain wants to see you for questioning."

"For what reason?"

The lieutenant grasped her hand, signaling her to come with him. The pressure of his grip warned her that he meant business. "*Stealing* supplies."

"Stealing? I have not made any supply runs since—"

"Your arrest. Tell that to the captain, Mrs. Graham. It's your choice. You come along peacefully, or I can throw you over my horse kicking and screaming."

"I have a young child inside."

The private snickered behind her back. "Bet you hid morphine in his nappies."

Prideful, she raised her head, refusing to give them the pleasure of seeing her make a scene. "Yankees," she muttered under her breath.

More snickering.

Amanda cast the thought of calling for Ezra from her mind. *Best to do as they say, for now.*

The lieutenant helped her onto the gray horse, before mounting behind her. With his body so near, the sultry day seemed hotter. Thankfully, he remained a gentleman and didn't take advantage of their proximity.

"I shall give your captain a piece of my mind," she said.

"I fancy you will." He cued the gray forward.

As they trotted toward the lane, Frieda stepped onto the porch.

"Frieda!"

The lieutenant clamped a hand over her mouth, and she bit the fleshy part of his palm. He swore, but his hand fell away.

"Frieda!"

But they had already traveled down the lane.

The lieutenant shook his bleeding hand. "Mrs. Graham, I assure you, no one will harm you."

Amanda turned slightly in the saddle. "You have already lied to me. Why should I believe you now?"

"The captain would see me in stocks if anything happened to you."

The sun sank beyond the horizon when they arrived at a camp near the river. No tents were pitched, alerting Amanda the regiment was an army on the move. The lieutenant helped her from the horse's back and escorted her through camp. Apparently the only woman, she grew self-conscious of men's eyes following her. She pretended not to notice the lewd stares.

A number of horses stood tethered among the breezes by the water. An officer slept on the bare ground. Her heart skipped a beat. *A scouting party.* Federal forces would soon be very near her home. In spite of the heat, she shivered.

The lieutenant halted by a wagon. *Oh God.* She nearly retched. Like some meat wagon, bloody bodies filled it. One dead soldier was missing an arm and leg. Another, part of his face. Agonized faces, grinning in the sightlessness of death. Hands. Feet. Even a disembodied head. Bile reached the back of her throat.

Amanda clamped a hand over her mouth, but someone grasped her arm and led her away.

"Amanda . . ."

"Sam?" The man rescuing her from the grisly scene was Sam, and he wore the shoulder bars of a captain. Since their last meeting, he had sprouted a beard. She touched his face to make certain he really stood next to her. "Why didn't your men tell me you were the captain? I would have come."

He straightened to a proper officer's stance. "I had business to tend to. I told Sheldon to use my name. I'm sorry if they frightened you."

"I don't envy the task of loading the wagons."

He rubbed his eyes. "You get used to it after a while."

"I don't believe that. I've been fretting you might be among them."

His blue eyes flickered, but his thoughts seemed elsewhere. "We've been through some heavy fighting. But as you can see, I'm unharmed."

For now. He didn't need to say the words. He showed her through camp, and men's eyes continued to follow her every move. "They don't mean any harm, Amanda."

"I reckon not, but I've heard talk of Yankee soldiers. Some farms near mine have been ransacked, and a neighbor's servant . . ." She couldn't say the words. "She put up a struggle, and my neighbor was able to frighten them off. I'm fortunate we're a little more out of the way."

"I won't deny what's happened. I'm relieved you haven't encountered any problems with foraging expeditions."

A couple of guards stood posted near the horses munching feed.

"Foraging? Is that what you call it?"

"Amanda, it doesn't happen here. I won't have them waging war on civilians. There's enough fighting already. Any man who doesn't pay for what he takes shall be brought up on charges. Are you satisfied?"

She hadn't meant to quarrel. "Why did you send for me?"

He ran a hand through his whiskers and looked out at the ripples on the river. "I wondered if you've been making any supply runs?"

Had he found out about Holly's letter? Not likely. Holly certainly wouldn't have informed him. And with death surrounding them, her heart sank. Selfish—maybe, but she had hoped he would ask about Rebecca. "Not since my arrest."

"Good." He turned to her, but his gaze fixed on a spot beyond her. "I'll see that you're escorted home." He stepped in the direction of the horses.

She thrust an arm in front of him. "That's all? I had hoped—"

"For what? Take a look around you, Amanda. None of us knows who will be here tomorrow."

Amanda dropped her hand to her side. "All the more reason to ask about your daughter. I shall walk home, Captain."

She turned toward the path leading away from the river, but Sam caught her arm. She shot him a piercing look.

He raised his hands in a truce. "If you had still been running supplies, I would have arrested you for your own goddamned safety."

"I will thank you kindly not to take the Lord's name in vain." For a brief moment, Amanda saw concern cross his face. She should have guessed he had been thinking of her safety. "Sam, let's not quarrel."

"You're right, Amanda. We should always speak as if it may be our last chance."

Did he have a feeling? She shuddered. He called for one of the guards, and Corporal Tucker hustled toward them. The girl soldier had blackened her face with charcoal for the effect of whisker growth. At the back of her mind lingered the dark thought that she was face-to-face with John's killer.

"See that Mrs. Graham gets home safely," Sam said.

"Yes, sir." With a salute, Tucker ducked under the rope to fetch a horse.

"Sam, I don't believe you brought me here just so you could ask if I'm running supplies."

"I was concerned for your welfare—and Rebecca's." He turned toward the main body of camp.

"She's talking. Says Mama. She doesn't even know she has a papa. I can bring her here if you're uncomfortable stopping by."

He halted in his tracks. "An army camp is no place for a little girl."

The corporal led two horses.

"I shall accompany Mrs. Graham," Sam said.

"Yes, sir. Is there anything else, sir?"

"No." Sam helped Amanda mount, then climbed aboard the second horse.

Although the horse wasn't the same crooked-legged bay as on their
first meeting, the gelding belonged to Sam. Of that fact, she had no
doubt. Tucker had somehow known he would make the trip. Amanda
squeezed her mount to a walk, and they rode out of camp in silence.

Lightning flashed in the distance. Thankfully, enough moonlight
filtered through the trees to see the road.

"When did you become captain?" she asked, attempting to break
the tension.

"At Beaver Dam Creek when Captain Pierson was killed."

"Oh—I'm sorry." A grave look reflected in the depths of his eyes—
something haunting. She had seen the same expression in John when
he recalled the war with the Mexicans.

"The Rebs blew off his head."

She bit her lip. "Sam, if you want to talk, I'll listen to whatever you
have to say."

"You're untouched by all of this. Why would I want to involve you?"

"Untouched? I saw the bodies."

"I saw them die."

Clouds spread across the moon. Glad for the cover of darkness so
he wouldn't see the tears filling her eyes, she brushed them away.

"Amanda, I often recall your laughter on the night we had dinner.
How you managed to laugh when you were mourning the loss of your
husband, I'll never know. But when my spirit sinks, the thought of
your laughter picks me up again. You told me not to say goodbye . . . "

Amanda's throat constricted. "Unless you mean forever."

In silence, they rode up the tree-lined lane to the farmhouse.
Lamps burned brightly inside. The scene was peaceful—no one frantically searching for her—almost as if she had spent the day visiting
Mama and Alice in Fredericksburg. Frieda must have sensed there had
been no danger. She slid from the horse's back and tied him to the rail.

With her walking stick in hand, Frieda came onto the porch.

"You must be Frieda," Sam said.

The old woman chuckled. "I is."

While Sam secured the horses, Amanda greeted Frieda. "The captain
has come to see Rebecca."

"Dulcie in da parlor with her. I'll set an extra plate on da table for
supper."

Sam joined them. "That won't be necessary. I won't be staying long."

"I coulda' swear diff'rent," Frieda muttered.

Inside the farmhouse, Sam removed his hat. His gaze was drawn to Rebecca, toddling across the floor. Amanda gathered the little girl into her arms, and she thought she saw a tear come into his eye. "This is your papa, Miss Rebecca."

He offered a finger, but Rebecca began to cry.

"I reckon the only menfolk she's used to is Ezra—and occasionally Wil."

"It's all right, Amanda. I don't expect to be greeted with open arms. I'm a stranger. I have something for her." From his pocket, Sam produced a wood carving—a horse polished to a fine finish, looking remarkably like Red. He gave it to Rebecca.

He did care.

Rebecca clutched the toy in a chubby hand.

"Tell Dulcie when she's ready to head north to contact my brother."

Amanda pointed to the carving. "You made this yourself, didn't you?"

"I've been a wretched father. I wanted her to have something from me." Dust flew as he replaced his hat on his head. "Bye, Amanda."

She barely could catch her breath as he retreated from the room.

Outside, Sam tightened the bay gelding's girth. The crooked-legged bay had died of distemper, and the sorrel had been killed at Beaver Dam Creek along with the captain and scores of others. He should have told Amanda about the week-long battle, but she had suffered enough. He hadn't meant for her to see the wagon carrying the dead either.

A lamp flickered on upstairs—probably Amanda's bedroom window. He must be tired. Even the thought of her readying for bed did nothing to arouse him. Not so long ago, he had been envious of Jackson and his relationship with Amanda. But dreams of dying, or maybe it was a feeling, were becoming more frequent. He only hoped Jackson treated her well.

In New Mexico, Jackson had kept company with an Indian woman. It wasn't that unusual for military men stationed so far from home, but he never thought of Jackson as the sort to settle down. War did strange things to men, including seasoned veterans of the Mexican War like Jackson.

With that thought, Sam untied the bay from the rail.

"Mr. Sam . . ." A cane's steady tapping traveled from the porch steps down the brick walkway toward him. Frieda propped her walking stick against the picket fence. "I know what you feelin', Mr. Sam."

"I doubt that."

"You think you goin' to die soon. Even if you do, how will hurtin' Miss Amanda make her feel better?"

"How am I hurting Amanda?"

"What will she tell Becca? Dat her papa brave on da battlefield, but he broke her mama's heart?"

Incoherent babbling—the old Negro woman must be mad. He put a foot in the stirrup. "I need to be leaving."

"Miss Amanda a good woman."

"I'm aware of that."

" 'Less you tells her, she won't fill in da part 'bout how much you love her. You went west so she don't find out. Da Colonel gone now. No need to hide it no more."

There seemed no way of fooling the old woman. He took his foot from the stirrup. "I thought she and Jackson—"

"Dat's what everyone thinks, but he ain't da kind to make promises. Before da Colonel die, I know it. I don't get da same feelin' with you."

"The last thing I want is to put Amanda through that kind of grief again."

"Da dreams could be a warnin', Mr. Sam."

How had she known?

"You da only one who can stop Miss Amanda."

"Stop her? From what?"

"She goin' to run supplies again."

"But she told me—"

"She ain't run no supplies since you last see her, but she got a note yesterday by courier. She say she goin' to make another run."

He clenched his hand. "If she makes a run anytime soon, she could get caught in the middle of things."

"Dat's why I tell you. I kept dat plate waitin' on da table for supper." The old woman meandered to the house with a chuckle.

Sam tethered the bay to the rail. Once he was inside the door, Dulcie pulled him into the kitchen. "Miss Amanda upstairs with Becca, but you make yourself to home."

Although he was intent on speaking with Amanda, he caught a whiff of fresh-baked bread and his will faded. The regiment was low on rations, and almost a week had passed since his last decent meal.

Frieda placed a loaf along with a mound of butter on the table. "I bake it dis mornin' afore it get too hot."

"But my men—"

"I give you some to take back." The old woman grinned and turned to the pantry.

Satisfied that his men would be able to share, he threw his dark-blue jacket across the chair. Dust went flying. Dulcie helped him brush the dirt away. He unstrapped his sword before taking a seat at the table.

"I detect a plot," Sam said.

As Dulcie cut the bread, his mouth watered. His stomach rumbled, and he resisted the urge to snatch the entire loaf from her hands.

"Why Mr. Sam, whatever do you think we be plottin'?" she said, giggling like a schoolgirl. She set a plate with the sliced bread and a thick pat of butter in front of him.

He bit into the crust. The sweet taste had been worth the wait.

Frieda brought over a platter of cold chicken and fresh vegetables from the garden.

"Is Amanda really going to make another run?" he asked.

"I wouldn't lie to you 'bout dat. I afraid. I raise her from a baby like she one of my own, and nothin' scare me like dis."

He polished off the chicken and briefly thought that he should feel guilt. His men had nothing but hardtack and a little salt pork left. But he felt no shame and devoured a raw carrot.

"Let me get somethin' to wash dat down."

"You're too kind, Frieda. You too, Dulcie. I will talk to Amanda."

"Talk to me about what? I thought you had left, Captain Prescott."

In a plain white robe, Amanda stood in the doorway with her yellow hair braided down her back. The meal must have revived him. The cotton material of her robe was moist with sweat and clung to her breasts. Sam didn't dare stand to greet Amanda. If he did, she would certainly realize how long he had been physically deprived of a woman. "Frieda invited me in for supper."

Dulcie scooted out the back door, and Amanda slid into the chair across from him. "I'm glad you changed your mind."

Her proximity was almost more than he could bear. He shifted his gaze to the empty plate.

"Sam, I was fretting something fierce after you said goodbye."

"It's a feeling I've had."

Comprehension filtered into her green eyes. "Did Frieda tell you . . . ?"

Hunched over her walking stick, Frieda traipsed across the brick floor to the door.

"Frieda!"

He grasped Amanda's hand and squeezed it. "It wasn't Frieda. It's a feeling I've had of my own."

"A feeling doesn't necessarily make it fact."

He caressed the back of her hand. "True."

She got up and began clearing dishes away. "Have you had enough to eat, Captain?"

Think—he needed to keep his head clear, and the more he thought about touching Amanda, the less he was able to concentrate. "Why didn't you tell me about the supply run?"

Plates clattered to the table. "Frieda had no right telling you."

"She's worried."

"I won't be arrested again."

"Amanda . . . " Frustrated that she had no concept of the danger, he blew out a breath. "I'm not talking about being arrested. You've already guessed why we're here. A few miles behind us is a corps of infantry."

"I won't be traveling near any fighting."

Sam pounded a fist on the table, and Amanda jumped. "I always knew Jackson was a scheming son of a bitch, but I never thought he'd risk a woman's life."

Amanda's eyes blazed. "I'll thank you to watch your mouth when under my roof, Captain. And what makes you think Wil is behind this?"

No matter what Frieda had said, Amanda was loyal to Jackson. "After our last meeting, it's easy to guess who's behind the smuggling. Promise me that you won't make the run. Amanda, it's not safe."

"Why is it womenfolk are supposed to keep their places and stay out of harm's way when we're perfectly capable of carrying out many of the tasks men say we cannot? If I can stop one mama, wife, or sweetheart from feeling the grief I have, then I have succeeded in my purpose. And quite frankly . . ." Her face flushed. "I need the money."

And he was partly to blame. With only a few cents in his pocket, he laid two dimes and a quarter on the table. "It's all I have."

"Sam, this isn't about Rebecca. I know the difficulty of getting mail across the lines."

At least she didn't question his lack of support—it had been down-right erratic since the war had begun. Sam stood and collected his weapons belt from the table. "Then I guess there's nothing left to say."

Amanda stepped in front of him. "I also know why you had to ask me not to make the run."

Stray locks clung to her damp neck. More than anything, he wanted to draw her into his arms and taste her mouth. Jo was right. It had been too long since he'd last kept company with a woman. Amidst all the death, how could he be thinking of such a thing? Easy—she was life. "Amanda . . ." He strapped on his belt and cleared his throat. "If I don't make it—"

"Don't think that way."

He picked up his hat. "We both know the possibility."

"If you keep thinking that way, it will become fact. We mustn't give up hope that the foolishness shall end soon."

When she spoke of hope, he believed. The feelings—maybe they were a warning as Frieda had stated. "I was going to bare my soul."

"Don't let me stop you from doing so, Captain."

During wartime, promises were empty. "It wouldn't be proper."

A cool breeze swept through the open window. The lace curtain fluttered, finally lending some relief to the hot summer day. With the storm growing closer, he needed to return to camp before it broke.

He shoved his hat on his head. "Until next time."

"Sam . . ."

Amanda stood so close that he was losing all sense of reason. Her scent. Her hair. Nipples pressed against the thin cotton fabric of her robe.

"Why did you request the transfer to New Mexico?" she asked.

All this time, she had known his feelings. He lifted her hand and gently kissed it. "I need to be leaving."

As he turned, Sam realized he should have been honest with her. A fool's time to fall in love. There was no sense in deceiving himself any longer. Even if she had been willing to reciprocate his feelings before the war, he cared too much to have placed her in such an awkward position. Now, promises were nothing more than wishful thinking.

Chapter Eleven

THE DUMFRIES INN, AN ELEGANT red-brick building framed by spreading oaks, had known better days before the war. At one time, it had been renowned for its social prominence. Amanda had stayed there with the Colonel on several occasions between home and Washington. Now, the crystal chandelier in the ballroom was cracked and missing pieces. Paintings had been stolen, along with the fancy lace doilies that had lent a special touch. But she had come to the inn to collect medical supplies, not reminisce.

Holly paced the length of the parlor, raising a brow upon seeing her. "I didn't think you were going to show, Amanda."

Dressed in a cheery floral print, as usual Holly had outdone herself for appearance's sake. With her black hair braided in a chignon at the nape of her neck, she was a stunning woman and seemed quite aware of it.

"I had to dodge Yankees. As you may recall, I used to get passes from Colonel Jackson."

"You haven't heard from Wil either?"

Amanda detected concern in Holly's voice. "No."

Bracelets clattered as Holly's hands went to her hips. "Then how shall I get paid?"

Definitely not concern, but greed. "Please forgive me, Holly, but how can you fret about money? There's been a lot of fighting. I haven't found Wil's name on any of the casualty lists, but they're not always reliable. He could be lying in a hospital somewhere—or dead."

"That thought has crossed my mind, which was why I hoped you had heard from him. My question remains—how shall I get paid?"

Why had she agreed to meet this woman? Aid for the wounded, and money, she reminded herself. She didn't like the fact that Holly had something in common with her. "I shall find a way to pay you if we don't hear from Wil."

"How soon?"

"I don't know. Aren't you the least bit worried about Wil?"

"Should I be? He doesn't lose sleep when I risk my neck. And he loves playing the role of a dashing war hero."

"War is no game. I've lost my husband and seen the mangled bodies."

"I'm aware of what war is like. I've visited the hospitals and nursemaided all too many sick and wounded soldiers. The sight of blood makes me ill, but I risk getting caught stealing supplies for the likes of you and Wil. He isn't here, so let's conclude our business and be done with it. I need to return to Washington before my husband gets back from inspecting troops, guns, or . . ." She twisted the pearl beads around her neck through her fingers. " . . . or whatever equally tedious job he's performing in the field."

Always able to find common ground to converse with anyone, Amanda decided Holly Prescott had proven the exception. Holly had a loving and caring husband, yet she lied to and cheated on him. Amanda's only consolation was that she doubted Wil fell for such a facade. Small comfort—where was Wil now?

After loading the supplies under the cover of darkness, Amanda started the journey home. Along back roads she crisscrossed war-torn fields to avoid Yankee patrols. Most of Virginia crawled with Federal soldiers these days—heading north and foraging as they went. Sam had tried to warn her. Blind determination as well as the knowledge that medical supplies would be a relief to many carried her through the miles.

Night gave way to a rosy dawn. Amanda brought Red to a halt at a stream. She let him drink before continuing on. A few miles from home, gunfire echoed ahead. She debated whether to stay put or continue on. This close to home, she decided to keep going.

A peal of thunder made Red jump. She looked to the sky—no clouds. Cannon fire. *How many had just died?*

A shell exploded overhead and fragments hit a tree. Red reared. Amanda intertwined her fingers in his mane to keep from slipping out of the saddle. She urged him forward.

Another shell burst and thick smoke surrounded her. Barely able to see, she kicked Red. The stallion took a hesitant step forward. Another step. *Good, they were making progress.* She clicked her tongue, and he picked up a trot. The rhythmic gait was ideally suited for moving through the dark woods.

The smoky cloud thickened, stinging her eyes. Then came the groans. A couple of bodies littered the ground. Straggling soldiers headed her direction in retreat. Although difficult to be certain in the smoke, she thought they wore blue. Yes, their uniforms were definitely blue.

A heavily bearded Yankee seized Red's reins. She swung a fist, but he held tight. He shoved her, and she barely kept her seat. The reins tightened. Red spooked and dodged to the side. She drew her pistol from the saddlebag. The soldier raised his hands and backed away.

She tucked the gun away and reined Red to the right, trying to shut the dreadful sights and sounds from her mind. The horse trotted up a gentle rise. Once on the other side, she should be clear of the death and destruction. She urged Red for more speed. His neck was lathered, and he snorted a protest but obliged. They topped the hill.

A single line of soldiers crossed the fields below. She decided to head in the opposite direction.

Amanda asked Red for everything he had and let the reins slide through her fingers. His legs glided across the ground with ease, leaving the gunfire in the distance. Thankful that she would be home before nightfall, the sound of drumming hooves came from behind her.

She glanced over her shoulder. A Yankee scout gained on her. She clicked to Red for more speed, but weighted with canvas bags full of supplies, he had nothing left to give. She passed a wooded grove and circled toward it.

The soldier kept his pursuit but started losing ground. As she neared the sanctuary, another horse and rider jumped from the forest, cutting off her access. She turned sharply to the left, but the fresh rider gained on her.

Wil's first warning had been to drop the supplies if she ever spotted a Yankee. After losing the last shipment, she mustn't let this one slip through her fingers. The Yankee pulled even. No escape—unless she dropped the heavy bags. She worked to free the taut leather.

An arm reached across. Amanda swatted her reins at the hand. Finally, she worked the canvas bags free. They fell to the ground.

Red kicked up his heels and burst forward.

By the time they reached the cover of the woods, Amanda had a terrible feeling in the pit of her stomach. Her skin prickled, and the air echoed in a shell burst.

Someone shouted.

A horse screamed.

Behind her, the scout's horse thrashed on the ground. Blood spurted from a gaping hole in its side. The soldier lay beneath the struggling animal. The horse collapsed onto its side, and its nostrils quivered in death.

She reined Red toward the helpless soldier.

A horse and rider in blue rushed in their direction. "Keep going!" he shouted.

"I have to help them."

"They're dead."

"You can't know that."

"I know what shells like that do to a body." Unable to think straight, Amanda let the soldier take the reins and lead her to safety.

Across the river, Sam waited with his command. The acrid scent of gunpowder lingered in the air. Except for the groans of the wounded on the field, there was an eerie stillness. He could hear his own ragged breathing. The calm meant the Rebs were near. Just before they reached the line, he'd hear that godawful yell.

Musket fire further down the line broke the stillness. The company next to them was engaged. Then he spotted them—gray and butternut, marching toward them. His boys fired. The unearthly yell made his skin crawl. Men were down, and holes gaped in the line.

Sam drew his pistol and motioned to one of the boys to fill a hole. He could barely see through the smoke. He fired. A Reb faltered and fell backward.

A bullet whirred over his head and thumped into a tree. Splintered wood rained like deadly projectiles. Another man was down. More Rebs poured from the dense smoke. *Too many.* The line wouldn't hold for long. Too many holes to fill.

He shouted at the men to close them up.

Sam's right leg crumpled from underneath him, knocking him flat on his back. Hit—but he couldn't make himself look down to see how bad. Thank goodness there was no pain, just an annoying dull throb.

"Captain . . . ?"

Sam withdrew his sword, nodding to the private that he was fine. *Finally a purpose for the damn thing.* Using the sword as a crutch, he regained his feet.

After another musket volley, the Rebs retreated to regroup. His line would break when they charged again.

The order came to withdraw. Double quick. *Too late.*

Rebs clambered over the breastworks. They were breaking through.

Lightheaded and weary, Sam aimed his pistol. He'd take a few Rebs with him before he went down. His vision blurred. A shadowy figure ran by. Then another. He couldn't tell whether they were his men fleeing or Rebs giving chase. If they were his own, he needed to get behind them—regroup. He couldn't think straight.

The pain in his leg seared.

He opened his mouth to bellow an order. Nothing came out.

A private with a face blackened by gunpowder latched onto his arm and helped him retreat through the woods. The soldier screamed and pitched forward.

Shot in the back. His family would draw the wrong conclusion that their son was a coward. He had been anything but.

Along the path, a horse twitched on its side. Blood bubbled from its nostrils, staining the fine gray hairs around its muzzle.

Sam's leg hurt something fierce now. Any movement made the pain worse. He hadn't looked yet to see how bad it was.

The horse groaned.

Sam swayed and aimed his pistol between the horse's eyes. Somehow he managed to hold the gun steady and fired.

The horse thrashed, then lay still.

He should have saved his ammunition for a Reb.

Disoriented, he stumbled through the smoke. Two men charged past and disappeared into a haze, but he had caught a glimpse of their uniforms—definitely blue.

Another soldier stopped near him and frantically loaded his musket. "They're coming, sir!" He aimed and fired.

A scream howled above the gunfire, and the soldier ran on.

Smoke swirled. All directions appeared the same. *Keep moving.* Sam limped through the dense cloud.

A soldier in gray lay on his stomach. Sam buried his sword in the ground and leaned on it to keep him steady. He turned the wounded man onto his back.

The soldier's face was covered in peach fuzz, and he wore the bar of a first lieutenant on his collar. Blood poured from a wound in his chest. Sam clamped a hand over it to stifle the flow. *Fighting time.* Even the surgeons wouldn't have bothered, but for some reason he felt compelled to stay.

The lieutenant's eyes fluttered open. They focused on him and widened in terror. The boy struggled to get up, but Sam gently pushed him back.

"What's your name?" Sam shouted above the gunfire. But his words circled back as nothing more than a whisper.

"Jimmy," he answered in a thick Southern drawl.

Although Sam was uncertain of the region, the accent was distinctly different from Amanda's.

Jimmy raised a bloody hand.

Sam took it in a truce and held it. "I'm Sam."

"Sam . . ." Jimmy licked cracked lips. "Save yourself."

"Can't." His hand went to his leg. He still hadn't looked, but his hand was covered in blood. No wonder he was lightheaded. Self-fulfilling prophecy, or was there hope as Amanda had suggested? He wouldn't know unless he looked.

For some reason, Sam thought of Kate on the night she had died. He had curled on the bed with her and held her lifeless body in his arms. As he slumped to the ground, he felt her presence.

The forest of Virginia faded to the lap of ocean waves. He detected salt in the air. *Maine.* He was home. How long had it been? Four years.

A well-worn path led to a rocky beach of rose-colored granite. It *was* the coast of Maine.

In an earlier time, he had taken long walks with Kate, talking and dreaming about the future. As a boy he had discovered a sandy spot nestled in behind the rocks and had kept the place a secret until he had courted Kate. With the memory, he smiled. He had been on leave from West Point, and her father had almost made him marry her then.

But it was dangerous to recall too much. Kate was dead because of him. Ocean waves crashed against the rocks. The sound hadn't been waves, but gunfire. He had never left Virginia.

Jimmy's face hovered over him. The pain was blinding. Unable to think straight, he suppressed the urge to scream.

"We can help each other, Sam."

Sam fought through the fog in search of the voice. *Jimmy?* Yes, Jimmy. "I was thinking of Kate."

"She your wife?"

He managed a nod. "She died over two years ago."

Jimmy clamped a hand over his chest. Blood trickled between his fingers. "Odd things a man sees an' thinks about in the face of death." He gasped for breath. "Sam, I ain't never known the love of a woman." He let out a ragged laugh, and tears filled his eyes. "Ain't goin' to now. I'll help you through the line—least as far as I can make it." He grasped Sam's arm and helped him sit up.

A wave passed over Sam, and he felt Kate's presence once more. *She didn't blame him.* He reached out, but it was Jimmy instead. "Jimmy—how bad is it?"

"If we get you to a doc, he might save the leg."

Might. Sam finally looked down. His right trouser leg was spattered with blood, but he was unable to see much else through the red stains.

"Don't look, Sam. It's best that way." Jimmy's eyes fluttered. "Don't seem quite real when it's your own flesh."

Jimmy swayed, and Sam caught him in his arms. "Jimmy, don't give up."

"If you don't." Jimmy leaned against him and started to cry.

Blue or gray didn't make a difference. He hugged Jimmy as if it could keep him from dying.

Jimmy brushed back his tears. "Why didn't you run? Dammit, I told you to run! I could have laid down an' died, if you hadn't happened by."

"Everything will work out, Jimmy. You'll find that woman and raise a family."

The young Confederate smiled. "Got any kids, Sam?"

"One—a daughter."

Jimmy's smile widened to a blissful grin. "Will you tell her about me? Ya know—the part of how I ended up savin' her pa's life?"

With Jimmy's aid, Sam gritted his teeth and got to his feet. After helping Jimmy up, they leaned on each for support. "No," Sam said, "you're going to tell her yourself. You'll bring your slew of kids to Maine for a visit, and they shall play together."

"Maine? This is the furthest north I ever been. Will you look me up in Georgia?"

"I've never been to Georgia, but of course I'll come for a visit."

As they made their way through the smoke, bodies littered the path. Jimmy studied one in particular. The soldier clad in blue had a wound in his chest—like Jimmy's. Large black birds with ugly pink heads roosted in the trees, waiting for them to pass.

"Sam—will you make sure the buzzards don't get me?"

Out here—how could he make such a promise? "You're not going—"

"Sam! We both know I ain't goin' to see Maine."

"I'll try," Sam answered.

Jimmy groaned. "Thanks. If I see your wife, I'll tell her . . . I'll tell her . . ."

The boy went limp. Sam lost his grip on Jimmy's sleeve. The Rebel lieutenant rolled down a hill, splashing into some water at the bottom.

Sam ran after him. His wounded leg slipped from underneath him, and he slid down the embankment. "Jimmy?" Bending down, he tried to pull Jimmy from the water.

A contented smile appeared on Jimmy's face. "I thought that was it, Sam."

Weakened by his own wound, Sam tapped some unknown reserve to hoist Jimmy up and prop him against a tree along the stream's edge. He had to find a way of getting Jimmy out of the waist-deep water.

Drowsy from blood loss, he'd never be able to haul him back up the hill.

With the growing darkness, only a stray shot broke through the sultry evening air.

Jimmy didn't move.

"Jimmy?" Sam shook him by the shoulders. "Jimmy! You goddamned Reb, wake up!"

Jimmy slumped, and his face fell into the water.

Unable to fight the tears, Sam closed his eyes. Nothing made sense. They went out of their way to kill one another, then risked their necks trying to save each other.

"Tell Kate that I love her."

Chapter Twelve

THE GUNS LAY SILENT. After arriving home, Amanda had heard bombarding cannon and the rattle of muskets from across the river. More fighting—to her dying day, she'd never forget the sound. Empty stillness surrounded the countryside as if mourning the loss of life.

Amanda greeted the misty morning, clutching Rebecca in her arms. In the dewy air, not even the birds sang. An acrid-scented breeze revived thoughts of gunpowder—and death. Long after her return, she had imagined agonized screams, calling out to her. She tightened her grip on Rebecca and sat on the porch steps and wept.

A gentle hand touched her shoulder. Ezra stood over her with his wizened face wrinkled in concern. "Miss Amanda, please don't cry. Everythin's goin' to be all right." He patted her on the shoulder.

She dabbed her eyes as Ezra sat on the steps beside her. "How can so much hatred exist?" she asked.

Rebecca smiled. "Mama . . ."

More than she could bear, Amanda scrambled from the porch, but Ezra caught up with her. "Miss Amanda, it's war. Yesterday, you see and hear it first hand. Ain't nothin' we can do to change it."

His words brought little comfort. Amanda crossed the lane to the barn for morning chores. Grief stricken or not, she couldn't ignore the farm work any more than when the Colonel had died.

She let Rebecca play in a clean bed of straw. The toddler trotted the wooden figure of Red through the air. What if Sam never saw her again? She had preached hope so often that she mustn't lose sight of it.

Amanda let Red into the outside yard to graze. The blood-red chestnut kicked up his heels and streaked across the pasture. After returning to the barn, she put the rest of the animals in another paddock and had barely finished mucking stalls when pounding hooves entered the bottom of the lane.

Whether they were Confederate or Yankee made little difference. Both sides robbed folks blind. Wishing she had lugged John's rifle along, she cracked open the barn door.

Ezra ambled down the porch steps to greet Colonel Jackson and two of his men.

Thankful to see Wil alive, she picked up Rebecca. The wooden horse—she couldn't find the figurine of Red. After a quick search through the straw, she gave up and went into the farmyard.

Wil tied the roan gelding to the rail and tipped his hat. "Mrs. Graham . . ."

Though his uniform was soiled and he had a week's worth of whisker growth, he seemed fit otherwise. "Colonel, you're alive."

"And you're a sight for sore eyes."

The men hooted.

When would she learn? She ignored the warmth filling her cheeks. "If you'd like to step inside, I managed to save a few supplies."

"Supplies?"

"Didn't Mrs. Prescott . . . ?"

"Perhaps we should discuss this in private."

After dropping Rebecca off with Dulcie, she met Wil in John's study. She lifted a floor board and dug out four saddlebags from the depression.

He checked through the bags. "I'm at a loss. I haven't been in contact with Mrs. Prescott for several months."

Amanda went on to explain the details of her strange encounter with Sam, as well as the meeting with Holly in Dumfries—and returning through a battle.

"I'm sorry you went through that," he said. "While we may be in desperate need, I wouldn't have sent you. Not now."

His reaction wasn't the one she had been expecting. "If you didn't come for supplies, then why are you here?"

"We're on reconnaissance—close enough that I could check to see how you're faring."

It was probably the closest he'd come to admitting that he was worried. "With all of the fighting, I was afraid you might have been killed."

Wil dropped the saddlebags on John's desk. "You should know by now that it takes more than a few dueling muskets to knock an old warhorse like me out of action."

As usual, he was downplaying recent events. "Wil—"

"Amanda, I haven't been paid in a couple of months. I don't have much spare cash."

"Pay me when you can. Have you and your men had breakfast?"

He rubbed bloodshot eyes. "That's very kind of you, but there's no need."

"I insist. Invite them around to the kitchen."

With a nod, he slung the saddlebags over his shoulder and strode for the door.

"Wil . . ." She had no recollection of moving but was in his arms, kissing him. She hadn't realized how much she ached when she thought he might have died in battle.

He lightly traced a finger over her lips, and down her throat, only stopping long enough to kiss her there. "We could let the boys tend to breakfast, while we nip upstairs."

Good reasoning almost abandoned her, and she nearly agreed. A broad grin spread across his face, returning her to her senses. "I can't. Not without—"

"Without what, Amanda? A vow? Should I remind you how foolish such things are these days?"

She stepped back, breaking their embrace. "I'm all too aware of our troubled times, but you resort to it as a convenient excuse."

"So be it. Believe as you wish." He picked up the saddlebags and vanished from the doorway.

Puzzled by his abruptness, she would definitely never understand his moods. By the time Amanda reached the kitchen, Frieda already had eggs scrambling in the skillet and popped golden brown cornbread from the oven. Hoping that she had large enough portions to feed three hungry men, Amanda added a slab of bacon to the griddle.

Only with high praise for her hospitality, the men gathered around the table. One scout had a boyish face with a cleft chin. The other—a lean man in his mid-twenties with a bobbing Adam's apple. They were a ragged, dirty bunch, and Amanda had no doubt Wil underplayed when any of them had last eaten.

Before taking a seat, Wil tucked a couple of bills and some odd change in her hand. "Between the three of us, we collected some compensation for the supplies."

"I can't accept this." But she saw it in his eyes. He wasn't about to take "no" for an answer. "Much obliged. All of you." She shoved the money into her apron pocket.

While the men ate, Wil spread a map on the table. He sipped a hot cup of coffee and paid little notice when she glanced over his shoulder. Cedar Mountain was marked prominently on the map. The battle sounds from the previous day had originated from there.

So close to home. Lord, if that was a skirmish, what must a full-scale battle be like? Amanda pointed to the map. "Wil, I wasn't near the battle. I dropped the remainder of the supplies over here."

"Sir," said the scout with the cleft chin, "we could check if there's anything salvageable."

Wil shook his head. "Most likely they've already been ransacked."

"If there's a possibility anything is left, isn't it worth the bother?" Amanda asked. "You're headed that direction anyway. I can show you where I dropped them."

"Too dangerous," Wil said.

"Sir." The young scout traced a finger over the map. "I can escort Mrs. Graham back to the farm, then cut a path across here to meet up with y'all over here by the river."

Wil checked his pocket watch. "Very well." The scouts headed for the door. "Amanda, I'm not overly fond of bringing you along, but Edmond is one my best scouts. He has a nose for danger. Make certain you're armed, and I shall meet you outside."

"Wil . . ."

As he left the kitchen, he nodded that he understood.

The steady tapping of Frieda's cane came toward her. The hunched woman halted beside her. "I worry, Miss Amanda. It ain't safe to go traipsin' about da countryside dese days."

"Colonel Jackson and his men will escort me."

"A handful of men cain't stop no horde of soldiers. No tellin' what a riled mob do to a woman."

There was no time to quarrel with Frieda. Dispensing with her apron, Amanda hurried to the parlor and gave Rebecca a goodbye kiss on the cheek. She collected the Colonel's hunting rifle from the mantel.

Outside, Frieda sat on the front porch, working on Rebecca's quilt. Even without vision, the old woman worked effortlessly. "Child, I warn you best as I can. Your papa should has taken you over his knee. Wouldn't be so full of sass."

Amanda ignored the reprimand and went down the steps. Red was saddled and ready to go when she met Wil by the picket fence. "My scouts have gone ahead," he said. "I have another two who should be reporting in soon."

She shivered slightly. Wartime reality—any of the men sitting at her breakfast table could wind up dead before the day was out.

"Amanda, you needn't go through with this."

"No, but if I can help . . ."

He exhaled wearily and helped her mount the stallion. They headed down the lane at a trot.

Once clear of the lane, she urged Red to a comfortable canter. An expert horseman, Wil easily kept the roan even with Red. They crossed the land once used as pasture for large cattle herds. The war had changed everything, and the fields were reduced to bare red earth from soldiers and wagons trampling them.

After crossing another field, they reached a hill. The gentle slope blended to woodland, and a flock of screeching, yellow-headed parakeets darted among the branches. The heat of the morning progressed, and a shaded deer path brought welcome relief.

"Wil, what's it like?"

Distracted by the task at hand, he glanced up from the trail. "What's what like?"

"Being wounded."

"Depends."

"You took a bullet meant for John. If you hadn't, I would have never met him."

"I'm fortunate it didn't hit anything vital." Amusement crossed his face. "I'd show you the scar, but you might think I had something else on my mind if I dropped my trousers."

"Wil . . ." Amanda reined Red ahead of the roan. "Can you ever be serious?"

"I am, Amanda." The gelding pulled even with Red once more. "I was hit in the hip. Took me nearly two years to recover, but it still troubles me on occasion. Why the sudden interest?"

All these years—he had been wounded over a decade before, and the wound still bothered him. "After John died, you told me that sometimes men get a feeling. When Sam visited me the other night, he had that feeling. Did you?"

Wil straightened in the saddle.

"So you did."

"I wrote to my family that I had been mortally wounded, but stubbornness prevailed." He laughed. "I'm still here." His face twisted in torment, but the wrinkles faded to an unreadable mask.

"You went to the Northwest after that. Is that when you met her?"

"You're very perceptive, Amanda." Wil cast his gaze to the trail once more. He obviously had no intention of talking further on the topic.

"After I show you where I've dropped the supplies, I'm going to help in the hospitals."

His coal-black eyes smoldered. "You're hoping to find *him*."

She couldn't help but snicker. "Wil, I never thought of you as the jealous sort."

"I'm not," he replied in a brusque manner. "I merely thought it would be an expedition in futility, not to mention plain foolhardy."

"Is that the colonel speaking—or the man?"

To this he gave no response.

The scout, Edmond, galloped to a halt beside them and saluted Wil. "There are dead and a few wounded on the field, sir, but no Yanks, except for a buryin' detail and ambulances. They're flyin' a flag of truce and won't be no bother." With another salute, he reined around and trotted ahead of them.

Before Amanda and Wil's horses stepped from woodland onto the open grassland, the stench of death assaulted her nostrils. A dead Confederate soldier sprawled face down on the ground, his corpse rotting.

She thought she was going to be sick. "Oh my . . . How do you ever get used to it?"

Wil placed a steadying hand on her shoulder. "You learn to block it out."

She kicked Red in the side and continued on. Two more bodies littered the way. One, still alive, twitched in death throes. Amanda gasped.

Like dark clouds, buzzards circled overhead. More buzzards gathered on the ground, squawking and fighting over human remains while flies buzzed in the heat. Men seemingly oblivious to the birds dug shallow graves. Their faces were covered with handkerchiefs. A wagon removed the living.

As they passed, a prone form sobbed. Amanda turned, but Wil placed the roan between them to block her view. "He needs help," she said. "The least I can do—"

Sobs turned to a wail.

"Amanda, trust me—he's dead. His body just doesn't know it yet." His eyes held her, pleading with her not to look.

"You can't just ignore it. What if it was you, Wil? Would you want me to leave you lying there to die alone?"

Wails became screams.

"Turn away," Wil said.

"How can I help if . . . ?"

A haunted expression crossed Wil's face as he drew his pistol. "I said turn away."

"Wil, you can't."

Too late—he aimed.

Amanda clamped her eyes shut, choking off tears. She prayed for the soldier's soul—and Wil's. No God-fearing man could . . . She jumped at the crack of gunfire and an unearthly scream filled the air.

Silence. The sobs were gone.

She slowly opened her eyes. Wil's gaze was fixed and his gun lowered. He bowed his head.

"Wil?"

He blinked and holstered his pistol. "I wish you hadn't been witness to that. It's not something a lady should see."

She touched the back of his hand. *So strong.* Underneath the gruff exterior was a truly compassionate man. If only he'd let others see that part of him. "It's something none of us should ever witness."

He grasped her hand and gave it a light squeeze. "Is it much farther?"

As usual, he changed the subject rather than admit to any emotions. Sick to her stomach, Amanda looked over at the men digging graves. The soldier Wil had shot would be buried here. Blue or gray—it didn't matter.

"No," she answered softly.

The scout galloped back to check on them but brought his horse to a trot when he saw what had happened. Amanda cued Red to a trot, and Wil pulled the roan alongside her. After crossing the bloody field, she brought the stallion to a halt where the Yankees had nearly overtaken her the day before. Trampled into the ground, a canvas bag was all that remained.

Wil dismounted and checked the bag. Except for some dirty linen, unusable for bandages, it was empty. "As I suspected. This is where we part company. Edmond, see that Mrs. Graham gets home safely." As Wil tossed the bag to the ground, even he couldn't hide his disappointment.

"Take care of yourself, Wil."

He remounted the roan. "You'll need to cross the river if you expect to locate the hospitals. Bye, Amanda."

"Never say goodbye unless you mean it."

He nodded in comprehension and touched two fingers to his hat. "Then I shall see you at a later time." He reined the gelding around and crossed the blood-soaked ground at a canter.

"Ma'am, if you'll follow me," said Edmond.

Thankful that the scout wasn't returning across the field, Amanda kicked Red in the side to quicken his pace but reined up sharply. The path took her past the area where the Yankee scouts had tried to overtake her. Both were dead. A horse rested on its side in the cold stillness of death with a man pinned underneath. His face was gone. She leaned over Red's side and retched.

A hand gripped her arm, making certain she didn't slip from the saddle.

She closed her eyes and waited for the dizziness to pass. "Thank you."

When he was certain she was all right, he reined his horse on. She squeezed Red to a trot to follow him.

Silently and briskly, Edmond escorted her to within half a mile of home. No wonder scouts could easily slip across the lines. Amanda reassured him that she would be fine and bid him farewell. Instead of returning home, she forded the river. More bodies—cautiously, she moved forward. She checked each one, half-expecting to see Sam's kind eyes staring up at her in the sightlessness of death. He wasn't among them.

In the middle of a stream she let Red drink. From her canteen, she quenched her own thirst. She capped the canteen and reined Red upstream. Well past where the worst of the fighting had taken place, she should have known better than to think she could find Sam. She turned Red in the direction of the main road.

Flaring his nostrils, the stallion balked.

"It's all right, Red," Amanda said with a gentle pat. She cued him to move forward. He took another step but swerved. She slid from his back and led him along the path.

Shadows from the dense forest grew long, and her dress caught on surrounding brush. She had let far more of the day slip by than intended. A large bird with an ugly pink head flew from one naked branch to another.

Red reared.

Amanda let out a relieved breath. "It's just a buzzard, Red." She stepped forward, but Red refused to budge.

She clicked her tongue, and the horse finally came along. The trail dipped down to another stream. Trickling water carried the distinct red color of blood. She looked up and down the bank. On the opposite side she spotted a Confederate lieutenant and ran toward him.

Already cold and stiff, he had been dead for several hours, but his body had been neatly arranged to give the appearance of sleep. A friend must have helped him.

Amanda gripped Red's reins and continued along the trail. She rounded a bend. A Yankee body stretched in front of her—an officer.

Chapter Thirteen

A MANDA'S HEART SKIPPED A BEAT. She inched toward the prone soldier. He looked dead. "Sam?" Her hands trembled, and she fought the urge to scream. She reached his side and bent down.

He swung around, aiming a pistol at her. His features were wild with pain, but the bearded face wasn't Sam's. He gulped for breath and lowered the gun. "Beggin' your pardon, but what are you doin' here?"

"I was looking for someone—a friend. Where have you been hit?"

"Don't matter none." He clutched his belly and whimpered. "Not goin' to make it."

Amanda nearly gagged at the smell of blood mixed with the foul smell of excrement. He was gutshot. "Let me get you to a hospital." She reached for his arm, and he howled.

"No use," he said in a ragged voice. "Would you . . . ? Pocket."

"I don't understand."

"Letter."

With some hesitation, Amanda reached into his frock coat and withdrew a bloodstained letter addressed to a woman. His wife or sweetheart, no doubt.

"See that she gets it."

Helpless, Amanda bit her lip to retain her poise. "I will."

He squeezed her hand in thanks and laid his head to the ground. At peace, he stopped breathing.

Amanda folded the letter and tucked it into Red's saddlebag. With the sinking sun, she had best return to the main road. Once reaching it, she heard wagon wheels turning, men cursing, and feet pounding the dirt surface. Around the bend marched a column of Yankee infantry—hundreds of men heading north. They watched her with interest.

Southern citizens jeered Yankees. Yankee intruders defiled the citizens. She refused to take part in the hatred. Such feelings had ignited the war.

Ignoring the leering stares, she reined Red over to the officer in front of the column and inquired about Maine units. The colonel was friendlier than she'd expected. His regiment hadn't been engaged in any recent fighting, but the column had passed several field hospitals.

After learning their whereabouts, Amanda thanked the colonel and let the creaking wagons and plodding hooves pass. Before she reached the first hospital, she heard the groans. Wounded sprawled across the churchyard, waiting to be tended. No Maine units were among them. Still, she checked the faces for Sam, whispering words of comfort and giving sips of water from her canteen to those she passed.

About a mile from the church, more men with agony-wretched faces covered the ground near a farmhouse. Night had fallen, and a young boy assigned to the medical unit carried a lantern to help her see. Although discouraged and ready to give up, she continued her search, until a hand tugged on her skirt. She bent to the dirty, bearded private. He licked his blackened lips. "Heard you're looking for Maine men."

"I am."

"Several—brought in after us." He laid his head on the ground.

"Where?"

"Barn," he groaned.

"Thank you." After a gentle squeeze to his hand, Amanda rushed that way.

The boy scurried alongside her to keep pace. She swung open the barn door, and he raised the lantern. Rows of wounded men covered the floor like a carpet. She spotted Lieutenant Sheldon and the red-haired private and gasped. "Sam?"

She motioned for the boy to raise the lantern higher, but was unable to find Sam. Maybe he had been spared. No, there he was—in the corner. His blackened face was barely recognizable, and he huddled on a bed of straw.

Her knees sagged, and she nearly stepped on a wounded soldier as she tottered over. Bending down, she said, "Sam, it's me, Amanda."

"Amanda? What . . . ? What are you doing here?"

Like most of the others, he had no blanket. "Looking for you. I'm here to help. Where have you been wounded?"

His answer was long in returning, and it finally came in a short gasp. "Leg."

His hand clutched his right leg just above the knee. Fresh blood trickled between his fingers. She motioned for the boy to move the lantern closer. "Let me see how bad it is."

She swatted away the buzzing flies. The wound was a gaping hole. *Oh Sam.* Suddenly lightheaded, she thrust out a hand to break her fall. She wouldn't be of much help if she swooned. She shook her head to clear it.

The Yankees called this disgusting place a hospital? Reminding herself that more serious wounds needed tending to first, Amanda ripped a section from her petticoat. She swabbed out dirt and bits of fabric, before wrapping a clean piece of cloth around Sam's leg. "You've lost a lot of blood." She had saved a little water from her canteen, and placed it to his lips.

The water trickled into his mouth. He gagged.

"Take it easy. Try again. This time slowly." She raised his head to help him drink. When his thirst seemed quenched, she said, "I'm going to fetch a doctor."

"Amanda—be realistic. What do you think they'll do?"

Amputate. She couldn't say the word and spotted fear in his eyes. "Then I shall tend you. Frieda will know what to do."

"Frieda? My leg is beyond folk remedies."

"Hush up. I said I'd tend you. That means I shall. Red's outside." She sent the boy to bring Red to the back of the barn. Amanda put her hands under Sam's arms but couldn't lift him. Frustrated, she clutched his hand and pulled. He didn't budge. "Sam, I can't help you if you don't help me."

He opened glazed eyes. "It's—no use."

"No you don't! I'll not have you think that way." She pulled his arm around her shoulder and helped him sit up.

He swayed and closed his eyes.

"Sam, you need to stay awake." She wasn't reaching him. What should she do now? Amanda raised her voice. "Sam!"

His hand went to his head. "You shouldn't have come."

"I was afraid I'd find you dead."

He closed his eyes again.

"Sam!" She grasped his shoulders and shook him.

His eyelids fluttered open.

"You're going to live," Amanda demanded. "Now get to your feet." Bearing the brunt of his weight on her shoulder, she helped him stand. "One step."

None too steady, he moved forward.

"Another."

Careful not to step on wounded soldiers, they made it outside. The boy waited with Red. Sam leaned against the stallion for support and clutched Red's mane. His gaze met hers. "You're a fool, Amanda."

"I want Rebecca to know her papa. If you lose the leg, we shall deal with that fact, but at least you'll be alive."

"Amanda . . . " He closed his eyes a moment. "You're a pretty lady. At least—my last sight shall be the prettiest lady I know."

"Sam, please don't give up. Now if I don't get you on Red, you're going to stand here and bleed to death."

Amanda gave a light push on his posterior, and Sam strained to pull himself up. A groan escaped him as he put his wounded leg over Red's back. Once in the saddle, he intertwined his fingers in the chestnut mane and slumped against the stallion's neck.

Leading Red, Amanda began the walk home. "Hold on, Sam. Think about home. If you let go now, you will never see it again."

His reply was sluggish. "Kate didn't either."

"That's no reason to join her."

"She died because of me."

"You can't blame yourself. She died in childbirth. More than anything, she wanted Rebecca to live." Amanda glanced back.

Extremely pale, he slouched across Red.

More determined than before, she had to find a way to keep him talking. "Sam, think about what I'm saying. You need to stay awake."

He focused on her. "I'm trying."

Good—he was responding. Leaving the groans of the wounded and the dim lantern light behind, she asked, "When was the last time you were home?"

"I don't recall."

With only moonlight to see by, she looked over her shoulder. "Then tell me what Maine is like. I have never been there. I'd like to see it one day."

Sam forced a smile. "You're a saint of a lady, Amanda. I know what you're trying to do."

"I'm trying to keep you alive." Amanda came to a stream and lifted her skirts to wade across. Once safely on the other side, she continued, "What happened?"

"The line broke."

She led Red across a long, narrow field that remained fallow.

"Kept filling holes. The damned . . . "

Her heart tugged. Like Wil, Sam knew how much she detested swearing. If the situation weren't so serious, she'd laugh. "That's all right, Sam. The last thing I'm going to do right now is scold you for cursing."

He laughed—weakly. "The Rebs got through. One of them helped me. His name was Jimmy." He reached for her. "Amanda . . . "

She brought Red to a halt.

With short, shallow breaths, Sam closed his eyes.

Amanda shook him—hard. "Sam, don't give up. We have a ways to go yet."

Peace entered his eyes, and she shook him again.

A faint sparkle of life returned to the depths. "Amanda, if—if I don't make it . . . "

More than anything she wanted to protest any notion of parting words. She gripped his hand. "I'm here, Sam."

"Will you let my family know?"

"Of course," she promised with a squeeze to his hand.

"I don't mean my death."

"Then what?"

"That I love you."

A nagging lump caught in her throat. He was giving up, and why hadn't she spotted the signs? She had, but she had chosen to ignore them. She quickened her pace. Although a good, strong horse, Red grew heavily lathered in the warm, humid night. She pushed him.

But Sam needed a rest. Amanda skirted a farm and stopped a good distance away in a glade. Most folks wouldn't understand her reasons for aiding a Yankee. She helped Sam from the saddle. Too weak to stand, he slumped to the ground.

She cradled Sam's head. "Let me get you something to drink." She retrieved the canteen from the saddle. "Drink this."

She put the canteen to his lips, and he sipped slowly.

"I need to keep you awake. I won't be able to help you if you lose consciousness." His eyes remained half-closed and his breathing shallow. "You were going to tell me about Maine."

Several minutes passed before he spoke. "Rebecca has never been to the ocean. I wanted to show her Maine."

"You will."

"I had hoped you might come with us." She squeezed his hand, and he touched a finger to her face. "The other night, I wanted to tell you about . . ." He groaned and put his head to the ground, closing his eyes.

Fearing the worst, she checked his pulse. While his heart rate was erratic, he was breathing easier. Amanda sat beside him and closed her eyes. Too tired to think—a few minutes rest, and she would revive. When she woke, it was still dark. Her heart pounded. Had she heard ambling hooves? She checked Sam's forehead—warm to the touch.

Light from a lantern flashed through the trees.

Alert and wide awake, Amanda reached for the Colonel's hunting rifle.

The light came closer, and she took careful aim as four Confederate soldiers rode into view. Shabby looking and coarse, they brought their horses to a halt. By the looks of them, she suspected they were deserters, but then much of the Confederate army wore nothing more than rags. Her hand trembled over the trigger.

"Ma'am," one of the men said, touching his hat. "This ain't a safe place for a Yank."

"I couldn't leave him to the butchers," she hissed.

After dismounting, he bent down for a closer look at Sam. He straightened and spat tobacco juice to the ground. "If you don't mind my sayin', he's a goner."

"I do mind." She waved the rifle in the direction of his horse. "Now get back on and ride out of here."

He chewed on the tobacco wad. "How far you got to go?"

"About three miles. He needed rest."

He shook his head. "Ain't goin' to make it."

"He will. I have no choice but to try."

"I'll help you get him on your horse."

Amanda lowered the gun. "Thank you. Sir, what is your name?"

He put his hands under Sam's arms. "Thomas. Sergeant Franklin Thomas."

Sam opened feverish eyes and groaned. He showed no awareness that someone was helping him onto Red.

"I wish you luck, ma'am."

"You're very kind. You shall be in my prayers, Sergeant Thomas."

He remounted his horse.

The soldiers rode on, and she started walking. "It's a good thing they happened by, Sam. I wasn't sure how I was going to get you back on Red."

Morning arrived by the time she returned home. Footsore and weary, she brought Red to a halt outside the picket fence. "Ezra!" When the old man failed to appear, she called again.

While buttoning his shirt, Ezra rushed from a rundown cottage in the walnut grove. "Miss Amanda," he scolded, "we expect you home long afore now."

"Ezra, I need your help."

Without being told, he helped Sam from Red's back.

Amanda drew Sam's arm around her shoulder while Ezra supported him on the other side. "Let's get him to the house," she said.

By the time they reached the porch, Frieda appeared at the door. The old woman followed them to the back room—the same room Amanda had shared with the Colonel.

Ezra helped her ease Sam to the bed when Dulcie ran in.

"Dulcie," Amanda said, "I need some water and cloth for bandages. Fetch some from my sewing kit."

"Yes'm." Dulcie disappeared from the room.

"Miss Amanda," Frieda said, "he's barely alive."

"What do I do to help him?" Amanda unwrapped the makeshift bandage from his leg and tossed the bloody cloth to the floor. "He was hit just above the knee."

"Da surgeons would—"

"I know what the surgeons would do. That's why I got him away from them. Frieda, I need your help."

"First, you need to see if da bullet's still in his leg. If it ain't too deep, you can cut it out."

Amanda examined the wound. Sam's muscles tensed noticeably when she touched his leg. "I know it hurts. I'm sorry. Ezra, can you fetch some laudanum?" As Ezra left the room, she took a deep breath before ripping the trouser leg for a better look at the wound.

"It's still in there," Sam gasped.

"Frieda needs to know how deep." Unable to continue, Amanda hesitated.

Frieda placed a bony hand on her shoulder. "Miss Amanda, you give him da laudanum, den Ezra dig da bullet out."

"Ezra can't see much better than you."

"Den Dulcie do it."

Dulcie returned with a porcelain pitcher and grimaced.

"She's little more than a girl. I shall do it."

Relief spread across Dulcie's blemished face as Ezra brought a tea cup.

Amanda breathed in the bitter scent of Frieda's home-brewed opium tincture and whiskey. "Drink this, Sam." She put the cup to his lips.

While waiting for the laudanum to take effect, she went into the kitchen and collected a sharp paring knife. Once back in the bedroom, she said, "I shall make it as quick as possible. Ezra, I need you to hold him down."

Sam closed his eyes, and the old man gripped his hands. Throwing an arm across Sam's shoulders, Ezra acknowledged that he was ready.

"Forgive me." Amanda said a silent prayer and went in search of the bullet.

Sam screamed. Ezra somehow managed to keep his struggles under control, and she probed deeper until Sam ceased fighting altogether.

"Please don't let him be gone. Sam, you've come too far."

Ezra relaxed his grip and put a hand in front of Sam's mouth to check for breathing. "He's still alive, Miss Amanda."

"Good." But she couldn't locate the bullet. No, there it was. She wiped her hands on her dress, staining the faded green fabric with

Sam's blood. "I think the bullet is right next to the bone, Frieda."

Frieda shook her head. "He's lucky it didn't shatters. You cut da bullet out, while I make a poultice. Miss Amanda, I has to be honest." The old woman's empty gaze rested on her face. "You should let da surgeon do da job. I's not sure we can save da leg—or him."

"Without our help, he'll definitely die."

The sightless eyes appeared to keep staring at her. "Dat true. Da leg bad. You wasn't thinkin' with your head."

The glaze of Frieda's blind eyes had never bothered her before, and a cold shiver ran down Amanda's back. She had been thinking with her heart. "Is there nothing you can do?"

"I try." Frieda tapped her walking stick in front of her as she left the room.

Amanda returned her attention to Sam and probed deeper into his flesh with the knife. Thank goodness he was unconscious. Finally freeing the bullet, she curled her fingers around it. The conical shape had flattened in his leg, causing the gaping wound. "He may want to show it to Rebecca someday."

"You do fine work, Miss Amanda."

"Thank you, Ezra." She shoved a stray hair from her face and checked Sam's breathing. It was steady again, but his forehead had grown dreadfully hot. First things first—she would worry about his fever later and set about to cleaning the wound. By the time she had washed and cleansed all bits of fabric and dirt from his leg, Frieda carried in the poultice. Amanda stitched the wound with Red's tail hair and applied the poultice.

Sam's hair was caked with Virginia clay, giving the sandy-brown color a reddish appearance. His tattered uniform was grimy and most likely lice infested. She'd have Ezra burn it. With Dulcie's assistance, she washed and dried him. Afterward, they changed him into one of the Colonel's nightshirts.

Too exhausted to wash herself, Amanda lowered her head. Sam's eyelids flickered. She waved a hand in front of his face. He didn't blink. Difficult to believe he was the same man who had visited only a few nights before, she managed a smile.

"Kate," he whispered.

Chapter Fourteen

MORE THAN A YEAR SINCE THE OPENING BATTLE, the war had come full circle. The two opposing armies were once again converging near Manassas Junction. Relieved of command by the mighty Stonewall, or "Old Jack" as he was often called, Wil lowered his pencil from the uneven writing surface of a tree stump. Against his better judgment, he had accepted a transfer to Tom Jackson's Corps at the division commander's insistence.

No longer a reclusive cadet from West Point, Old Jack had grown more stubborn over the years. "Jackass," one cadet had referred to him at the Point, and it was an apt description of any commander who sought the aide of Providence to wage war.

One of the boys strummed a tune on the banjo, reminding Wil of another way of life. Tired of war. Tired of bloodshed. Twice wounded. This war was going to kill him. He felt it. Was that what held him back from telling Amanda his true feelings? Or was it as Amanda suggested—an all-too-easy excuse?

The reason didn't matter. Wil forced himself to commit the words to paper. He lowered the pencil and read over the letter. But he had made a vow to himself—long ago. To never let anyone see that part of him again. Resigned to his fate, he crumpled the letter and tossed it into the fire.

"Colonel Jackson!"

At the sound of General Hill's voice, he snapped to attention, but Powell motioned for him to remain at ease.

"If that was your resignation, Wil, you did the right thing."

Wil had been friends with the red-bearded division commander, who shared an equal dislike for Old Jack, since West Point. "It wasn't my resignation."

Snorting back a laugh, the general offered him a cigar. "I didn't think Old Jack could get to you that easy. Care to tell me what happened?"

Out of cigars days ago, Wil rolled it between his fingers and savored the aroma. "The boys got rambunctious. Tore down a fence for firewood. They agreed to pay for it, but our esteemed commander saw it as a violation of orders."

Powell rolled his eyes. "You should be commanding a brigade."

It was Wil's turn to laugh as he struck a match to the cigar. "Not likely. Old Jack trusts me less than he does you."

Tapping a foot, Powell took a drag on his cigar before dropping the butt to the ground. "It may not be a brigade, Colonel, but I expect you to lead your command."

With the order, Wil straightened. "Jack will have your head."

"He'll find some meager cause anyway. Wil, if we're going into battle, I need fighting men that *I* can trust."

"At your service, sir."

Wrinkles formed around the general's eyes as he grinned. Old men—the war had aged them beyond their years.

"If it wasn't your resignation, why did you burn the letter?" Powell asked.

Almost in ashes, the letter smoldered on the fire as if refusing to die. During the Mexican War, he and Powell had wooed the lovely *señoritas*. Afterward, the general courted a lady and lost her favor to a Yank—another West Pointer, George McClellan. But then, Powell cherished the notion of being in love, which was a foreign concept to Wil. He realized he had nearly slipped and almost allowed a woman to steal his heart.

"It shouldn't have been written in the first place, sir. My judgment momentarily lapsed."

* * *

Although pockmarked, the gold pocket watch had survived. Amanda flicked it open and studied Kate's picture tucked inside. First Kate, then John. Would Sam be next? Not if she could help it.

"Miss Amanda . . . " Frieda's stooped form hovered beside the bed, shaking her head. "His fever ain't comin' down. Gangrene has set in."

Weary from the day and night vigil, Amanda shoved stray hair away from her face. "But there's no infection."

A bony finger went to Frieda's nose. "I smell it. It's da leg or him. I'll get Ezra."

"Frieda, I can't do what you're asking. Even if I could, I don't think he can survive it."

Frieda shuffled toward the bedroom door. "Dat's why I tell you da doctor should do it. Now it prob'ly too late."

Amanda returned the pocket watch to the dresser. She sat on the edge of the bed and dipped a cloth in the wash basin. After wringing the cloth, she placed it on Sam's forehead. If gangrene had set in, she would have noticed. She unwrapped the bandage.

Sam opened feverish eyes. Sweat beaded on his forehead and rolled down the side of his face. "I won't let you."

"I'm only checking the wound." Amanda finished unwinding the bandage.

Puffy and swollen, his leg remained an angry red. Then she spotted tiny blackened edges around the sutures and drew in a sharp breath. Gangrene—the first stages, but as Frieda had claimed, it was definitely there.

"I won't let you take my leg," Sam repeated.

"Gangrene has set in."

His brows furrowed, and he groaned as he sat up. The cloth on his forehead tumbled to the floor.

Amanda grasped his shoulders to keep him from leaving the bed. Although ill, he was strong and struggled against her grip.

"Think of home." She retrieved the watch from the dresser, and his struggles ceased. "You told me you wanted to visit the ocean—with Rebecca."

He glanced at Kate's picture and trembled. "She's buried in Maine."

"Kate lives on through Rebecca."

His fingers clasped the pocket watch. "No!" He tossed the watch across the room and clenched the bedpost for support. Crying out in pain, he stood.

"You'll split your stitches." Amanda's arms encircled his waist, and she struggled to get him back in bed. Droplets of fresh blood spattered the floor.

Ezra charged into the room and clamped a vise-like hand around Sam's arm. Sam's resistance ceased, and they helped him return to bed.

Amanda sat on the edge and inspected his leg. The stitches were torn, and the stench was frightfully overpowering. Frieda *was* right. "The wound is open."

"Miss Amanda, dere is one thing we can try," Frieda said, entering the room.

Amanda spotted fear in Sam's eyes. She squeezed his hand. "Try it, Frieda!"

"You ain't goin' to like it."

"Will it save his leg?"

"It might."

"Then do it." With her words, Sam closed his eyes. He trusted her. She couldn't betray that now.

The touch was a gentle one—a woman's. She placed something cool on his forehead. The invigorating feeling spread down his neck to his chest, but the pain . . . Sam bit his lip to hold in a scream.

"Here, drink this."

Her voice was soothing as she put a cup to his lips. Bitter liquid trickled down the wrong way. He choked, but the woman helped him.

Another face joined the woman—a dark one.

"He still doesn't recognize us," one of the women said.

He felt as if he should know them—the woman with the green eyes especially. Weariness and worry registered in those beautiful eyes. Was he the cause? At the back of his mind something told him she was important in his life. But he couldn't think straight. If only he could be rid of the pain.

Sam clenched his teeth and closed his eyes.

Water dripped into a pan, and her touch returned. The cloth was cool and wet, and the pain faded with her deep, tender strokes. Someone grasped his arms and massaged his back in long and soothing strokes. Once flat on his back again, her touch reached his groin. In fond remembrance, he smiled. He had wanted to make love with her.

"Goodbye," she whispered.

Goodbye? Goodbye meant forever.

"Noooo!" Sam sat up and seized her wrist. "Don't go!"

"I'm not going anywhere."

Her hair was blonde, not dark brown like Kate's. When he tightened his grip, she moved closer. Definitely a pretty woman, she beamed and her green eyes sparkled like emeralds.

"Where am I?" he asked.

Clad in a clean, cotton nightshirt, he glanced around the room. Besides a chest of drawers and the woman's rocking chair, there was no furniture. She had a porcelain basin and pitcher to wash him with, and a chamber pot rested on the floor beside the bed. Gunfire echoed in his head. Rebels had broken through the line.

"Where am I?" he repeated.

The woman gently pushed him to the bed. "You're safe."

"I heard Kate."

"Kate died over two years ago."

Kate was *dead*? "But I heard her just now."

"No, Sam. She died giving birth to Rebecca."

"Rebecca?"

Tired—so tired. He closed his eyes, and the woman patted him on the shoulder. Kate had died because of him. No, Kate lived through Rebecca.

"You shall recall everything in time."

At the sound of her comforting Virginian accent, he remembered her sweet scent and how much he wanted to hold her. Her brow had been beaded with sweat and her braided hair was damp against her neck. In the hot summer evening, he had longed to caress her, whispering words of love for a tomorrow that might never arrive. He dressed in blue, even though her heart remained with the gray. With that thought he drifted.

When he woke, she was slumped in the rocking chair next to the bed with her chin to her chest. "Amanda?"

She opened her eyes, exposing the beautiful emerald color. "Sam—you recognized me." A hint of pink entered her cheeks, and she quickly brushed a tear away.

"What happened?"

"You were wounded."

There had been hesitation in her voice. "Wounded?"

"I brought you here to tend you. You were hit in the right leg."

Wounded in the leg? Although unable to recall what had happened to him, he had witnessed more leg injuries than he cared to think about. Aware of the usual outcome, he couldn't bring himself to look down. "Amanda..." His parched throat scratched.

Seeing his need, Amanda placed a cup to his lips.

When his thirst was quenched, he tried again, "Is my leg...?"

"We saved it." Amanda sat beside him and lifted the sheet. Under the nightshirt was a heavily swathed leg. "It's not a pretty sight, and it's going to give you trouble for some time to come."

Sam let out the breath he hadn't realized he was holding in as she raised the nightshirt to his thigh.

Amanda unwrapped the bandage and rubbed some sort of salve on his leg.

"What's that?" he asked.

"A mixture of yarrow and root of indigo. Dulcie collects the materials for Frieda's potions. Frieda had to use all of her resources to save you—and the leg."

"I thought someone mentioned gangrene."

Amanda winked. "Frieda knew an old treatment."

"For gangrene? More folk medicine?"

"Not quite. When I found you, flies had already got to the wound. Think about what their offspring eat."

Maggots and decaying matter. He didn't want to think about it too much.

"Sam, the important thing is that it worked. Until now, you haven't spoken a coherent sentence in over a week."

"A week?"

A grin appeared on her face. "And I must say you've been quite talkative during that time."

He frowned.

"Don't fret," she continued, "you haven't revealed any military secrets."

"After a week, I doubt I have any current ones to give. What did I talk about?"

"You talked about the war, Maine, and Kate."

She pressed the pocket watch into his palm. With Kate's voice fresh in his mind, he clutched the watch to his abdomen.

"I know how much you cared for her."

"Amanda—there's something more, isn't there?"

"You needn't explain."

Explain what? His memory was full of holes. She must have seen the confusion on his face.

"You don't recall?" she asked.

Sam flipped open the pocket watch. The glass was cracked down the center, but Kate's face stared back at him. "Recall what? Did I say something that hurt you?"

"On the contrary." She wrapped a clean cloth around his leg. "I had Ezra burn your uniform. Between the blood, dirt, and graybacks, it was beyond saving."

Sam snapped the pocket watch shut. "I can't know what it was if you don't tell me."

"It wouldn't be proper."

As she returned to fixing the bandage, pain shot through his leg. He tightened his muscles, only making the pain worse.

"It's a deep wound. It will take a long while to mend." Finished with the bandage, Amanda started to rise.

He grasped her hand, and her green eyes lit up.

"I have some of the Colonel's clothes beside the bed. I won't swear to the fit, but if you care to try them on—"

"You keep changing the subject. What could I have said in a feverish state that has you in such a mysterious mood?"

"It's something you must recall on your own. I shall try to get a message through to Charles. No promises, but I think your family would appreciate knowing you're alive. Meanwhile, you need rest. I'll check on you later." She stood.

"Was it about you?"

Amanda exhaled a tired breath. "Get some rest. We shall talk later."

Recalling his recent thoughts, Sam hoped whatever he had said hadn't been indecent. Frieda entered the room as Amanda was leaving, and they exchanged a few words. He couldn't recall a time when exhaustion had been so overwhelming—not even after many hours of picket duty. He settled his head against the feather pillow.

"Miss Amanda say da fever fin'ly broke." The old woman suddenly loomed over him, startling him.

He glanced around the room, but there was no sign of Amanda.

"Miss Amanda need sleep. She be nursin' you day and night."

"I owe you my life. Thank you."

"You owe Miss Amanda, not me." Frieda's walking stick guided her back the way she had come.

Only then did he notice the pocket watch remained clenched in his hand. Opening it to Kate's picture, he realized how close he had come to joining her in the grave. That's why he had dreamed of her. It was past time to bury his guilt for Rebecca being the survivor, and he whispered a silent goodbye.

Chapter Fifteen

WITH EACH PASSING DAY, Sam grew stronger. Progress was slow, and there were times when he lapsed. Nights were especially bad, but he no longer called for Kate. Day and night Amanda toiled, but she was relieved he had been spared from the recent wave of fighting. "There's been another battle at Manassas. The Yankees lost. Rumors from town say that General Lee has crossed over into Maryland."

He grimaced as she pinned the fresh bandage. "That should make you happy."

"I will be happy when this foolish war is over and not a moment before. I have already sacrificed enough and count my blessings you weren't at Manassas. But what about a month or two from now? Have I patched you together only to send you to the front again?"

"With Bobby Lee in the North, maybe the war will be over by the time I regain my feet."

Was he reassuring her or poking fun? "If General Lee's actions bring an end to this nonsense—"

He sent her a harsh glare, warning her of the latter.

Sam grasped her hand. In spite of being wounded, his grip remained strong. His gaze turned intense. "I'm a captain in the U.S. Army. I have a duty to uphold. There's a rebellion in this country. One which needs to be put down."

For some reason, he was patronizing her. "Does that include old friends?" she asked.

He let go of her hand, and his eyes narrowed. "I presume you mean Jackson?"

"As a matter of fact, yes. Wil's regiment was in the thick of the fighting at Manassas. So what if he's among the dead *Rebs*? That makes one less to kill."

His voice softened. "You know that's not what I meant. If anyone can survive this war, Jackson can."

While his words were meant as comfort, she thought of the past. "If he isn't fool enough to take another bullet intended for someone else. I would have never met John—or you—if he hadn't."

"Amanda, I respect Jackson. We were never the best of friends, but we shared a few times—good and bad—in New Mexico."

Awkwardness and not knowing what to say had returned. She resorted to straightening the folds in her dress.

"Do you love him?" Sam asked.

Her eyes widened. "That's a highly improper question, Captain."

His gaze met hers. "But an honest one."

Like the time she had asked why he requested the transfer to New Mexico. "I'm not certain how I feel about Wil. He has helped me come to terms with John's death. I don't know what I would have done if he hadn't been here, but love...?" She shook her head. "He doesn't exactly make such a feeling an easy one."

Sam touched an index finger to her cheek. "An honest answer. I didn't expect anything else. You let me think there was more between the two of you as a cover for smuggling supplies."

Had it been more? With Wil, she could never be certain. "I never meant to deceive you, but I feared you wouldn't understand my reasoning."

He clenched his left hand to a fist. "Your reasons are all too clear. You needed the money. Damn this war. Damn it to hell!"

"What happened to your fine talk of putting down the rebellion?"

Her question only made him angrier, and he pushed himself to a sitting position with a groan. When his face contorted, Amanda resisted the urge to help. Whatever he was attempting to prove, he seemed more at ease with the pain. He latched onto the bedpost, and she backed out of his way. His forehead wrinkled, and he clamped his eyes shut as he gingerly put his leg over the side of the bed.

"You'll tear the stitches open again," she said.

Using the bedpost for support, Sam stood. The color drained from his face. He bowed his head and swayed. "Amanda, I'm not certain I can make it by myself."

The plea was all she needed to hear. Her arms encircled his waist, and Sam sank into bed. Careful not to cause him further pain, she lifted his legs under the linens and drew the quilt over him. "Let that be a lesson to you. You could still lose the leg."

His face had gone ashen. "I'm well aware of that, Mrs. Graham. I've passed the hospitals where they butcher men like livestock."

Maybe someday she'd understand the moods that men suffered. Sam relaxed his head to the feather pillow. His whiskers had grown shaggy. In her vigil to keep him alive, she had forgotten to shave him. "I'll fetch one of the Colonel's razors."

Sam lifted a hand to his face. "It is getting rather scruffy. Maybe I should keep the beard. I'd look more like one of your Rebel boys."

In protest she raised a finger, but he gave her a teasing smile. Amanda lowered her arm. "I will thank you kindly if you wouldn't refer to them as *my* Rebel boys. After I fetch the razor, I'll help you wash up."

"I think I can manage."

"I suppose you were feverish the last time I bathed you." Only when his cheeks flushed a gentle shade of pink did she realize what she had said. "I'm a widow. There's no cause for embarrassment."

A mischievous grin formed on his lips. Although thick whiskers gave him a rugged look, gentle kindness remained in his eyes. Before now, she hadn't allowed herself the luxury to think. Tirelessly, she had washed his feverish skin. Day and night, she had tended him. Day and night, she had closed her mind to anything but his survival.

"Tell me, *Mrs.* Graham, what does a proper widow think when she washes the body of a fallen soldier?"

"Captain Prescott, I was under the misguided notion that you're a gentleman. I'll not have you speak about such things while under my roof."

"I see. More than cleanliness."

Such brashness she had come to expect from Wil, but Sam had always been cordial and proper. Afraid to care for anyone during such difficult times, Amanda hurried from the room. Gulping back her breaths, she slammed the door behind her and leaned on it.

"Miss Amanda . . ." Frieda entered the hallway.

What would she do without her beloved servant? Frieda always sensed her moods. "It's the wrong time to love. I've already lost the Colonel, and for all I know, Wil could be just as dead."

"Mr. Wil ain't dead."

"But what about the next battle? Frieda, how do I choose? I can't relive what I've already been through."

A bony hand went around her wrist. "I cain't answer all your questions. What happens will happen, but you're a stronger woman dan you think."

"Thank you, Frieda." The old woman scuffed back the same way she had come.

With continued rest, Sam would regain his strength. Through long days and nights, he had slipped in and out of consciousness. The threat of death was past, and she allowed herself to think.

As she grieved for John, she had drifted from one day to the next. Cold and indifferent, he had rarely taken the time to satisfy her needs. After eight years of marriage, she had respected him but wondered if she ever truly loved him. Taken in by the dashing lieutenant when they had first met, she had been so young and foolish until sharing intimacies had dissolved to nothing more than satisfying his own need or attempting to provide the child she had never conceived. While Wil's strength had revived her, Sam's presence had reawakened her to the world of the living. Eventually she would be forced to choose between them.

Like a grinning buffoon, Charles dragged Holly to the sofa and waved a message in the air. After reading the slip of paper from Amanda, Holly narrowed her eyes. Why couldn't it have been the money Wil owed her? "Sam's alive?" she asked, pretending she was properly thrilled. "We must wire the family."

She wrapped her arms around Charles's scrawny neck and kissed him on the cheek.

"We had better wait until I have the opportunity to check the circumstances. The courier disappeared before I could ask questions. He did sound Southron though."

Southron? As widely traveled as Charles was, he wouldn't recognize a fine Southern drawl if it bit him on the derrière. She twisted her pearl necklace between her fingers. "You have doubts?"

"Let's just say I want to be certain before getting my hopes up."

"Charles, don't be ridiculous. It's Amanda's handwriting. She's as pure as gold. Why, I bet she sent it through that friend of hers, Sam's old commander—what's his name? Colonel Jackson."

Charles raised a skeptical brow. "*Colonel* Jackson? As I recall, he was a captain in New Mexico."

She tugged on the necklace. "Was he? I only met him the one time at the general's reception several years ago. Amanda has spoken about him on occasion."

Charles gave her a slow, appraising look. After five years of anything but wedded bliss, she doubted that he believed her, but she could care less. He lacked ambition. Most men did, including Wil. Most of his West Point buddies were generals. If she ever saw him again, she'd remind him of that fact.

Holly snapped her fingers in front of his face. "Charles?"

He blinked. "Colonel Wingate has agreed to let me go."

"Go where?"

"To Virginia."

Sad frown. Surprised by his initiative, she couldn't have scripted it better. "But Charles, we might lose both of you."

"I can't leave my brother stranded in Virginia if he's been wounded."

She feigned interest. "Of course not. When do you leave?"

"First light."

"So soon?" To hide the drudgery her life had become in recent weeks, she curled her lip to a pout. Although it was bad enough that she hadn't heard from Wil in reference to the money, she was feeling as restless as hell. While Charles was away, she'd find another officer capable of tending to her needs.

At thirty, Charles was nothing more than a has-been. No drive—no desire. He certainly didn't know the first thing about keeping a wife content.

He traced a finger down the curve of her neck, and his hand came to rest on her throat. She felt light pressure. Daring him, she smiled sweetly. "Why Charles—I didn't know you had it in you."

"Do you think I won't?" More pressure on her throat. "Tell me about you and Jackson."

"Which part? Smuggling supplies to the Rebels with the kind-hearted Mrs. Graham as the go-between or ..." She tasted revenge. "... sharing the enemy's bed."

"Bitch!" A vein in his temple bulged. Delighted with the reaction, she raised her skirt. Men were such simple fools. Maybe she had finally made him angry enough to satisfy her.

Chapter Sixteen

CRITICAL OF THE MIRROR'S REFLECTION, Amanda sighed. While she hadn't lost as much weight in the past year as she had feared, the blue silk dress was loose in the shoulders and, much to her surprise, about the waist. She replaced a stray lock of hair. Deciding to cover the bagginess with a belt, she twisted to see her back. What had possessed her to try it on?

Certainly not a day dress, it was impractical and slightly off the shoulder. With farm chores to tend to, she would need a hat while working in the sun. She scanned her appearance and nearly changed. She knew perfectly well why she had chosen it. She felt like a woman again, and with Sam regaining his strength she wanted him to take notice.

When Amanda reached the back bedroom, she met Ezra as he was leaving. He bid her good morning, politely pretending he hadn't noticed her dress. As she knocked on the door, she felt more like a flirting schoolgirl. Surprisingly unashamed, Amanda smoothed the folds of the dress before opening the door.

With the aid of a crutch that Ezra had constructed from pine wood, Sam was on his feet. He took a wobbly step, then another.

"What are you doing out of bed?" she asked, forgetting about the dress.

"I've been lying around long enough."

"I have warned you to take it easy. You could start to bleed again. You should have waited for Ezra or me to help."

"I'm doing fi . . . " He glanced up, and his mouth dropped open. "Amanda?"

His eyes traveled the length of her body, and she found herself enjoying it. She suppressed a smile. "Since you are on your feet, you might like to join us for breakfast in the kitchen."

Nodding, he shifted his weight to his wounded leg and yelped. With outstretched arms, Amanda rushed over to help. He latched onto her arm but tumbled to the bed, bringing her with him.

"It's my fault," Amanda said. "I distracted you."

His face contorted in pain.

"Sam, are you all right?"

His eyes cleared, but he remained frozen in place. "What do you want me to do, Amanda?"

Her head spun, and she sat up. First, Wil—now Sam. "I don't know."

"I won't press you, but I'll be the first to admit that I might not get back for months at a time."

If at all. At least he thought beyond the moment. She swallowed hard.

At the nape of her neck, Sam unpinned her hair. Loose strands tickled her skin as his fingers combed through it. After a long, tender kiss, she thought of Wil. Good Lord, she was doing it again. Self-conscious and shaking, Amanda pulled the quilt between them. "I've lost sight of my senses."

"When it comes to you, my sense of reasoning went out ages ago."

He stopped short of saying the word love. Unless they thought they were on their deathbeds, maybe all men were stubborn that way.

"It's best if I leave," she said. As she got to her feet, he grasped her hand, kissed it lightly, then tugged her back to him.

"Amanda, please don't go. I like sharing your company."

She refused to look at him. "I have chores that need tending. Join us for breakfast when you're ready."

Out in the hall, Amanda pinned her hair. Before entering the kitchen, she checked for stray hairs. After readjusting another, she crossed the brick floor.

Frieda sat on a stool, churning milk. "Mornin', Miss Amanda."

"Frieda . . . "

"How Mr. Sam doin' dis mornin'? Ezra say he drop da crutch by."

It was mighty unusual the old woman hadn't noticed her confusion. "Sam shall be joining us for breakfast."

"Dat good to hear." Frieda's wrinkled face remained expressionless. *Did she know?*

"Dat a fine perfume you wearin'."

She did. "Oh Frieda—I'm so afraid."

Frieda placed thin arms around her. "I know dat, Miss Amanda. I also know what it like to be young. You won't question yourself when da time right."

Comforted by the old woman's words, Amanda tied an apron around her waist and set about to fixing breakfast. The scent of Frieda's cornbread baking a golden brown drifted from the oven while she cracked eggs for the griddle. Popping and sputtering, they began to fry.

With the crutch under his arm, Sam hobbled into the kitchen. He eased himself into a chair, and their gazes met. Amanda shied away and looked to the floor.

"Mornin' Mr. Sam," Frieda said. "Miss Amanda, I smell eggs burnin'."

Amanda flipped sunny-side up eggs onto plates and set them on the table. She sat across from Sam and watched him eat.

He looked across at her and beamed. "You're looking radiant this morning, Mrs. Graham."

She wrung her hands. "It was unfair of me to lead you on."

Frieda left the kitchen, leaving them to their privacy, and he grasped her hand. "Amanda, you needn't apologize. I want to say all the things you want to hear and promise you everything that you deserve, but during war, those promises may turn up empty."

She had criticized Wil for resorting to the same excuse. Avoiding unproductive thoughts, she checked the cornbread.

Outside the window, a figure in blue lurked near the barn. Amanda glanced over her shoulder at Sam. "There's a Yankee outside. I haven't seen any for several weeks—not since they went north."

Sam struggled to his feet. "If Lee is in Maryland, you can guess where most of the Army of the Potomac is."

"Maybe it's Charles. I sent him a message that you're here."

"Charles has better manners than to stalk around the yard. He'd knock on the door." Sam limped over to her side. "He could be a deserter."

Amanda had overheard stories about deserters. Lawless, with no respect for authority, deserters were even worse than regular army men stealing what they wanted from civilians. They preyed on their victims with terror. She ran to the parlor for the Colonel's rifle.

"Amanda, my gun. Let me help."

"You're in no condition, Captain."

"I can still shoot. He might not be alone. I've seen firsthand what these shameless bastards do."

Unsure whether she could actually shoot a man, Amanda hurried to John's study. She searched through the desk drawers and placed Sam's pistol on the polished oak surface.

Extremely pale, Sam hobbled into the room.

"Sam?"

He waved that he was fine and checked the pistol. "Four rounds. Do you have any ammunition?"

Amanda withdrew a cartridge box—the one Wil had given her for the .44. With the rifle in hand, she led the way from the study. Unable to keep up, Sam trailed behind. She pressed forward, only stopping when she came to the kitchen door.

Two red hens strutted across the farmyard, but there was no sign of the soldier. She opened the door a crack and heard a whinny from the barn. *Red!*

The chickens fluttered as Amanda bolted across the farmyard. Inside the partly ajar barn door, Ezra sprawled face down in the dirt. A red stain covered the back of his head. *Was he dead?*

Two men in faded blue were outside Red's stall.

Keep calm. Her hands were clammy, but she raised the rifle. "What can I do for you gentlemen?"

The nearest man had a jagged scar running down his left cheek. He touched two fingers to his hat. "We're hungry, ma'am."

The nasal twang was definitely Northern but more rural than Sam's. Disgusted by the vile men, Amanda clenched her teeth. "Beating my servant is a poor way to ask for a meal."

"Sorry, ma'am. We thought he had a gun." The man with the scar stretched his hands as proof that he carried no weapon.

They were trying to gain her confidence. *Steady.* She must not let them see fear. "Step away from the horse." She waved the gun, and the two men edged away from the stall. "There's not much to be had, but I will feed you. I expect you to be on your way then."

"Thank you kindly."

A man's shadow crossed in front of her. Thank goodness, Sam had caught up with her.

A rough hand seized her arm and twisted it behind her back. The rifle clattered to the floor, and she faced harsh, dark eyes. An unshaven, heavy-set man in dirty blue with whiskey on his breath snatched up the gun. "We'll take that meal, ma'am," he said with a lewd leer, "then we'll see what comes after."

Amanda fought a growing panic and struggled against his grip.

He touched a grimy finger to her cheek and stroked it. "You're a mighty purty lady."

As she turned, she heard a pistol's hammer being pulled back.

"Let the lady go." Sam aimed the Colt directly at the man's head. "Or I'll blow off your head."

The beefy Yankee loosened the grip on her arm.

"Hand the rifle to the lady—slow and easy."

He obeyed the order and raised his hands. Still with his back to Sam, he said, "You don't sound Southron."

"I'm not."

His leer returned. "Didn't know this was a loyal household. Bet she's worth the kickin' an' screamin'."

Sam's gaze hardened. Amanda recognized the look—the same one Wil had when putting the dying soldier out of his misery. "No Sam."

Sam blinked. His face paled, and he leaned on the crutch, looking like he might faint. "Amanda, do you have something to tie them with?"

Ezra groaned and rubbed the back of his head.

Thank God, her servant was alive. "I have some leg irons at the back of the barn."

The man with the scar hissed. "Treat us like one of your damned niggers."

Amanda ignored the insult and kept the two men in rifle sight as she passed Red's stall. They didn't budge. At the back of the barn, she searched through the straw for leg irons. A haunted frenzy came into their eyes—one similar to that of battle-weary soldiers. The same as she had witnessed in Wil and Sam's—only these men were out of control and more frightening than the war itself.

Her hand trembled, but she continued to search. Probably long rusted, the leg irons hadn't been used since before Papa had died. Straw scratched her hand, and a thunder clap rocked the barn. "Sam!"

Hands were locked around the pistol as the Yankee struggled with Sam for possession. The other men fled.

After saying a silent prayer, Amanda fired, and they scurried for the back door. The scarred man dropped to his knees and clutched a bloody arm. As she reloaded the rifle, they vanished out the door.

Up front, the Yankee had wrestled Sam to the floor. A flash of silver caught Amanda's eye. *A knife.*

The ramrod was back in place, and she aimed the rifle. Unable to separate the mass of flying arms and legs, she couldn't take chances. The Colt went off. Both men lay on the floor, unmoving.

Her finger twitched over the trigger as she waited to see which one got up. "Sam?"

"I'm fine." With a groan he struggled from under the prone, heavy-set body. "See to Ezra."

Unconvinced, Amanda lowered the rifle. Sam waved her on, and she scrambled over to Ezra. She helped her servant sit up.

Ezra rubbed the back of his head. "They took me by surprise, Miss Amanda. Hit me on the blamed head."

She buried her fingers in the curly, gray hair and felt a lump. "You've got a goose egg. Get up to the house, and I shall see to it."

Ezra clambered to his feet, and she handed him the rifle. "Just in case the Yankees return. Sam?"

Though he had managed to sit up, Sam's head was bowed, and his face, ashen. Amanda stepped toward him, but the Yankee's lifeless eyes stared up at her. A crimson stain spread across the front of the man's checked shirt.

With a groan, Sam grabbed the crutch. Finally looking away from the dead body, Amanda helped steady him. He leaned on her for support and wobbled when she took a step. "My leg."

"Let's get up to the house where I can see what I'm doing."

"The deserter?"

She helped him with another step. "He's dead. Ezra and I will bury him later."

"Now I'm killing both sides."

"He would have killed you if you hadn't."

Halfway across the farmyard, he clenched his hands and screamed. His hand went to his head as if he were in pain. "You know I was ready to kill him before he had me down. At night, I see their faces. I hear their cries. A part of me dies with each of them."

"I know." Even in the name of war, he could never wash the blood completely from his hands. Understanding what Wil meant by the words, she wanted to comfort Sam. But a growing patch of red on his trouser leg warned her that medical attention was her first priority.

"I understand your concern, Captain," the major with a drooping moustache said, "but I don't have any men to spare. The wires have gone crazy. Harper's Ferry has fallen."

Charles let out a frustrated breath. After playing Holly's calculated hand, he had informed her to be moved out of the brownstone by the time he returned to Washington.

Near the Maryland border he had haggled through military protocol for more than an hour, and his luck wasn't getting much better. Mid-September already, it had been over a month since Sam had been wounded. Charles feared what might have become of his brother. "I only need one scout—someone familiar with the terrain."

The major sucked on a cigar, before blowing out a smoke ring. He straightened. "One scout," he finally agreed. He called to his aide.

The lieutenant hurried from the tent. When he returned, he was accompanied by a lanky sergeant.

Probably underage, Charles thought to himself as the sergeant saluted.

"Captain," the major said, "this is Sergeant Tucker. You can tell him the news. Dismissed."

They saluted, and the major gave them an impatient wave to get out.

Charles ducked out of the tent. Once out of earshot, he asked, "Is he always that cranky?"

"He ain't been feelin' well lately, sir. Old soldiers' disease." Tucker's voice was high-pitched and wheezy. And his size—definitely underage, and too young to know about women and marriage.

If Charles guessed right about Jackson, he doubted that the Rebel colonel would have Holly either—except in bed.

"You have some news for me, sir?" Tucker asked.

"Right. Allow me to introduce myself—Captain Charles Prescott."

The sergeant's eyes widened. "Prescott? You must be the captain's brother."

"I am."

Tucker lowered his head. "He was wounded, sir. We know that much. Wandered off. Probably in a daze. Ain't no one found a body, but the captain's probably dead. You got my sympathy, sir."

"Hold your sympathy, Sergeant. I have every reason to believe my brother is alive."

"The Rebs would've let us know if they'd captured him."

"I didn't mean to imply he was captured." Charles handed the sergeant the note from Amanda, but Tucker gave it right back.

"Can't read, sir. The captain used to help me with my letters."

Charles now understood why the major had chosen Tucker. "What's your given name, Sergeant?"

"Jo."

Charles held out his right hand. "I have never cared much for military protocol. I expect you to call me Charles."

The sergeant shook his hand. "Yes, sir—Charles. You said Sam is still alive?"

Just as he suspected. The young sergeant was a friend of Sam's. "You're going to help me find him." Jo grinned as he explained Amanda's note, detailing the best route to her farm.

Chapter Seventeen

Near Sharpsburg, Maryland
September 17, 1862

MANY OF THE BOYS WORE BLUE, courtesy of the Yankees at Harper's Ferry. The rumble of cannon grew closer, and the day got hotter. Men were dropping from the ranks like flies. Wil had no time to order a detail to pick up stragglers. Proceed to Sharpsburg—best possible speed. Powell Hill wore his red battle shirt, signaling they would engage upon arrival. No rest—not until the fighting was over.

In the dust and heat, Wil led Poker Chip along the snaking column to Sharpsburg. He considered himself lucky. Not many men had the same mount from the beginning of the war. But the Nez Perce had developed the Appaloosa as sturdy warhorses. He shouldn't think about that time. But he always did—just before battle. It helped him channel his killing urge toward the Yankees.

Wil wiped the sweat and grime from his eyes. Buzzards circled in the air up ahead. He wondered how many were already dead.

The guns grew louder. The boys knew to save their energy, and few spoke. All were hardened veterans now. Feet trod and hooves plodded against the sunbaked surface.

Wil hated winter's cold and should have been rejoicing in the heat. It had been mighty cold when Benjamin had died. She had come to him in the night and announced that he was dead. There had been no emotion in her voice, and he lingered on her message. *Their son was dead*.

No one comprehended how much he covered his feelings with the soldier's mask of duty, except for *her*. Then Benjamin had died. Yet, he had been unable to take her in his arms and give her comfort when she needed it most. From that time on, he drifted—making certain he never cared that deeply again. Until he had met Amanda.

But she had peered behind the mask and sensed the insanity within him. He should tell her how it had got there. Like with the letter, he was thinking foolishly. He would reveal a part of himself that he hadn't wanted anyone to know. *Stop thinking*.

A private sprawled spread eagle on the ground. Wil prodded the freckle-faced boy with his sword. The private got to his knees, swayed, and sank to the dust. He fought the urge of running the boy through. *Not yet*. Control the fury. The guns were close. *Soon enough*—he would draw the enemy's blood. Leave the boy be and give him the chance Benjamin had never received.

Wil sheathed his sword and continued marching. A flurry of riders and lathered horses ahead caught his attention. He felt the presence of Yankees beyond the next hill. The order would come. *Might as well ride the last mile*. He mounted Poker. The gelding felt the excitement and pawed the ground.

A courier brought the dispatch to advance.

Wil faced the boys and shouted the order. Muskets readied as the order went down the line. He raised his sword. *Forward*. As they moved closer to the battle, the guns became deafening.

Another dispatch—form the regiment to the right. Second nature—Wil gave the commands. At the top of the hill, Yankees were near a cornfield. Through the smoke he couldn't see the gray line. Confused by the blue uniforms, the Yanks hadn't fired on his boys yet.

Several heads bowed in silent prayer. Others urinated their nerves away. A private watched him—the freckle-faced boy. Somehow he had managed to catch up. Wil nodded to a job well done, and a wild-eyed look gave way to courage as the private gripped his musket with confidence.

Wil sent Poker to the back and waited for the order to attack. It wasn't long in coming. After a seventeen-mile march with no rest, he had discovered a body could do more than he thought possible. He bellowed the order at the top of his lungs and waved his sword.

With a roar and a yell, the regiment charged forward. The Yankees realized their mistake—too late. A volley fired into the blue ranks and delivered deadly lead.

In a state of confusion, some Yanks returned fire. Others ran. Smoke clouded the field. Another volley. More Yankees withdrew.

Heat from a bullet grazed the side of Wil's face. Unharmed, he gave the order to fire at will. Dead and wounded covered the ground.

Two soldiers in blue struggled in hand-to-hand combat. Wil drew his pistol and fired at the man on the left. The Yankee dropped, and the freckle-faced boy continued forward. With cold calculation, he sighted targets and fired. More Yankees turned tail and fled. Some threw their muskets down and shoved their hands in the air in surrender.

Leave them for someone else to take prisoner. Wil pressed on. Smoke filtered past. The old wound began acting up, and the dull throb in his hip slowed him.

A bluecoat stumbled over a leveled corn stalk. Wil aimed his Colt, and the boy started reciting the Lord's Prayer. Wil pulled the trigger. *Click.* Empty chamber. As Wil raised his sword, the boy saw his chance. He retreated—triple quick.

More Rebel yells, more guns firing. Proud of his boys' bravery, Wil could no longer see the cornfield beneath the bodies. He hadn't seen the Yankees skedaddle like this since first Manassas. After another wave of firing, smoke clouded the field. Muskets were so hot, the boys hammered ramrods with stones.

The smoke drifted, and the cloud lifted. After reloading his pistol, Wil raised his Colt. His chest blazed with pain, and he slammed to the ground before he could shoot. He couldn't think straight. For a brief moment, he thought he heard *her* voice. She spoke halting English, but it was lyrical nonetheless. She *had* known the depth of his feelings—just before she died.

Sweat beaded on Sam's forehead. Longing for a Maine autumn, where days would be cooling with brisk evenings, he sat on the porch steps and whittled a block of wood. The thought that he might not see Maine again intruded. His leg wasn't mending properly, and amputation was never far from his mind. Fewer soldiers survived when the operation had been delayed.

After Amanda's tender nursing care, he couldn't fault her for trying to save the leg. A man missing a leg on a farm was only so much use. *A farm?* Neither of them had professed undying love. In fact, she seemed downright hesitant. So why was he so hopelessly entangled that he already had thoughts of making Virginia his home after the war?

If he kept the leg, he might entertain the notion. He had once passed a makeshift hospital in a farmhouse. Glistening white severed arms and legs had been tossed out the window. The body parts formed a mound ready for burial. *Morbid.* But then, the whole war was morbid.

He was an even bigger fool than he thought. Though he had been unable to admit it, he had always loved her.

He pared a section from the wood block, never knowing what a carving would be until it was nearly finished. This piece vaguely resembled a horse.

Ezra led the stallion, Red, to a nearby pasture.

Sam held up the figure to compare them. That's what this piece was—Red. He shaved another flake away.

"Good afternoon."

With Amanda's greeting, the knife slipped, slicing into his index finger. "Shit . . . " The oath was out of his mouth before he had time to think about it.

"I didn't mean to startle you." Amanda examined his bleeding finger. "I shall fetch some water to clean it up."

She lifted his hand for closer inspection, and he became distinctly aware of her touch. After the deserter's death, she had become subdued. *A killer's hand.* She knew him for what he was now. Sam withdrew his bleeding forefinger from her grip. "I'd rather you didn't."

"If you're certain that it's all right."

"It is." Sam returned his attention to the carving, while Amanda watched curiously.

"It's Red," she said. "Rebecca lost the last one you made for her."

Although awkward in his role of a father, he made certain to spend a few minutes with Rebecca each day. "I'll give it to her when I'm finished." He glanced over at Amanda and came close to cutting his finger again. *Pay attention.*

Dressed in a faded yellow skirt that had been laundered and mended once too often, she looked particularly appealing. Then again, she always looked that way. Damn, now he couldn't concentrate.

"Sam?"

The whisper of his name increased his arousal. "Amanda, my behavior was unbecoming as an officer and a gentleman."

"Kate was right."

He stole a glance. Instead of ranting, she arched her lips in a smile. "About what?" he asked.

"That you're conscientious about a lady's feelings."

He nearly dropped the carving. So much for the belief that women never talked about such things. He diverted his attention to whittling.

"I meant it as a compliment," Amanda said. "The Colonel tended to be rather stern."

"That may be, but . . . Amanda, why did you come looking for me?"

She crossed her arms as if suddenly cold. "After you came to me that night, I knew I had to do something to help. Wil said it would be an act in futility, but I had to try."

With the mention of Jackson's name, he bristled.

"And I just said something that I shouldn't have," she said.

"No, you've been honest with me. I think you have an inkling of how I feel. If you prefer Jackson, I'll step aside."

Amanda laughed and clapped a hand over her mouth. "I'm sorry Sam, but how different you are from Wil."

"Is that good or bad?"

She crossed her arms again. "It wasn't meant as anything—only that you're different."

"Amanda . . . " Life was too short for too many these days. None of them could turn a blind eye to it. He cleared his throat. "You wanted to know why I requested the transfer—"

"Miss Amanda . . . " Frieda appeared in the doorway.

Amanda straightened her faded dress and backed away from him as though the old woman could see. "Yes, Frieda?"

"Dere a carriage comin'."

With a tug on Sam's arm, Amanda shot a nervous glance down the lane. "Hurry. They'll know you're a Yankee from your accent."

The wood carving tumbled down the porch steps, and Sam groaned getting to his feet. "I can't move that fast, Amanda."

Carriage wheels creaked, and the clip-clop of hooves entered the lane. Amanda snatched up the carving from the bottom step. "You must. Unless it's Charles, they will turn you over to the authorities."

And Charles wouldn't have been out for a Sunday drive in a carriage. When visions of emaciated forms from Confederate prisons entered Sam's mind, he hobbled up the stairs as fast as he could. "I don't care to find out if the rumors about Libby are true."

Frieda reached out a thin hand. "I will help him, Miss Amanda. You see to our visitor." The old woman's sense of direction was uncanny as she helped him to the back bedroom. "Da leg has stopped gettin' better, Mr. Sam. If it get worse, da doctors ain't goin' to have no choice. Miss Amanda talk me out of doin' what's best."

Sam sat on the edge of the bed. He bit his lip, hoping to take his mind from the pain. "I appreciate everything you've done."

"I make a poultice and pray it does da job dis time. I need time to prepare, but I get somethin' for da pain."

Breathing out, he said, "That would be most welcome, Frieda."

As Frieda left the room, he sat back. He unpinned the section of fabric near his knee and unwound the bandage around his leg. Jagged and an inflamed red, the wound continued to drain.

"Mr. Sam . . . " The old woman carried a tea cup. "I know it don't look good."

"How did you know?"

She smiled a toothless grin, and the wrinkles appeared to etch deeper in her lined face. "I know just about everythin'." She handed him the cup. "Now drink it down. My mammy taught me da ways of Africa. She taught me well. Da white doctors could learn if dey take da time."

He smelled the heavy aroma of whiskey—good Southern whiskey. From experience, he was all too aware the whiskey was a cover for Frieda's bitter-tasting concoctions. The fiery drink tingled his throat. "I wonder where your mammy found Southern whiskey in Africa."

Frieda's grin widened. "I adapt my potions to my needs."

"Have you always read minds?"

"Don't read minds. Just have a way of knowin' what people think."
Her smile vanished. "Da massa thought I was possessed and try to beat
da devil from me."

Slavery—such an ugly institution. He had thought Kate a bit of
a radical with her extreme abolitionist views, but Frieda's firsthand
account proved she had been right.

"You don't need to feel sorry for me, Mr. Sam. All dis happen afore
I come to live with Miss Amanda. Her papa buy me, and I raise her
as if she was my own young 'un. She give me my freedom when da
Colonel die. Never thought I'd see da day, but you doin' right by tryin'
to set my people free."

"But . . . "

Frieda raised a finger. "You already has doubts 'bout it bein' to save
da Union. You know dat it wrong to keep my people slaves."

Sam gulped the last of the drink. "Sometimes I wonder what we're
fighting for." As drowsiness overwhelmed him, the cup fell from his
hand to the wood floor, and he heard the sound of clattering glass.

"Da cost is high, but it right." Frieda's sightless eyes came to rest
on him. "Miss Amanda, she ain't got no one to depend on, except us,
and we gettin' so old dat it don't matter. We ain't goin' to be 'round
much longer."

The pain had vanished, and Sam stretched his legs on the bed. "I
don't understand."

"She ain't goin' to get da Colonel's pension 'cause he fight for da
rebellion. He bin gone over a year. Ain't nothin' holdin' you back from
askin' Miss Amanda to marry you."

Marry Amanda? "Maybe you've forgotten Jackson. If I ask Amanda
anything, he'd most likely challenge me to a duel."

Frieda chuckled. "I already tell you, he don't make no promises."

"That won't stop him . . . " The old woman's image blurred, and
Sam rubbed his eyes. "What did you put in the drink?"

"I told you. It help da pain. It should be gone."

"It is."

"It should also make you honest with yourself."

"In what . . . " Blackness enveloped him. " . . . way?"

"Like how *you* feel 'bout Miss Amanda."

Drowsy, Sam closed his eyes. He heard Frieda shuffle over to the door. "Is that why you gave me the drink? You already know I care. It's not enough during these troubled times."

"I sorry for not tellin' da truth. Miss Amanda need time to get rid of our visitor. You rest, but don't forget what I say. Miss Amanda ain't got no one."

The tapping of Frieda's stick retreated from the room, and he thought of Amanda in his arms. Wartime was a dangerous time to love. When faced with battle, other men had lost their nerve because of a woman waiting at home. But no matter how hard he tried, he couldn't rid Amanda from his mind.

Chapter Eighteen

"ALICE." AMANDA GREETED HER SISTER WITH A SMILE.
A black servant helped Alice from the carriage. As always, she was dressed in the latest foreign fashion—whalebone crinoline, a striped dress with frilly trim on the skirt, and a bonnet to match. With everyday items growing scarce, Amanda wondered where her sister bought such luxuries.

Alice arranged the hoops of her skirt and unfolded her silk fan to break the afternoon heat. She pointed to the house. "Amanda, who was that?"

"Who?"

"I saw someone with Frieda—a man. And he certainly wasn't Ezra."

There would be no hiding Sam now. Thankful that her uninvited guest had turned out to be Alice, Amanda said, "You must mean Captain Samuel Prescott."

"Prescott, isn't he . . . ?"

"Rebecca's papa."

"But Amanda . . . " Alice's voice squeaked. "He's a Yankee!"

"I'm well aware of that. He was wounded in the recent fighting. I couldn't just leave him to be hacked to bits by the butchers commonly referred to as surgeons, now could I? After all, his wife was my friend."

"I suppose not."

"I was on a supply run just before the captain was wounded."

"Oh." Alice stopped fanning herself. "Amanda, we were beginning to fret. You haven't been by to see Mama in over a week. We're so relieved the fighting went north. With all the scalawag Yankees milling about, we were terrified."

In her own recent encounter, Amanda had helped Ezra bury the Yankee in the bottomland. She hoped a rainstorm didn't go washing up his body again. "Yankees?" she asked, pretending innocence.

Alice's lashes fluttered. "Thank goodness, we haven't been affected, but we have heard the troubles of you country folks. With rifles so heavy, I wouldn't even be able to defend myself. Poor Mama is fit to be tied."

Not as helpless as she let on, Alice used the ploy to gain men's attention. She would one day meet her match. The way she had dallied with Wil, maybe she already had.

Amanda strolled the brick walk toward the house. "You know how to shoot, Alice. Papa taught both of us."

Alice joined her. "But I have given up my tomboy ways."

"You may have convinced others that you have, but not me."

"Amanda, I was only trying to say there aren't many women who have helped the Cause like you, so pray tell, how could you help a good-for-nothing Yankee?"

Amanda climbed the stairs to the porch. "My reasons for making the supply runs have never been to help the Cause. It was for the sake of the wounded, and I will help the wounded on either side. So I will thank you not to speak any further about it. If the Yankees get wind that I have made another run since my arrest, I could be hanged for treason."

"Even the Yankees wouldn't hang a woman."

"I suppose not, but I'd rather not take the chance of them finding out."

She opened the door, and the frantic tapping of Frieda's cane came from the back room. "Miss Amanda, he's taken mighty sick."

"Sam?" Forgetting about her sister, Amanda rushed to the back bedroom.

Sam rested on the bed with a curious smile. Like most men, he was probably dreaming of their venture and wishing it had been more intimate. She bent down and checked his heart rate and breathing. Normal. Puzzled, she felt his forehead. Also normal. Yet Frieda wrung a cloth and placed it over his brow. Had she detected something unusual in the old woman's manner?

With crinoline hoops shaped like a church bell, Alice barely fit through the bedroom door. "What can I do to help?"

"He's been fighting a fever for days now, but I thought it was beaten."

Frieda straightened. "I'll make a poultice."

Amanda thought she detected a hint of a smile as the old woman left the bedroom. Frieda must have given Sam one of her potions. If only she could be sure. She went ahead and checked Sam's wound.

Suddenly pale, Alice fanned herself. "Oh my . . ."

"Alice?" Amanda clamped onto Alice's arm to help support her. "Why don't you go sit in the parlor? I shall be with you as soon as I can."

Alice waved her outstretched arms and weaved from the room.

Certain her sister would be fine, Amanda returned her attention to Sam. "So help me Sam, if this isn't Frieda's doing . . ."

As if in answer, his eyes opened.

She pressed a fist to her chest and sat on the edge of the bed. "Please don't ever do that again."

Unable to focus, he raised a hand to his temple. "Tell Frieda. She didn't warn me that it would knock me out."

Amanda placed two fingers to his lips. "Frieda knows how to get Alice's sympathy. I told her the truth. It won't set well if she tells Mama."

"Amanda, you can't risk it." He grimaced as he rose on an elbow. "I don't know where you think you're heading, but as long as Alice remains sympathetic, it buys you time."

"Time for what?"

"Time for Charles to get here. I would feel more comfortable if you waited for his help."

"You're assuming he got your note." Sam pushed to a sitting position. "I won't put you in danger. What if she alerts the authorities?"

"The only one she's likely to tell is Wil, and I haven't heard from him. I suspect he's gone north."

He shook his head. "I don't like it."

"We'll discuss it later. Now, let me hurry Alice along." His eyes reflected concern, and she squeezed his hand. "I'll be fine. You get some rest."

He returned his head to the feather pillow.

In the parlor, Alice was seated on the tapestry sofa, fanning herself. "I'm sorry, Amanda, but when I saw the wound—"

"I almost swooned the first time too. Before I had a chance to stitch it, it was covered in flies." Leaving the gory details to Alice's fertile imagination, Amanda tugged on her sister's arm. "I hope it explains why I had to help."

"Of course." Alice smiled slyly. "I suppose harboring a Yankee isn't much different from teaching the servants to read. Papa would have given you a licking for this as well."

Amanda guided Alice toward the door. "Probably. Just like when he caught you cursing or smoking behind the barn. A proper lady—you have all of your suitors fooled."

Alice's hands went to her hips, and Amanda worried that she might have pressed too far. Their gazes met.

Alice burst out laughing. "I helped with the servants' lessons too, but I didn't get caught." She sobered. "Amanda, I won't tell Mama. I shall make an excuse as to why you haven't dropped by. After that, she'll demand to visit. You had best make certain your captain is gone before then." She reached the door and stopped. "In all of the commotion, I almost forgot why I came. There's been a terrible battle in Sharpsburg, Maryland. Colonel Jackson's regiment was heavily involved, with Colonel Jackson listed among the missing."

Suddenly dizzy, Amanda swayed. Her knees buckled, and she grabbed a peg to keep from falling. Her burgundy cloak tumbled to the floor. Missing usually meant dead—or deserted. Wil wasn't the sort to desert. "Not Wil too."

"Missing doesn't mean that he's dead. Hasn't your Yank been reported missing?"

That's right. It would be just like Wil to charm a dazzling Northern lady. While she fretted, he probably frolicked in some woman's bed.

"General Lee has retreated."

Amanda blinked. "Leaving Wil in the North?"

"Amanda, you know as much as I do. We can only wait and see."

When would the waiting end?

* * *

Amanda picked wildflowers near the stream in the bottomland. The daylilies were in bloom. The Colonel had always liked the orange blossoms brightening the rooms. On the hill behind the house, she kneeled beside the headboard marking the Colonel's grave. "John, I try to visit more often, but there's so much to do these days. Most of the work falls on me. Ezra helps as much as he can. He's still strong, but he can't work the long hours like he used to. And even though it's been a struggle, Sam is getting stronger—well, he will be leaving soon."

She bowed her head and listened to a chorus of crickets. Tears pooled in her eyes. "Sam's a captain now, and you're probably having fits in your grave from the way I've helped him. But since you were friends before this foolish war began, I thought you would be able to see past the uniform."

She stood and brushed away the tears. Her only answer was the echo of crickets. *Colonel John Graham—loving husband.* Loving indeed. While she had admired his resolve, he had rarely taken her in his arms or given her a tender kiss to show that he cared. And she had chastised Wil for speaking the truth. Wil—dear Lord, she prayed he wasn't buried in some unmarked mass grave in the North. *Don't think like that.* He had been reported as missing, not dead.

Darkness had settled by the time she returned to the farmhouse. With the clear evening, Amanda shoved contrary thoughts from her mind and counted stars. So peaceful. She could almost forget the ravages of war.

Ezra's laugh drifted from the front porch. She moved toward the sound. Smoking a corncob pipe, he sat in a rocking chair next to Sam. She climbed the steps, and both men fell silent.

Ezra leaped to attention.

"Am I interrupting?" she asked.

"No, Miss Amanda. We was just talkin'."

Even through the scant light filtering from the lamps in the parlor, she could see that Ezra's eyes glowed with pride. "What is it, Ezra? You have always been able to talk to me."

He lowered his head. "Mr. Sam—he say—"

"I told him," Sam replied, "that in Maine, he would be able to vote."

A vote—she couldn't have dreamed of a more inviting enticement to drive Ezra from the farm if she had tried. Her world was crumbling apart.

"If you want to lay a broom to someone, I'm the one to blame, not Ezra."

Skeptical that even Maine would allow a Negro to vote, she asked, "Is it true?"

"Yes."

She faced Ezra. "You're a free man. You can leave anytime you wish."

Ezra's eyebrows wiggled in relief. "Miss Amanda, you know I can't leave you and Frieda, but imagine dat—I could vote." He grinned and kept shaking his head. "Me... If you don' mind, I like to say good night." After they bid Ezra good night, he crossed the farmyard toward the cabin sheltered in a grove of walnut trees.

When the old man's form disappeared in the darkness, Amanda grew curious. "Did you have a reason for telling Ezra about being able to vote?"

"That things change." Sam seemed solemn.

"Then you have given him something to dream for."

"I had hoped you wouldn't be angry."

"I've never considered knowledge a bad thing."

"Amanda, it's time I leave. This afternoon made me realize that I must."

She suddenly understood why he seemed melancholy. "You're not properly mended."

"What if next time it's not your sister? I'm leaving in the morning."

First the news of Wil, and now Sam. He extended a hand and slipped a wood carving into her palm—the one he had been whittling earlier in the day. It was finished in the likeness of Red. Her throat went dry.

"Amanda, Frieda told me the news about Jackson. The battlefield is a mighty confusing place. He could have been captured."

Captured? Instead of bringing her hope, the thought unsettled her further. Wil would prefer to die as a warrior, rather than languish in some Yankee prison. "Thank you for trying, but even if he were the sort to surrender, Yankee prisons aren't faring any better than Confederate."

Sam sighed. "Then you do love him."

Love Wil? Uncertain, she felt numb. Was she clinging to false hope? And there was Sam. He was very much alive—for now. Traveling on foot, he'd never make it to the nearest Yankee lines without being captured or killed. "I'd like to show you something before you go."

Amanda turned, and Sam grasped the crutch resting against the porch rail and struggled to his feet. She crossed the farmyard, but he was unable to keep up. She slowed her pace. By the light of the moon, she saw his face furrow in pain with each step.

Once inside the barn, she lit a lantern and led Red from his stall. "An officer needs a good horse."

He shook his head. "I can't take Red."

"I have managed to keep him this long because I was running supplies. My mare is in foal to him, and it's only a matter of time before someone steals him. He's a strong horse that will serve you well."

Sam hobbled closer and patted Red on the neck. He examined the horse. "He's everything you say, but I can't."

"I would rather he goes to someone who I know will take care of him."

"I've lost two horses in the fighting."

"He would face the same risk with the Confederates. There's no escaping the danger. Sam, please take him. He shall give you a chance of making it back to the lines alive."

"I know how much he means to you. I can't." He adjusted his weight on the crutch and limped for the door.

"Don't do this to me. You won't make it without a good horse. And I can't face losing anyone else."

Without turning around, he halted by the door.

Amanda dropped Red's lead line. "Sam?"

"Don't say any more," he said in a shaky voice. He straightened his shoulders before facing her. "I'm finding this hard enough as it is."

"So you distance yourself. Take Red. At least I know you shall have a chance, and ... " She forced a smile. "When the war is over, he will make certain you remember where I live."

Sam shifted his weight on the crutch. "I requested the transfer to New Mexico because I cared for you more than I should have back then."

Finally, the confession she thought she might never hear. "That's what you were going to tell me before you were wounded."

Like a shy schoolboy, he lowered his head. If it hadn't been for the crutch, she imagined him shuffling.

"I was going to tell you that I love you, but your heart already belonged to another."

"You thought I loved Wil. But I . . . " *Had she loved Wil?* The question no longer required an answer. He was gone, without ever telling her how he might have felt. Her throat constricted. She had comforted Sam when Kate died, and Wil had consoled her after John's death. Life was fleeting.

She failed to notice Sam's arms going around her. He held her. Like a child frightened of the dark, she clung to him and nearly toppled him from the crutch. With a shudder she fought the tears. For ages, she stood there, hanging on tight.

He kissed her. "Amanda, I meant what I said."

He loved her. She couldn't think about that now. So lost and alone, she clasped him tighter and listened to the galloping rhythm of his heart. With so many friends and loved ones cold and lifeless in their graves, she absorbed herself in his radiating warmth. His fingertips stroked her cheek, then his hand traced the length of her body.

One by one, their clothes dropped to the straw floor. Bare flesh touched bare flesh. As she breathed in the sweet scent of hay, the single lantern cast an intertwined shadow on the barn wall.

Chapter Nineteen

A BULLET SAILED BY, AND CANISTER WHISTLED overhead. Sam woke to a scream with his heart racing.

Amanda stroked the stubble on his chin. "It's all right," she murmured.

He glanced around Amanda's bedroom. The battle had been nothing more than a dream. His fear faded, and he huddled next to her with his head coming to rest on her breast. Her fingers went through his hair. Breathing deeply, he closed his eyes.

Throughout the night, they had comforted each other. He never wanted to leave the safety of her arms, but he must. His presence jeopardized her safety. During the night, she had made him promise to take Red. "Thank you," he whispered.

A hint of pink appeared in her cheeks. "I was thinking of when the Colonel left . . ."

He pressed his fingers to her lips. "Good thoughts only. Promise me, no tears."

Bravely, she agreed. Amanda snuggled into the crook of his arm, and Sam brushed her blonde hair away from her shoulders, revealing her pale, white breasts. She shyly lowered her head.

"There's no reason to be embarrassed."

She met his gaze. "The Colonel used to say proper women didn't—"

"I'm not the Colonel." *Or Jackson.* He left that thought unsaid. "Amanda, I hope you don't regret what happened."

"I don't regret anything."

But she had looked away. Maybe she wasn't even aware of her doubts. In spite of his own misgivings, he wasn't satiated either. With

Amanda, he doubted that he ever could be. When he kissed her on the mouth, angry wails filled the room. Caught in the moment, he had forgotten that Rebecca slept in the crib not more than two feet away.

Amanda slid to the edge of the bed, but the toddler quieted. Sam scooped Amanda into his arms, and they rolled over with her head coming to rest on the feather pillow.

"Your leg," she reminded him.

"I'm fine." Out of the corner of his eye, he spotted a figure crouching over the crib. Sam drew his pistol from its holster at the top of the bed and aimed.

A young colored girl screamed and shoved her hands skyward. "I didn' know you was here, Mr. Sam. Honest. Miss Becca cry, and I come get her."

Dulcie. Not a Rebel blackened by gunpowder. He blinked back the image and lowered his gun.

"Dulcie, go ahead and take Rebecca," Amanda said.

"Yes'm." After gathering the toddler in her arms, Dulcie scooted from the room.

Amanda's lips curved to a grin. "Everyone in the household will know the nature of our relationship very soon."

His gaze locked onto hers. "I could have shot her."

"But you didn't. She wasn't harmed. Dulcie had no reason to think we were in here carrying on like a couple of newlyweds."

She touched the back of his hand, and he closed his eyes, trying to shut out the image of Dulcie lying on the floor covered in blood.

"Sam, it wasn't your fault."

"No? It's a sign of what I've become."

"I don't believe that."

He held out the revolver. "This is what I live by now."

"Men who live by the gun are incapable of morals." Amanda tucked the patchwork quilt to her chin. "If our time together has meant nothing more than satisfying your needs, tell me now, while I can still recover with some dignity."

Sam holstered the gun. "I meant it when I said I cared." As he drew her to him, the rumpled quilt fell to the surface of the bed. "Were you trying to convince me or yourself?"

"I didn't meet the Colonel until after he fought the Mexicans, but he had dark moods every once in a while. He refused to talk about them. Same as you, he had dreams. No one can see what you have and not be affected by it." She placed a hand over his heart. "You need to find some way of holding onto yourself. If necessary, find a small place in here where you won't allow the war to reach and hang on. If I can be of any help, let me know."

Content just holding her, he tightened his grip. A beam of light passed through parted curtains. "I need to be leaving."

"I shall make breakfast." She rose from the bed.

Sam grasped her hand. "I'm not hungry."

"Then I'll fix something to take with you."

"Amanda—you're trying too hard."

"You didn't want me to cry. If I don't keep busy, I'll break the promise."

He let go of her hand and watched her dress. The contentment of the night gave way to empty reality. War was a hell of a time to love, but he had loved her from the beginning. Near the dresser she combed her tousled hair, and he struggled with his trousers.

"I shall pack enough supplies to last a couple of days," she said. "Hopefully, that will see you through."

Sparkling green eyes followed him in the mirror as he limped over to her. He ran his fingers through her freshly combed hair and felt a tremble beneath his fingertips. She pinned her hair into a knot. When he kissed her exposed neck, she closed her eyes, but he had already seen the tears filling them.

She dabbed her face with her sleeve before turning to him. "Come back to me—please."

"I will."

A promise—well intentioned, but meaningless during these terrible times. A nagging lump formed in her throat. He was leaving. Unable to delay any longer, she watched him tug on his boots. His face contorted. Pain—she felt it as if he had voiced it.

None too steady, he got to his feet, gripping the bedpost for support. Amanda reached for the crutch, but he waved her away. "I can't take it with me."

Though shaky, he straightened and strapped the pistol around his waist. Weapons to kill—or with which to be killed.

"The wound hasn't mended completely. If you're not careful, you could still lose the leg."

"I'm well aware of that."

She must have sounded like an old mother hen. Deciding to leave him be, she faced the mirror. "Ezra can saddle Red."

His foot scuffed the wood floor when he walked, and she wondered how he would ever manage to ride Red.

"You haven't changed your mind about taking Dulcie?" she asked.

"I'll take Dulcie."

"Good, she will be able to help you."

Sam stepped behind her and unpinned her chignon. He pulled her pearl-handled brush through her hair and smoothed her hair with his hand. "You worry too much."

She watched his mirror image and realized he was left-handed. Rebecca showed the same preference. Turning around, she said, "On the contrary, you are trying to protect me."

"A fault of mine. I would protect you to the ends of the earth if I could find a way." He twisted her hair through his fingertips and smiled slightly. "Would you mind wearing your hair down this morning?"

She shook her head. "Sam—"

"We said everything there is to say last night."

"Then do we count the number of times we say goodbye?"

"You warned me not to say goodbye unless I meant it. I've learned my lesson, Amanda."

As he kissed her on the mouth, Amanda threw her arms around his neck and hugged him. So many had departed without returning. She never wanted to let go.

Sam kissed her once more. "It's time."

Determined not to break her promise, she clasped his hand and led the way from the room. His brow furrowed with each step. He gripped the rail for support. Her heart went out to him, but he needed to make it on his own. He would never make the trip to Yankee lines if he didn't.

At the bottom of the stairs, he let go of the rail and nearly fell. Amanda caught his hand. "You need to be extra careful riding Red. He will take advantage of your weak side if you don't."

"I shall remember that."

They reached the parlor, and Dulcie plucked Rebecca from the floor. Amanda couldn't blame the servant girl for being upset. With a firm grip on Sam's arm, she helped him to the kitchen. Biscuits straight from the oven changed his mind about not staying for breakfast. Grateful for an extra few minutes with him, Amanda sat across from him, watching his every move. When their gazes met, a sly grin crossed his face. All too aware of what he must be thinking, warmth rose in her cheeks.

"You had best . . ." She cleared her throat. "Eat something before your food gets cold."

He shoved his plate to the middle of the table. "We should have put our time to better use."

With Frieda puttering about the kitchen, Amanda placed her fingers to her lips to hush him.

The old woman doddered over to the table and set the coffee pot on it. "I go hurry Dulcie up."

The lump at the back of Amanda's throat returned. "You should go through the bottomland. It's the direction I mapped out for Charles."

"I'll be fine."

Fighting tears, Amanda got up and shouted out the back door for Ezra. He was on the stoop chopping wood for the increasingly chilly nights. After asking him to saddle Red, she reseated herself at the table. At least Sam was eating. Or pretending to.

"I appreciate all that you've done for me—and Rebecca," Sam said, sounding more like a departing houseguest than a lover. He finally stopped playing with the food on his plate.

Dulcie appeared in the doorway, holding Rebecca's hand. "Miss Becca wants to say 'bye to her papa."

Rebecca waved. "Bye-bye."

With a groan Sam got to his feet and swept the little girl into his arms. She giggled and pulled on his moustache.

"She won't forget her papa—not this time." Amanda turned to Dulcie. "I wish you the best of luck up north."

Dulcie gave a worried frown. "Miss Amanda—how's you goin' to explain my disappearin'?"

"In a couple of days, I'll inform Oakcrest that you've run off. By that time, you shall be far enough away. They'll never find you."

"Da massa blame you for fillin' my head with ideas."

"I shall pay him. He'll fuss and fume but will let it pass."

"When I get north, I pay you back."

Amanda hugged Dulcie. "You have already paid me through your help with Rebecca."

"I always remember you, Miss Amanda. Ain't no one ever treat me da way you do."

Sam cuddled Rebecca. "Dulcie, it's time to fetch your things."

"Straight away."

Dulcie scampered from the kitchen, and Sam lowered Rebecca to the floor, keeping hold of her tiny hand. He limped toward the door.

"I think you need more help than she does," Amanda said. She hooked her hands under his elbow, lending him support. His eyes expressed their appreciation as she helped him outside to the back steps.

Ezra stood on the other side of the picket fence, holding Red steady.

A few minutes later, Dulcie dashed across the farmyard with a dirty cotton bag slung over her shoulder.

Bile rose in Amanda's throat. She pressed a hand to her stomach to keep from getting sick. *Everyone who left never returned.*

Sam strapped Dulcie's bag to the saddle. Her worldly goods—even less than he carried on marches. Wearing civilian clothing and traveling with contraband, he could be branded a spy. He wished he had a uniform. Federal blue would be more difficult to wear the next time. After being wounded, he must have been losing his nerve. Other soldiers had.

Frieda handed him a bag containing rations. "Ain't much, but it should see you across da line."

He squeezed Frieda's withered hand and mumbled his thanks, before tying the bag alongside Dulcie's.

Amanda picked up Rebecca and pressed against him. He kissed them goodbye, gritted his teeth, and climbed into the saddle. When the worst of the pain passed, he extended his hand to Dulcie, pulling her on behind him. "Amanda . . . " He let the thought go, reining Red on. After last night, she knew how he felt. There was no need to announce it to everyone else.

His right leg hung limp in the stirrup. He intertwined his fingers in Red's mane to help him remain steady in the saddle. Dulcie circled her arms about his waist, and he guided the horse across the farmyard. He brought the stallion to a halt and waved to Amanda.

She held Rebecca's hand in her own and waved with her. Tears rolled unashamedly down her cheeks.

So much for promises. He buried the feeling and sent Red across the pasture. The horse trotted along the path until reaching the top of a hill. Indecision gripped him. Should he look back for a final glance? He might turn around. Unwilling to risk it, Sam sent Red down the grassy slope to the creek.

"I scared."

Thankful for the company, he had all but forgotten Dulcie. The distraction helped free his mind from Amanda. "We'll make it."

"Dat only partly what I scared of. Even if I get north, what do I do?"

The creek meandered through the bottomland. "I'll help you find a job."

"Miss Amanda right. You very kind."

The bottomland gave way to poplar and sycamore woods. "Do you have any family?"

"I don't know where dey are, except my baby. He buried in da slave plot. He sickly from da start, but give me da milk I need for Miss Becca."

Sam muttered his condolences. "But you seem so young."

Dulcie tightened her grip, and he let the subject drop. At a bend, Sam studied the steep hill in their path. With no direct route through the trees, he would need to lead Red. "If you go ahead, I'll see to Red."

As Dulcie slid from the stallion's back, her dark eyes darted back and forth.

"No one else is around," Sam said.

Reassured, she began climbing.

Gingerly, Sam got off Red and muffled a cry when his foot hit the ground. Halfway up the hillside, his leg crumpled underneath him, and he slid several feet. Luckily Red stepped over him, but rocks jabbed his arms and legs. He sucked in his breath against the pain.

"Mr. Sam!" Dulcie stood over him, while Red calmly munched tender shoots farther up the hill. "You bleedin' again. I don't know how to help!"

Fresh blood stained his trouser leg. "Damn . . . " He had seen other wounds like this. The unfortunate individual always ended up losing the limb. *Keep focused.* Sam struggled to stand. "If you . . . " He couldn't think straight. "If you will help me up."

Dulcie latched onto his arm, and he wobbled to his feet. "I'm not going to make it unless Red carries me. If you can hold him steady . . . "

"I can do dat."

Sam caught a hand in Red's bridle and positioned the horse on lower ground. Once in the saddle, he clicked his tongue. With Dulcie alongside of them, Red started up the hill. Progress was slow. The stallion stumbled and almost went to his knees. Red backed a few paces, but Sam kicked him. Finally, they reached the top.

He caught his breath and allowed Red a moment to do the same. Thankful for Frieda's supplies, Sam uncapped the canteen and sipped cool water. He held the canteen out to Dulcie.

Her eyes widened, and she backed away.

"What did I do this time?" he asked.

"A darkie ain't supposed to drink from da same canteen as a white man."

"You'll get mighty thirsty, since we only have the one." He held out the canteen. "I can't imagine Amanda abiding by such folly."

Dulcie sipped water like deer at a pond, watching for predators.

"I'm not going to hurt you."

Her dark eyes darted around as if making sure they were truly alone. "Foolish thinkin'."

"It's not foolish, if you've been hurt." Judging by Dulcie's diminutive size and blemished face, he guessed her to be fifteen or sixteen at best. As fidgety as she was, he also had a good idea who had probably fathered her baby.

She drank her fill and expressed her thanks.

After recapping the canteen, Sam surveyed the area.

A trail cut through the woods. The dirt road was a familiar one. Full circle—the army had camped along the Rappahannock River. When he arrived at the banks, he would head north. Sam helped Dulcie aboard and guided Red parallel to the road. As morning gave way to afternoon, he circled a rundown farmhouse with a rickety porch. A few hundred yards beyond the outbuildings was a peaceful pond with plentiful grazing.

After dismounting, he hoped he would be able to climb back in the saddle, especially if the need to move quickly arose. Once Red was watered, he relaxed. He tied the horse securely to a sycamore tree and carried a few provisions to the edge of the pond. "You're welcome to join me."

Dulcie lingered beside Red, hunching behind the horse, while Sam stretched by the pond. With a clear view of the water and the path leading in, he doubted anyone could take them by surprise.

The day had grown hot. Wiping the sweat from his brow, he longed for Maine. But Virginia was Amanda's home. A woman with a small child—alone and unprotected. No matter how many warnings he sent of approaching armies, she would never leave. That fact made him downright uneasy.

Sam checked the provisions—hard rolls and some dried meat. It beat army rations. After satisfying his hunger, he checked his leg. The wound wasn't festering. A good sign according to Frieda, and she had been very specific about keeping it clean. Just the opposite of what the doctors would say. What did they know? They would have unceremoniously lopped it off.

Out of the corner of his eye, he saw tall grass rustle near the pond. There was no breeze in the air. He glanced over his shoulder. Dulcie huddled near Red's feet with her knees tucked to her body. He drew his pistol and aimed at the waving grass.

"Don't shoot!" a small voice shrieked. With arms raised high and eyes widened in sheer terror, a young girl with red curls stepped from the long grass.

Sam lowered the pistol. "I won't hurt you. Are you alone?"

She nodded, and her hands returned to their sides. "You sound funny—like you got a nose full. Are you a Yank? My mama says Yankee bluebellies like to burn an' kill. Why would you want to kill my papa or brothers?"

Always the innocent. "I don't want to kill your papa or brothers."

She moved closer but didn't politely avert her gaze from his wound. "My papa is very brave."

"I'm sure he is."

"Mama says he's the bravest man in the Rebel army. 'Course now that my brothers are with him, there ain't no one but me to help on the farm."

If her brothers had recently joined the fighting, they were most likely boys. Boys didn't belong in a war, and it certainly was an unjust way of growing up.

She took a hesitant step toward him. "Did you fall off your horse?"

"No."

Comprehension filtered into the childish eyes. "Did my papa do that?"

"Your papa wasn't there."

She cracked a smile. "You don't look so diff'rent. Do you have a name?"

"Sam."

She curtsied. "Louise."

"Pleased to meet you, Louise." She held up a tiny hand, and he kissed it. "I have a little girl of my own."

Louise giggled. "In the North?"

"As a matter of fact, in Virginia—near Fredericksburg."

"You're the first Yank I've met—up close I mean. Does it hurt?"

"A little."

Sam finished wrapping his leg. Blood seeped through the already crimson cloth. He quickly pinned the trouser leg.

"Are you goin' to die?" she asked.

"I don't think so. I need to be moving, Louise." With a groan, Sam got to his feet. He hobbled over to Red.

Dulcie was no longer huddled beside the horse. He glanced around. Where was she? This was no time to be hiding. Suddenly lightheaded, he dropped the canteen and clung to the horse's side for support. Louise picked up the canteen. Welcoming her help, he strapped the canteen to the saddle.

From the far side of the pond, a woman called, "Louise"—her mother, no doubt. Fraternizing with a Yankee wouldn't likely set well. She'd get the wrong impression. Sam untied Red from the tree.

"Louise?"

The call was closer than before. Sam put the brunt of his weight on his wounded leg. *Wrong move.* He was eating dirt. Almost comically, the little girl grasped his arm and tried to help him up.

"Louise!"

Sam latched onto the stirrup and pulled himself to his feet.

"Sam's my friend," Louise said to her mother. "He's not so diff'rent. He's a Yank, Mama."

"Get up to the house!" Louise scurried past her mother, and the woman swatted the little girl on the back of the legs with a poplar switch. Her eyes blazed as she raised the stick in the air. "As for you, Mr. Damnyankee—if you've touched her, I'll have your stinkin' bluebelly hide."

"I didn't hurt her." Sam shoved a foot in the stirrup.

"Then you've filled her head full of your good-for-nothin' damnyankee lies."

He swung in the saddle.

She hurtled after him, waving the switch over her head. "I hope in all tarnation, you burn!"

The switch cracked across Red's flank. Sam fought the stallion, barely managing to keep him under control. Again the switch crashed down, smacking him on the leg. A dull sting—luckily it hadn't hit his wounded one. Eager to put some distance between them, he reined Red around and splashed into the water. Never again would he underestimate the determination of an angered mother.

Once safe on the other side, he scanned the area around the swamp for Dulcie.

"Sam," came a whisper from behind a willow tree. Louise stepped into the open. "There are Rebels the way you're headin'. They were through yesterday." She counted on her fingers. "Five—I think. They were hungry. Mama fed them some bread. They slept in the barn last night."

"Louise!"

Sam waved her on. "Go before you get into trouble again."

She scurried up the hill toward the farmhouse that he had passed earlier. Halfway up the path, she halted. "Sam, if you meet my papa—or brothers—please don't kill one another." With her curls flying behind, she charged up the hill.

He cued Red forward. As soon as he was out of the farm woman's sight, he circled the pond. Near the spot where he had watered Red, a dark shape huddled in the reeds.

"Dulcie?" Sam slid from Red's back. Using the stallion for support, he moved toward her.

Wide-eyed, she swung flying fists. "Don't you touch me."

Sam caught a clenched hand, and she screamed.

"Dulcie, it's me. Sam." Beneath his grip, her hand trembled. He let go. "Dulcie, I can guess what someone has done to you, but I'm not going to hurt you. We don't have much time. If you don't want to go back to that life, then we need to move on."

Swallowing hard, Dulcie got to her feet. "I afeared dey send me back."

"They're gone."

With her hands clasped behind her back, Dulcie smiled shyly. Was it the first time he had ever seen the young colored girl smile? He reached for Red's reins and managed to remount. Tired—so tired, but they still had many miles to go.

Dulcie climbed on behind him.

As they traveled the length of the woods, his energy drained further. The woods thinned to a trampled meadow. Little was left but wagon ruts gouged in the red dirt. An army had marched through, stripping the grassland bare. He brought Red to a halt.

Even under normal circumstances, he was nervous crossing a clearing. With the threat of Rebs in the area, he was more tense than usual. His hand was uneven on the reins, and Red jumped at a squirrel scampering up a tree.

If he circled the treeline, they might go miles out of the way, making it necessary to backtrack. Not a good plan, especially with Rebs near.

Sam searched through the provisions. While Dulcie hadn't eaten anything, accounting for her portion, there might be another day's food supply.

A brilliant orange glow spread over them as the sun slipped in the western sky. Twilight would be the best time to cross.

Sam relaxed in the saddle, and Red bent his head, nibbling on sapling leaves. The sun sank, and he thought of long blonde hair draped over him, tickling his chest. Her soft cries. He wished he could get such thoughts out of his mind. If Dulcie suspected, she would certainly think he was about to take liberties with her.

Gunfire popped in the distance. All of Sam's muscles tensed, and he gathered Red's reins. Dulcie straightened, but the countryside fell strangely quiet. The sun dropped low in the sky, and he scanned the horizon. "Rebs are near. I can feel it. Be prepared to hold on for dear life. We may be moving mighty fast if they show their ugly faces."

Dulcie tightened her grip around his waist, and he cautiously sent Red onto open ground. Cattle bellowed in a nearby field, but no more guns discharged. When they came to a stream, he let Red drink. Twilight dimmed to near darkness, and every nerve in his body screamed. He yanked Red's head from the water and drew his pistol. If there was a fight, he would make his ammunition count.

Not a twig snapped. Maybe he was beginning to imagine things. Sam listened for sounds, any clue of where the Rebs might be.

Red's ears pricked forward, and the stallion nickered.

To Sam's right, a horse responded.

He reined Red sharply to the left at a full gallop.

Dulcie squeezed the grip around his waist to a stranglehold. Pounding hooves chased after them, and the whir of a bullet flew overhead. He ducked low against Red's neck and urged Red for more speed. Carrying two, the stallion had nothing more to give.

Two riders appeared in front. Sam veered to avoid a collision. Instead of joining the pursuit, they raced after the Rebels.

Sam expected to hear a round of gunfire, but the Rebels fled. He cued Red to a walk, and one rider turned back to greet him, grinning from ear to ear.

"Charles?"

"I wasn't sure we would find you alive, little brother." Charles brought his horse even with Red and thumped Sam on the back.

"You obviously received Amanda's message."

Charles gave him a brotherly hug. "We did. It seems we're constantly in that courageous woman's debt."

Lightheaded, Sam put a hand to his temple. "This is Dulcie."

Charles tipped his hat. "Captain Charles Prescott."

The second horse drew near, and Sam acknowledged the rider. "Corporal."

Jo pointed to her sleeve with the extra stripe. "Sergeant," she corrected. "The Rebs had no belly for fightin'. Captain, I'm pleased to see you in one piece."

"Since when have you been so formal, Jo?"

Cracking a smile, Jo nodded at Charles. "Sam." She shoved out a hand. "Good to see you."

So Charles hadn't discovered her true identity. Respecting her privacy, Sam grasped the outstretched hand. "It might be wise to put some distance between us and the Rebs before they return with reinforcements."

"Right," Charles agreed. Concerned, he checked Sam over. "Are you up to it? Amanda said you had been wounded."

"I'll be fine."

"I know that tone, Sam."

"Mr. Sam, hurtin' somethin' fierce," Dulcie said.

Sam gasped. "An understatement, but worry about me later. Right now, let's make a hasty retreat." He slumped over Red's neck. Each step took him farther from Amanda. He must have been delusional again. He heard her voice whispering in the evening chill.

Lower and lower he sank. Charles reached for his arm but missed as he slipped from the saddle.

Chapter Twenty

FINALLY RID OF THE SICKENING STENCH of blood and death from the hospital, Sam was relieved to be released. Long into the nights, he had heard cries for home or the name of a loved one on final breaths. For a fortnight, he had been in his own delirium with fever, longing not for home, but for the mist-filled mornings of Virginia and Amanda.

After leading Red from the barn, Sam tied the horse to the hitching rail behind the brownstone. He curried the stallion's coppery coat until it gleamed like a newly minted penny. If he had any conscience, he would send Red north and buy another horse for the coming campaign. Amanda's argument to the contrary echoed in his mind—an officer needed a good horse. Normally, he wasn't the superstitious sort, but along with Red came Amanda's blessing. That might keep him safe long enough to see her again.

With General McClellan's dismissal, the new leader of the Army of the Potomac, General Ambrose Burnside, could not afford the luxury of waiting to make a move on Richmond unless he wished to follow in his predecessor's footsteps. In spite of the prospect of heavy fighting, Sam welcomed crossing the river into Virginia. In the one place Sam truly felt a part of Amanda, Red would guide him back to her.

"Sam." Charles joined him in the saddling yard. "I hope you approve."

"You did a fine job caring for him." Sam held out his hand in appreciation.

Charles shrugged. "It's the least I could do. I've heard congratulations are in order." His brother grasped his hand and shook it. "*Major* Prescott."

"Brevet," Sam reminded him.

"I know. A fancy way of saying more responsibility for the same pay." Charles patted Red on the neck. "I'm going with you on this one."

Uncertain he had heard right, Sam stared at his brother. "Going with me?"

"I've resigned my post and accepted a field command."

Throughout the years, Charles had made a competition of their achievements, most notably finishing ahead of him in class standings at West Point. "If this is some effort to prove yourself—"

"It's not."

"You don't know the first thing about command in the field."

"My brother will teach me what I need to know."

"Charles, this is no longer the Point. It's war, and there's no glory."

"I realize that. Remember, I nearly lost my brother. What's done is done. Accept it as something I need to do for myself. I'm bringing Holly along too. She can cook and launder for a little extra money."

Now he *was* confused. Holly wasn't the sort to carry out everyday household chores, let alone play servant to an army. "More likely she'll entertain a few lonely officers," he grumbled.

Before Charles could respond, he ducked into the barn for his saddle.

Charles followed him inside. "I'll pretend I didn't hear that. You're not exactly guiltless. Or didn't you know Holly was involved in smuggling supplies to the Rebs?"

Sam pulled the saddle from the top rail of the stall but replaced it before he dropped it. "Smuggling to the Rebs?"

"It appears Mrs. Graham never informed you who her Washington contact was."

Sam swallowed. "She didn't."

Charles's gaze softened. "I'm sorry to break it to you this way, but I thought you should know. Holly met your old commander, Jackson, at General Evan's reception a few years back."

He laughed at the irony. The general's reception was where he had met Amanda.

"Holly made the rounds of the hospitals, pretending to visit the wounded. It was nothing more than a cover to steal supplies for Jackson. Amanda was a go-between."

Sam seized the tack and stepped into the brisk morning air, where Red stood waiting. All along, he had guessed Jackson was the mastermind behind the supply runs. Even in New Mexico, Jackson had always held an ace. He had ways of knowing which Indians could be trusted, and only his former commander would have thought of using women to smuggle supplies. Unsuspected by most soldiers, women could travel more freely between the lines. And Amanda had only turned to him because she thought Jackson was dead.

As Sam tightened the girth, a cold wind blew, reminding him that autumn would soon turn to winter. Virginia beckoned him, but the opportunity to see Amanda wasn't likely in the coming days. He adjusted the bridle and gritted his teeth, before mounting Red.

His leg hurt like hell. When the pain passed, he bent over to place his foot in the stirrup. He straightened in the saddle and saluted Charles. "See you in hell, brother."

Late November brought the influenza season. Amanda had taken ill during the week. After spending the night bent over the chamber pot, she found the simple task of dressing daunting. There had been no word from Sam or Wil. Unable to afford a private courier, she had no way of smuggling a letter across the lines to Sam, but she had written to Wil's family in Charleston. They hadn't heard anything about his status either. Any hope that he might have survived slipped from her grasp.

On the bed beside her, Rebecca opened her brilliant blue eyes with a smile. The toddler resembled Sam, so much that sometimes the likeness pained her. *What if Sam didn't return either?* "Good morning, Miss Rebecca," she said, struggling to sound cheerful.

"Mama." Too little to understand Amanda's deepest fear, Rebecca babbled.

The child's cheer grew contagious. Amanda tugged off her nightdress. Influenza or not, she was going to get dressed. Over by the wardrobe, she took out a faded cotton dress in need of mending under the arms and in the hemline. These days she had so few dresses to choose from that her only other work dress was mottled with Sam's blood. Although she had scrubbed and scrubbed, the stains never washed out. Perhaps she should pay Alice a call. Her little sister might have something she had grown weary of.

On the bed Rebecca galloped the wood carving resembling Red through the blankets. Amanda didn't have the heart to tell the toddler the horse was upside down. "That's a unique horse, Rebecca. Your papa made it especially for you."

"Papa." Rebecca held up the toy with a grin.

"That's right." Tears brimmed in Amanda's eyes. Determined not to let them fall, she started to dress and continued, "Why is it menfolk can't see what they're doing? They keep saying it's for what they believe in, but a loved one's death is final."

Finished changing, she dressed Rebecca and gathered the toddler in her arms. When she reached the bottom stair, she suddenly felt hot. Amanda fanned herself and wiped her beading forehead. Lightheaded, she called for the servants. She grabbed the rail to keep from falling, and Frieda tapped her walking stick into the parlor.

"Frieda, could you take Rebecca? I think I might swoon."

"Miss Amanda, you bin workin' too hard." Frieda supported Amanda's arm and helped her to the tapestry sofa.

Amanda's stomach knotted. She clasped her hands until her knuckles turned white. Burning nausea rose in her throat.

"Take a deep breath. You rest. I see to Becca."

"I thought I was feeling better."

Frieda vanished to the kitchen with Rebecca.

Amanda's stomach settled, and she got to her feet. She swayed. Reseating herself, she leaned her head against a cushion and closed her eyes. *A few minutes rest—that's all I need.*

Frieda offered a plate of freshly toasted bread. "Miss Amanda, you need to eat somethin' to keep up your strength. You done eat so little dese past few days. Just sittin' dere frettin' 'bout da way things are ain't goin' to do no good."

Amanda's stomach churned again, and she shoved the plate away from her nose. "I shall start my chores in a few minutes."

"You do no such thing." Frieda wagged a finger. "You ain't well, and it ain't no flu. It's bad enough dat you work so hard you make yourself sick, but now you riskin' da baby's life too."

"Baby?" Sweat trickled down Amanda's neck. She pushed loose strands of hair from her face. "Rebecca is hardly a baby anymore."

"I ain't talkin' about Becca. Why, if you ain't figured it out— Think child, when was da last time you wash rags?"

"Rags? Last . . ." Amanda hadn't washed rags since before Sam left. "I missed my monthly because of influenza. Now stop talking foolishness. You know I can't have any babies."

Frieda patted her on the shoulder. "You can when you does what you has bin with Mr. Sam."

Frieda had finally gone daft. Such a silly notion. "I was married to the Colonel for eight years and never got in a family way. The doctor said—"

"You ain't made love to da Colonel in a long time. Da white doctors forget dat it take two." Frieda held up two fingers. "Dey blame da woman so it don't hurt manly pride. Miss Amanda, like it or not, you goin' to have a baby."

"But I can't have a baby now."

"Dat choice long gone. 'Less you wants me to makes some yew tea."

Frieda's medicinal knowledge was well known throughout Stafford and Spotsylvania Counties. Other women had come to her for yew tea. Usually unwed, they hoped to save their families from embarrassment and shame. A baby—growing inside her? Her baby—Sam's baby. All these years hoping, but it was never meant to be. One time with Sam . . . Suddenly frightened, Amanda touched her belly. "What should I do, Frieda?"

Frieda smiled, making her wrinkled forehead more pronounced. "All you need to do is write Mr. Sam. He come back and marry you. Dat will make things nice and proper."

Marriage? What had she been thinking? Definitely not with her head, and she refused to hold any man in such a manner. "I don't want him marrying me out of some misplaced honor."

"Miss Amanda, he's cared for you from da beginnin'."

Amanada slouched. Too much was happening in such a short time. She needed fresh air to think more clearly. Tears streaked her face as she meandered outside and across the farmyard, straight to the gray mare's stall. She rubbed the horse's shoulder. "It looks like you won't be the only one having a baby next summer."

A baby! After all this time, why now? She touched her abdomen. It certainly explained why no one else in the family had got sick. How many years had she longed for a child? And now, she was going to have Sam's.

She threw a blanket and saddle over the mare's back. "A fine fix I'm in. I'm going to have a baby, and the man I was married to is long dead." Sensing someone behind her, Amanda turned to Ezra loitering by the door. "How much did you hear?"

"Whatever you want me to, Miss Amanda."

His devotion was so simple, yet complete. The servants really were her family. "So what is your opinion, Ezra? Frieda thinks I should write to Sam and tell him."

His thick lips widened to a grin. "He come back and marry you if'n you do."

Tired of everyone wanting to marry her off, Amanda finished tacking the mare and led her from the stall. "That's just it. I don't want him marrying me out of duty."

Outside in the wintery air, she mounted, reining the mare toward the lane. She reached the main road. Deserted—not a soul stirred. The mare's hooves clip-clopped against the hard-packed red dirt. Clicking her tongue, Amanda gave the gray her head. They took off at a gallop. Dirt clods flew in the air. Leaving nothing in reserve, they streaked across a frozen field. Frosty wind nipped her face. Tears entered her eyes and nearly blinded her. Under the steady rhythm of pounding hooves, they bounded up a gentle rise.

Almost too late, Amanda spotted the stone fence directly in their path. Before she could prepare the mare for the jump, the gray swerved. Her arms flailed, and she sailed over the fence. A brush pile softened her landing, but she lay there a long while without moving.

What had she been trying to prove? Had she been trying to rid herself of the problem? The mare could have stepped in a gopher hole and broken a leg. Unable to hold back any longer, she broke down sobbing.

After a good cry, Amanda regained her feet. Her body ached, and she checked herself for injuries—a few cuts and bruises. She was fortunate that she hadn't broken her fool neck. She began the walk back to the house.

On the road, she met Ezra aboard his mule. "Miss Amanda, we got worried when da mare come back to da barn without you."

She assured him that she was fine but suddenly felt cold. The brisk air hinted at snow.

Each day after the spill, she took the mare out for a morning ride. Though she kept the pace under control, being alone with her thoughts helped her ponder her predicament. Still no answer came to her.

Nearly a week later, Amanda rounded the bend and brought the gray to a halt. Down the road, a blue roan trotted toward her. Her heart pounded. Wil had a thick beard, and she almost hadn't recognized him. "We had given you up for dead, Wil."

He halted Poker Chip beside the mare and tipped his hat. Dust went flying. "Good morning, Mrs. Graham. Fancy meeting you at such an early hour."

"I was, uh . . . " She caught herself. His coal-black eyes twinkled at seeing her. He hadn't really expected an explanation. "Colonel Jackson, you startled me. If you would like to accompany me back to the house, I shall have Frieda serve up some breakfast."

"Thank you kindly. I would appreciate it."

As she reined the mare around, his expression changed to weariness. *Oh Lord, what am I going to tell him?* "Wil, you were missing—"

"From where?"

Not in the mood for his games, she said, "You were listed as missing at Sharpsburg."

They arrived at the lane, and his eyes danced. "Don't believe everything you read, Amanda."

"Then you weren't missing?"

He grinned. "I got lost for a while." His smile vanished as quickly as it had appeared. "I didn't come here to exchange idle pleasantries."

And he wasn't going to talk about the months of no correspondence. He hadn't changed.

"I had a notion you were here for a reason, but I can't run supplies again."

Wil brought Poker Chip to a halt in front of her, making her stop so sudden that she was nearly unseated. "I wouldn't ask you. The war has changed."

Her gaze met the dark, penetrating eyes, and she looked away. She couldn't possibly tell him the truth.

"Is everything all right?" he asked.

"Yes, why do you ask?"

He regarded her curiously. "I thought you might have encountered Yankees. Many citizens have been vandalized. With you being alone—"

"I'm not alone." Uncomfortable under his constant gaze, Amanda guided the mare around Poker Chip. "I had a touch of influenza earlier in the week."

The roan easily caught up with the mare. "Then you should be resting."

Wil had never been the sort to dote, and she suddenly wished he would go away. Close to blurting out the truth, Amanda clenched her teeth to retain her poise. "After my bout with influenza, I tire easily. Getting a breath of morning air is better than lying on one's back with my feet propped up."

They entered the farmyard. Wil brought his horse to a halt. After dismounting, he helped her from the mare's back. When her feet touched the ground, she found herself staring into his eyes. She shimmied from his grip and tethered the mare.

"Amanda, the Yankees are moving. You may find yourself on Federal ground soon."

The brisk morning suddenly got colder, and she tightened her cloak. "It won't be the first time."

They ambled up the walk together. "No, it won't," he said. "Alice tells me that Prescott was here."

"She had no right."

"She hadn't intended on saying anything, but it slipped." He laughed tiredly. "Your sister does like to talk."

Amanda leveled an accusing finger at him. "Especially with a handsome gentleman caller. I bet Alice wouldn't be so smitten if she knew about your Yankee trollop. How dare you, Wil Jackson—using my little sister like that. I'm not harboring any Yankee."

"I don't think I implied you were harboring a Yankee. Was Prescott seriously wounded?"

"I thought *Mrs.* Prescott would have kept you informed."

"What has got into you? If it is any of your business, I've had no contact with Mrs. Prescott since spring. Perhaps *you* have some guilt that needs to be dealt with."

She slapped his cheek. To her regret the beard softened the blow.

His gaze grew harsh. Wil reached for her but lowered his hands. Without uttering a word, he retreated down the walkway.

He's leaving. "Wil . . ."

Outside the gate, he mounted the roan.

A little louder, she called again, "I didn't mean it."

The gelding fought the bit, but Wil kept a firm grip on the reins.

"I'm sorry," she said. "I shall try to explain."

With the apology, he slid from the roan's back and tied Poker to the rail. As he joined her, he removed his hat. "I do recall what it was like being wounded."

"Sam wasn't in very good shape when he left here. I was hoping you had heard something from Holly."

"Then I apologize for not making the arrangements for a rendezvous with Mrs. Prescott."

For some reason, his directness still bothered her. She felt the warmth in her cheeks. Clearing her throat, she said, "I promised you breakfast."

After hanging his hat and weapons belt on the peg inside the door, she showed him to the kitchen. The smell of flapjacks on the griddle made her stomach knot. She motioned for Wil to have a seat at the table and held her breath until the queasiness passed. "Frieda, we have a guest." Before she could be seated, Wil was behind her, helping her. "Tell me, Wil, what happened at Sharpsburg?"

He sat across from her. "I was hit."

"Then you were wounded?"

"No, I was hit squarely on the chest but walked away unharmed."

Frieda brought a pot of coffee over to the table.

"How is that possible?" Amanda asked.

He helped himself to the coffee. "Anything is possible on the battlefield. By the time I regained my senses, the division had already retreated and there were three Yanks standing over me. They were as lost as I was but insisted on taking me prisoner. I waited until they got drunk and slipped out under the cover of darkness. Not a walk I'd recommend, but I returned to the valley in plenty of time for more fighting."

"That can't be a true story."

"I swear on my honor that it is."

"Why didn't you write to say that you were all right?"

His face brightened. "I hadn't realized a pretty damsel was fretting about me."

"Wil . . . " She had to find a way of telling him. *Not yet.* "Now you say the Yankees are coming here? How many?"

He leaned back in the chair and tugged on his moustache. The gesture was a nervous habit that didn't help her wits any. He opened his mouth to answer, but Frieda placed a stack of flapjacks on the table. While Wil filled his plate, the scent of sickly sweet syrup made her stomach churn.

After a few ravenous mouthfuls, Wil replied, "Burnside has replaced McClellan. If he marches with the intent of taking Richmond, his path will go straight through Fredericksburg."

"Oh . . . " *What would become of them?*

He cleaned the plate and stuffed the last forkful in his mouth.

"Wil, when was the last time you had a decent meal?"

"A while." He filled the plate a second time.

"As in days—or weeks?"

"It was a rough march. We encountered sleet crossing the mountains."

If he wasn't going to give a straight answer, he had to be half-starving. The smell of flapjacks and maple syrup made her queasy. Covering her mouth, Amanda ran for the back door. Barely reaching the steps in time, she leaned over the porch rail and retched. Someone patted her on the back as she threw up again. Expecting to see Frieda, she turned and found Wil behind her. She placed a hand over her stomach, and he grasped her elbow to help steady her.

"I got too much sun," she said, sitting on the steps.

"You're not a very good liar. The first excuse was a touch of influenza, and there hasn't been much sun in recent days. I *know* when something is wrong."

"You should be ashamed of yourself. How dare you call *me* a liar. But I wouldn't expect you to understand. You've never truly cared for anyone." Amanda got to her feet. Dizziness swept over her, and she swayed.

Wil gave her a steadying hand. "You're a little flushed again. Amanda, if I didn't know better, I would guess that you had been nipping the brandy." He helped her back to the steps and sat beside her. "As for not caring for someone, you know that's not true. After taking the bullet intended for *your* husband, I was assigned to the Northwest. I should have taken more time to recuperate, but I was even more stubborn then. A local woman tended me, and I married her."

The confession she had waited so long to hear caught her off guard. "You gave me the impression you were never married."

With a shrug, he laughed. "According to the church, I never have been. I married a Nez Perce."

An Indian woman—her suspicions were confirmed. "What became of her?"

His beard effectively hid any expression. "She stayed behind."

"And you have proven my point. If you truly loved her, she would have returned with you."

"You, my good woman, are a romantic." Wil clenched his right hand, then opened it again. "Sometimes Amanda, love is not enough. If she had returned with me, she would never have adapted to our way of life. And who, pray tell, would have accepted a squaw as my wife?"

"I would."

With the mask falling ever so slightly, the muscles around his mouth twitched. "That may be—"

"Wil, with your social standing, you can sway others' thinking. Things won't change unless we make a stand for them."

He clapped his hands and stood. "Beautiful speech, but what about her? People would have regarded her as something less than a field nigger." He straightened his stained gray jacket with the dirty gold embroidery on the sleeves. "Forgive me for bringing it up. I've told you it isn't something I like to talk about."

Shame? Embarrassment? She couldn't be certain what he was feeling. "It still hurts, doesn't it? Were there any children?" Sadness entered his eyes. He did understand—probably better than anyone. She choked back a sob. "Wil . . . I'm with child."

His tall frame loomed over her without moving. "Prescott?"

His voice had been even, but she detected rage simmering underneath. Amanda nodded weakly. Still, he didn't move. A smoldering frenzy entered his eyes. He seized her arms, nearly hoisting her off her feet. She let out a yelp, but his fingers held her so tight that they dug into her flesh. She tried to wiggle free. "You're hurting me."

"How did you expect me to react? Good day, Mrs. Graham, I hear you've been whoring around with my former lieutenant while I put my life on the line for the ground you live on, but that's fine. We'll just overlook the little indiscretion."

"How dare you treat me in this manner after the way you carry on. Then you have the gall to tell me that you abandoned your family in the Northwest."

"Amanda, my son died when he was three years old—from a white man's disease. None of the doctors cared to treat a half-breed."

She now understood why the supplies had been so important. "Did she die of measles too?"

He loosened his grip, and the lines around his eyes were etched with grief. "No. After our son died. I got sick. She was caught stealing supplies."

Her hand flew to her chest. Caught like she had been. Wil was ready to storm the Yankee camp. *Dashing to the end*—wasn't that what she had taunted him with? "Forgive me."

"They left her for me to cut down."

Cut down? Amanda clamped her eyes shut. All this time, she had accused him incapable of loving one woman. "I'm so sorry."

Strong arms went around her, drawing her close. After a long while she brushed away the brimming tears. Wil reached into a pocket for a handkerchief. Like the rest of his clothing, it was soiled. But his anger had faded.

"I thought you were dead," she said, "and you hadn't told me how you felt."

"I did—in a letter."

"But I never received it."

"Because I never mailed it. You were wise to choose Prescott, Amanda. When I could do nothing to help Peopeo, I died right along with her. I'll collect my hat and sword and be on my way." He started down the steps.

She dabbed her eyes with the dirty handkerchief. "Wil, don't leave. I'd like for us to remain friends."

"I don't see how that's possible."

He *did* love her. "Sam doesn't know. Couriers capable of getting a message across the lines expect to be paid in Yankee greenbacks or gold. After paying Oakcrest for Dulcie, I don't have that kind of money."

Without turning, Wil came to a halt. "Are you asking me for money?"

"I've never asked for anything and wouldn't now, but I don't know who else to turn to."

With deliberate slowness, he faced her. "All you ever needed to do was ask. I'll get a message through for you," he said, taking charge. Bold and in control, he had retreated behind the mask again. "If Prescott is less than honorable, I will challenge him to a duel."

"I don't think a duel is the answer, but I don't want Sam marrying me out of duty either."

"I thought you didn't like the word bastard. Weren't you the one just a few moments ago telling me that love can solve all problems? Or are you afraid he doesn't love you?"

At a loss on how to answer, Amanda looked to the sky. Clouds were building for an afternoon thundershower—unusual for so late in the season. Ever since finding herself in the middle of a skirmish, each thunder clap reminded her of cannon fire. Not until the guns were silenced once and for all would any of them be free to lead normal lives.

"I was wrong—terribly wrong. And Colonel Jackson, I believe that gruff exterior of yours a sham. For underneath there seems to be an honorable gentleman."

He raised an eyebrow. "Gentleman? My dear, Mrs. Graham, I can assure you that I am no gentleman and never have been. It's no wonder I lost your favor to Prescott. Fancy that, a Yankee abolitionist."

Detecting his sense of humor returning, she finally realized that it was a front to hide his feelings. "He's not an abolitionist."

"One mark in his favor." He returned to her side. "Amanda—now if you don't mind, I would like to return to my breakfast before it gets any colder."

With Wil's aid, she no longer felt so frightened.

Chapter Twenty-One

"**D**ULCIE!" HOLLY DRUMMED her fingers on the desk. Charles would have assigned the dim-witted servant girl to the leased hovel for only one reason—to keep an eye on her comings and goings. It was bad enough that she was chained to Charles in name—now the house, too. With the prison her life had become, he might as well have gone ahead and arrested her. But then, he lacked evidence of her Confederate dealings. At least he spent more time pretending to be a soldier these days than pestering her. It usually saved her the bother of feigning breathlessness when he whined for his marital rights. "Dulcie!"

The servant girl entered the study and lowered her head. Careful not to make eye contact, Dulcie approached the desk. "Yes'm."

Holly held up an envelope clearly marked for Captain Prescott. *Oh, what was the use?* It wouldn't make an impression. Darkies couldn't read. "Did no one inform your former mistress that Sam is a major now?"

"Miss Amanda?"

"Yes, Amanda. Who else do you think I meant? And to think, if President Lincoln has his way, more darkies will be wandering the streets of the major cities after this war is over. It's bad enough with the contrabands already."

"I expect no one tell her, ma'am. If dat a letter for Mr. Sam, I take it to him."

Holly held the envelope up to the light. Since it was addressed to Sam, she doubted it was the money Amanda owed her. She ripped open the envelope. "If Charles seriously thinks I will cook and launder after filthy, louse-ridden soldiers, he shall soon discover the contrary."

She read through the letter, and her jaw dropped. Amanda carrying Sam's child? *My, my—what had happened to propriety?* Amanda—always so proper—but it was nothing more than an act.

Holly crumpled the paper and tossed it in the bin. "It wasn't important. Now Dulcie, I'm certain you have chores to tend to."

"Yes'm. I do."

"Then see to them." She waved a dismissal, and the servant girl ran from the room.

On the other hand, with such important news, she should deliver it to Sam personally. She fished the crumpled paper from the bin and stuffed it into her skirt pocket. If she couldn't squeeze the money out of Sam, at least she would have the satisfaction of seeing the look on his face when she told him.

The division would be near Fredericksburg soon. More than anything, Sam wished Amanda would abandon the farm and retreat to safety. As he studied maps and field reports, his eyes blurred. He reached for a tin cup from the field desk and gulped. He sputtered. *Cold coffee.* Once recovered, he checked his pocket watch. "Lieutenant!"

An officer stepped into the tent and removed his hat.

"I gave an order to report ten minutes ago!"

The officer saluted. "I'm a captain, sir, and I never received the order."

Sam blinked. "Charles?" Holly stood beside his brother with a coy grin. He gritted his teeth and stood to greet them. With the onset of colder weather, the leg was bothering him more than before. "When did you arrive?"

"A few hours ago, sir."

Sam waved a hand. "Enough of the sirs. We're alone." Relatively speaking—Holly's grin hadn't vanished. Scheming, no doubt. He extended a hand. "Good to see you."

Charles approached the field desk and shook Sam's hand. "Thank you, Sam."

"Charles . . ."

Charles held up a hand. "I know what you're going to say, little brother. You wish I hadn't come. I've already told you that it was something I had to do. Now that Mac is gone, the folks in Washington are expecting a fight soon."

The folks in Washington weren't the only ones expecting a fight— a big one. One the Union couldn't afford to lose. Yet he didn't hold much faith in Burnside. He had certainly performed ineptly at Antietam—a battle Sam had missed due to the leg wound. "What can I do for you, Charles? I don't have time for social calls."

"Right. I'll talk to you later."

"First duty—see that Mrs. Graham has a guard. I don't want her victimized by foragers."

Charles saluted and left, but Holly lingered behind.

"What is it, Holly?" he asked.

Her grin widened. "Why Sam—you could be a little more polite. I agreed to accompany Charles to tend the wounded. Such a sacrifice, when I get dreadfully ill from the sight of blood."

Sacrifice indeed. He raised a finger. "If you go anywhere near the medical stores, I will have you brought up on charges so fast, you won't know what hit you."

"You needn't fret. I never got paid from the last supply run. The Confederates can rot for all I care." She withdrew an envelope from a crocheted bag. "However, dear Mrs. Graham promised that she would personally see to my payment. I've never known Amanda to renege a promise. Did she use any of those supplies for your benefit?"

So that was her game. "You're not getting the money from me."

She fanned her face with the envelope. "Then you're not responsible for Mrs. Graham?"

Two could play this game. "Weren't the two of you working with Jackson? From what I hear, he's across the river. Get your money from him."

Holly wrinkled her face in annoyance. "Sam—I came on an errand of mercy and you tease me. I have a notion . . . " She held up the envelope, poised to rip it to shreds. "It's from Amanda."

Through the days since his departure, Amanda had never been far from his thoughts. He regretted not having secured a pass for her while he had been in Washington. And now that the army drew closer to her home, there was no time. "Why would Amanda send you a letter?"

"The least you could do is offer a lady a seat." Spreading the folds of her dress, Holly made herself comfortable on a camp stool. "She addressed it to Captain Prescott, and the courier thought that meant Charles."

He reached for the envelope, but she snatched it beyond his grasp. "Is Amanda or Rebecca ill?"

A grin spread across Holly's face. "Rebecca's fine. Amanda's another matter. Seems she did more than tend your wound."

Sam's knees went weak, and he eased himself onto the stool behind the field desk.

"What's the matter, Sam? You're looking a little pale. I'm sure it was just one of those little indiscretions. After all, Kate's been gone a long time, and Amanda—she's a mighty fine-looking woman. Why, I bet neither of you gave a thought to the consequences since she's been barren all these years."

Barren? She shoved the envelope across the desk, and he broke out in a sweat. The days had grown too cold for sweating. With the letter finally in his hands, he trembled. He unfolded the crinkled paper. Through his shaking, he could scarcely make out the words. The letter was brief and to the point. Rebecca was in good health. But Amanda . . . His heart thumped. She was going to have a baby—his baby.

"I thought I should deliver it personally. You never know who might read it and spread rumors. Of course, *I* wouldn't do such a thing."

"Holly . . . " His voice cracked. He cleared his throat. "You've had your fun. What do you want?"

Her eyes widened with insult. "You're so suspicious of anything I do."

"With good cause."

"I didn't realize I had given you that impression."

She sounded so serious, he couldn't help but laugh. It must be the confusion of the moment. He couldn't think of any other reason why he might be laughing.

"Are you going to marry her?" she asked.

"Leave, Holly. Before I throw you out. Do remember one thing—I'll be watching hospital supplies. If anything turns up missing, you'll be sitting behind bars."

Indignant, she gathered her skirts together and hustled from the tent.

Sam pounded a fist against the field desk. He hadn't said goodbye because in Amanda's mind it meant forever. That would be an admission of sorts. While he didn't get the same feeling as when he had been wounded, there was something deep in his craw that didn't set right. He pulled a cigar from his pocket and chewed on it a short while before lighting it.

He flicked the ashes, and hot embers fell on a map, scorching the center. He was lucky he hadn't set the whole tent afire. "Dammit." In his mind, he heard Amanda chastising him for cursing. He needed to pull himself together or others might die as a result. His mind would be at rest if he knew she were taken care of, should he not return from the upcoming battle. Charles—he'd ask his brother to tend to the details.

Finally registering that Amanda was going to have a baby, he hoped she wasn't too sick. He longed to see her. Kate had been dreadfully ill the first few months.

In need of some air, he stepped outside into the brisk evening. Winter was coming. He checked the stars in the clear sky and wondered if Amanda might be gazing at the same ones. He wished she were beside him, so he could tell her everything was going to be all right. Even he had doubts during these troubled times. He took a draft on the cigar. For some reason, he had been purposely avoiding goodbyes lately and couldn't help but think it must mean something.

A week later, soaking wet and chilled to the bone, a Confederate lieutenant escorted Holly to the tavern. She thanked him and entered the smoke-filled establishment. Officers played cards, while painted harlots waited for the winners to buy them a drink and retire upstairs. She barely recognized the bearded colonel sitting at a table near the windows.

From a distance, she watched Wil play his poker hand—smooth and collected. Would she have expected anything less? Gold—and he was doing his fair share of winning.

Strong hands twirled her around. "I'd like to buy you a drink." Through slurred words, a drunken captain jabbed a finger to her breast. His hand lingered.

Disgusted, Holly flipped his hand from her person before his breath
intoxicated her. "I'm with the colonel this evening. I'm certain he'd
understand if you went over there and explained to him, but I'll warn
you about his jealous streak."

The officer bowed his regret and nearly fell.

Southern gentlemen to the end—even to their whores. Holly neared
the table where Wil played poker and peered over his shoulder. "Wil,
you have an extraordinary poker face. No one would guess you hold a
mere pair of threes."

Other bids raised, and Wil tossed his cards to the table. His dark
eyes looked her way. "Mrs. Prescott—a pleasant surprise."

"Colonel, it's been a while." Her arms went around his neck, and
she wriggled into his lap. A crooked smile formed on his face. She
shimmied closer and felt him harden. "Don't tell me that you weren't
expecting me?"

"As a matter of fact—"

She kissed him on the mouth. "I'm sure you can find somewhere a
little less noisy."

"It seems the little lady has a more pressing need."

The men around the table hooted. Holly sprang to her feet, but
kept a grip on Wil's hand while he collected his winnings. At least five
gold pieces. She hooked her arm through his.

Outside the tavern, he faced her. "You can stop pretending. What is
it you want?"

She batted her eyelashes. "Everyone has become so suspicious lately.
I missed you, Wil."

He lit a cigar. "Missed me? I rather doubt that."

She shivered. "Can you at least take me somewhere so I may warm
myself? The river crossing was extremely cold and frightening."

"Not to mention foolhardy."

"Now I'm a fool. I fretted that you'd been killed last spring. When
I found out you were still alive, I was so eager to be by your side that I
came at the first opportunity. I had to wait until Charles was officer of
the day to get away."

Wil clapped his hands and bowed. "A very good performance, Mrs.
Prescott. I have another engagement this evening, but I'd be honored
if you'd accompany me."

Not simpleminded like Charles, Wil Jackson was not an easy man to deceive. "As long as we understand one another. I refuse to be treated like one of your tavern harlots."

His hand went to his chest as if he were wounded. "Do you think I have lowered my standards that much?"

"Then I would be delighted to accompany you. A lady must be properly wined and dined."

After he collected the horses, they rode from the edge of town to a brick mansion. Using a servant's entrance, Wil gave the excuse that she had taken a spill from her horse. Busy with guests, the hostess pointed to a room upstairs.

Holly took Wil's hand. They ascended the stairs. Once in the room, she stripped off her wet dress and petticoat in front of the fire.

Wil's arms went around her and warmed her. He kissed her full on the mouth, gently tracing a hand down her side. She *had* missed him, but she mustn't let him get the upper hand. "Since when have you treated me like a porcelain doll?"

He kissed her again, harsher. She felt him unleashing the other side of himself and wondered how much he held back.

Holly broke his vise-like grip and grinned sweetly. "But I haven't been wined and dined yet, Colonel."

In one swift move, he had her flat on her back, drawers open and legs spread wide. His black eyes seethed.

"What's the matter, Wil? Nothing left for the performance?"

He rolled to the side and started laughing. He picked up his hat and got to his feet. "Almost—I'll grant you that. A dangerous game, my dear. One I assure you that you don't wish to win."

As he closed the door behind him, she heard his laughter in the hall.

Chapter Twenty-Two

WITH EACH PASSING DAY, AMANDA FELT the baby growing inside her womb. Morning sickness came less often as time went on, but her breasts had grown tender. She wondered how long it would be before there was movement. Her thoughts turned to Sam. The day before, a Yankee guard had appeared outside her house. She had no doubt it was Sam's doing, but he hadn't sent word that he had received her letter.

"Amanda? Amanda!" Mama clapped her hands inches from her face. "Try to look like you're having a good time."

Amanda smoothed the emerald satin gown Alice had loaned her. Due to her condition, she had left the stays of her corset loose. At least she could breathe freely, but no matter the occasion, she hated crinolines. Fashion or not, they were hardly practical. "You know I don't like parties, Mama. Especially when there are chores I could be tending to."

"Chores will wait. It's time you actively supported the Cause."

"I suppose my supply runs meant nothing."

"Shh . . ." Mama fidgeted with the glass beads around her neck and smiled at another guest. "Who knows, you just might find yourself another husband here."

Amanda glanced across the room, where Wil danced with her sister.

"If you don't pay him some notice soon, he may choose Alice instead."

Wil led her sister in a slow waltz across the dance floor. As usual, Alice had outdone herself. Her navy taffeta gown had pearls on the bodice, and her auburn hair was arranged with ringlet curls and dried black-eyed Susans. With the arrival of winter, she looked like a breath of spring air. With a pang, she recalled Wil's strong arms around her, and her heart tugged. *Jealousy?* No, she had made her choice. She loved Sam. "Colonel Jackson is much too worldly for Alice," Amanda finally said.

"There were twelve years between you and the Colonel."

"I'm well aware of that, Mama. My point is . . ." What was the use? Amanda let the matter drop.

The string band stopped playing, and Wil bowed to Alice. Her sister rejoined them with her hands clasped together. She sighed. "I think I'm in love."

How quickly Alice had forgotten their little talk about Wil. "You were in love with your last beau too. And the one before that. Need I continue?"

Dewy eyed like a puppy worshiping his master, Alice cast a glance at Wil, who now danced with another exquisitely gowned woman. "They were mere boys."

Even Amanda knew how easy a woman could be swayed by his advances. She wondered which woman present would be his bed partner that evening. "He's definitely not a boy," she agreed.

The curls in Alice's hair shook, and her grin widened. "Amanda, you're blushing. Is there something you haven't told us about yourself and Colonel Jackson? If you sashay over there right now, he will stop dancing with the *girls.*"

Her cheeks got warmer. "The only thing Wil Jackson wants is under a woman's skirt. And you, my little sister—should be careful."

"Amanda, I'll thank you to hush your mouth," Mama said sharply. "Or I shall forget you're a grown woman and take some soap to it."

"It's true, Mama."

Mama waved her fan. "Amanda, I thought you had been married long enough to realize that's what all men want."

"You don't understand. Colonel Jackson is a dear friend, but he has a tendency to toy with women. His latest dalliance is married."

Mama's fan pumped faster, and Alice looked more like a sad-eyed puppy, instead of an adoring one. "He comes from a good family," Alice said.

"With many skeletons in it."

Alice smiled a wicked grin.

Instead of discouraging Alice, Amanda's tirade had the opposite effect. "Fine, but don't say I didn't warn you."

"Stop fretting. I've already told you that I don't wish to court a military man. But they are so dashing when dressed in their finest."

Destined to fall for military men, Amanda knew the feeling—all too well. She did love Wil—and Sam, in different ways.

"Amanda, there is someone in your life, isn't there?" Alice giggled. "You're pining for that Yankee captain."

Mama glared, then paled when she offered no denial.

"I'm in love with Captain Prescott," Amanda admitted.

Mama swayed on her feet, and Alice rushed her to the nearest chair. Her sister grabbed the fan and waved it furiously in front of Mama's face. "Amanda, what has got into you? You fuss at me for innocent flirtations with a respectable Confederate officer, and you've been dallying with—with a Yankee."

Amanda raised her skirts and scurried across the dance floor. She neared the door, and Wil stepped in front of her.

"Let me pass!" she said.

"Amanda, what's wrong?"

"Nothing! Now let me pass."

She poised a hand to strike his face, and he held up his hands in surrender. "I don't need another wallop to remind me that you mean business." He tucked her arm under his and stepped into the marble foyer. "Amanda, we have known each other a long time. I know when something is wrong. No matter what happens, I do care as a friend."

"You said we could no longer be friends."

"I reacted in haste."

But he couldn't hide his feelings. He loved her and would have never shared the tragic story of his Indian wife otherwise. He studied her thoughtfully. "Now you know all of my dark secrets and why I never married again."

"I doubt I know *all* of your dark secrets. And doesn't it bother you that your mistress is married?"

Wil shrugged. "Should it? I don't wish to marry her, and I doubt her husband is fool enough to trust her. At least your Prescott had the good sense not to marry her. Another point in his favor."

Amanda frowned.

"What's the matter, Amanda? Did Prescott never share the details of his courtship with his brother's wife to you? Perhaps, you should like to ask her about it. She's upstairs, resting."

Holly was present? Amanda no longer needed to guess which woman Wil would share his bed with. She reminded herself to remain calm. "Sam has told me all that I care to hear. The past is just that, but *you* never change. When you told me about your wife and son, I grieved for your loss. But it's an excuse, so you don't get close to anyone. You knew I was vulnerable after John's passing. You also knew you could take advantage of it. So why didn't you? Because you were afraid, Colonel. Yes, I said *afraid*. You were afraid that you might fall in love. As for Mrs. Prescott, that woman has no morals. Maybe the two of you deserve one another." In disgust, Amanda headed for the door.

"She may have news of your Prescott," he said in a low voice.

Before reaching the door, Amanda halted. While she couldn't trust Holly, any scrap of information might be worth something.

"Mrs. Prescott's visit was unexpected. The river was rough. She's resting."

Sheepishly, Amanda faced him. "I was under the impression . . . "

He arched a brow in amusement. "You jumped to conclusions."

"I would like to speak with her. That is, if you're still speaking to me after the way I carried on."

Wil bowed slightly. "I shall fetch her."

He disappeared up the stairs, and Amanda peeked into the ballroom. Alice danced with another young officer, while Mama was on her feet socializing again. She feared she might have said too much by blurting out the truth to Wil. Yet, if he came to terms with the past he just might settle down. Probably a foolish notion. At the same time, his eyes flickered in a different manner when he mentioned his Indian wife. He *was* afraid, and knowing she wouldn't return his love, he had pursued her.

Murmurs came from behind her. Holly descended the stairs with her arm hooked through Wil's. Her maroon velvet gown accented her dark hair. For having just experienced a rough river crossing, she seemed no worse for the wear.

Holly reached the bottom step. "Mrs. Graham, fancy meeting you here."

"I was thinking the same thing. Not many Northern women make appearances at Confederate social gatherings."

Holly gave a curt smile. "Oh, really? I was under the impression that you didn't support the Confederacy. As I recall, your supply runs were merely for the dear, sick boys. Isn't that what you told Charles? He put his career on the line and got you released because you promised not to make any more runs."

Amanda gave her credit. Holly knew exactly where to attack an opponent. "You may recall my last run was at your bidding."

"For which I've never been paid."

Wil regarded Holly with interest. Amanda could easily guess what he was thinking, and it had nothing to do with supply runs. "Holly, do you have any news of Sam?"

"The poor dear. He barely made it. He must have been weakened from that terrible wound. Is it really any wonder that he came down with one of your Southern fevers?"

Nearly dropping to her knees and pleading, Amanda asked again, "How is he?"

"Much better. As a matter of fact, he's nearby. I think he's busy preparing for the battle."

Amanda thought her heart had stopped. "Battle? What battle?"

Holly's grin widened. "Don't look so worried, Amanda. I'm certain he will honor your good name before the baby arrives."

Amanda glared at Wil. "How dare you, Wil Jackson!" She rushed for the door and slammed it behind her. Reaching the front steps, she realized she shouldn't have made such a hasty retreat without her cloak. A winter wind blew, and there was an icy nip to the evening. She hugged herself to keep warm. A popping like the sound of corn frying in a pan came from somewhere along the river.

The door opened behind her. Wil stepped out and placed his wool jacket over her shoulders. "I didn't tell her, Amanda. You must believe that. I don't know how she found out."

The popping got louder, and her anger faded.

Wil waited for the guns to stop firing. "The Yankees are preparing to make a move. Our sharpshooters are positioned along the river."

Shooting at Yankees—he didn't need to clarify. Snuggling into his jacket, she welcomed the warmth. "So there is a battle brewing?"

He blew out a weary breath. "Yes." He uncurled her fingers and dropped some coins into her hand.

"What's this for?"

"Mrs. Prescott reminded me that you never received payment for the last supply run."

Five coins—and they looked like gold. In the darkness, she couldn't be certain. "I never delivered them, and this is far too much."

"If anything should happen, I want you . . . " He folded her fingers over the coins.

"Wil, do you have a feeling?"

"You have other things to worry about." He returned to the house.

"Wil?" She started to follow him, when another rifle fired, halting her in her tracks. Fredericksburg was the next target. Shivering, but no longer from the cold, she realized her family might need to flee their home. She hoped the farm was far enough from the beaten path. And if Sam was across the river preparing for battle, would she ever see him again?

In the winter cold, Wil heard shrieks and whoops of joy at catching a thief. Dazed by fever, he struggled to the cabin door. A crowd had swarmed, laughing and staring at a squaw perched on a spotted horse with a rope around her neck. She bravely recited a prayer as he shoved through the mob.

The horde brought him down and pinned his arms to the ground before he could reach her. The crowd hailed a roaring cheer, and he heard galloping hooves. *Then thrashing.*

He had witnessed death countless times, but nothing could have prepared him for hers.

"Wil?" Holly leaned on an elbow, and the linen fell away from her, exposing a full, ripe breast. "Your mind is elsewhere."

After cutting the rope, he had lowered Peopeo's lifeless form to the ground and screamed. He focused on Holly's face. "I've serviced you like the two-bit whore you are. What more do you want?"

"Bastard." She swung at him, but he caught her wrist.

The fingernails of her free hand raked across his bare back, and he pinned her to the bed. She smiled up at him, daring him. He envisioned her face beaten to a bloody pulp but restrained himself. He released her and rolled to the side.

"When we first met, you were able to last more than a couple of rounds. You're getting old, Wil."

Bored, Wil pulled a cigar from his jacket on the floor. He struck a match and exhaled. "I've grown tired of your incessant games. I presume you can find another officer of suitable rank to satisfy you."

The sting of her hand struck the side of his face. Anger was all they had ever shared.

"Be serious," she said. "We're too much alike." She nestled closer and twisted the deerskin cord of the Nez Perce medicine pouch between her fingers.

Peopeo had said the medicine pouch would bring him luck. At Sharpsburg, the bullet had struck him senseless, torn a hole in the fabric of his shirt, and fragmented the mountain lion's tooth inside the pouch, but he had been unharmed. "We're nothing alike."

He snuffed the cigar and got up to dress. Once finished, he threw several bills on the bed. "For your time and the supplies. I apologize for only having Confederate."

With a wild shriek, she tossed the bills to the floor. He turned, but she hailed him. "Colonel . . ." Stark naked on the bed, Holly leveled a pearl-handled derringer at his chest. "I'd rather not kill you. I'm squeamish at the sight of blood, but if it's for a good cause, I can say you forced yourself on me. No one will question a woman defending her honor."

Wil choked back a laugh. "Women like you have none."

Holly narrowed her eyes. "Don't test me. I will shoot."

As she got to her feet, black hair tumbled the length of her back. The unclad form stirred familiar feelings. Danger only added to the excitement. Across from him, she motioned with the derringer to open his jacket. When he obliged, she rummaged through his pockets and withdrew two Confederate bills.

"Satisfied?" he asked.

"I saw gold. What happened to it?"

With a shrug, he held out his hands.

She lowered the derringer. "So calm. Do you fear anything?"

Unlike the gentle Peopeo, Holly thrived on danger—the same as him. "If I did, do you think I'd share it with you?"

He gave a sharp tug on her hand, and she was in his arms. Her naked body molded tightly to him. The derringer pressed between them as their mouths met. "I should shoot you," she murmured.

Instead of being appalled by her greed and hostility, he felt formidable hunger. "There will be plenty of time for that—later."

Her arms went around his neck, and the gun thumped to the floor. No ties—no demands. Amanda was right. He and Holly were equally corrupt. They deserved one another.

Chapter Twenty-Three

CHARLES DIDN'T HAVE THE BACKBONE TO WAIT at the ford along the Rappahannock River. The air was getting colder, and it felt like snow. Sam rubbed his hands together, hoping he had guessed wrong. If Holly crossed, he might learn Amanda had been involved in supply running again. He slid from Red's back. If he didn't keep moving, he'd give in to the cold—something that had never bothered him before being wounded.

"I'd give just about anythin' for a hot pot of coffee right now, includin' my soul."

The cold had numbed his mind as well. He had forgotten Jo.

"Sir, what if she ain't comin'?"

"She will." Sam blew on his hands and listened to the choppy waves. There was no sound of a horse in the water, but he hadn't expected Holly until just before dawn.

"Sam . . ." Jo straightened in the saddle.

He had heard it too—voices on the other side of the river. "Hold tight, Jo."

With only the two of them, he hoped Holly hadn't brought Rebel reinforcements. The voices grew louder as they neared the ford on the opposite side. One was feminine and mighty angry—Holly's.

All of Sam's senses snapped to attention, and he remounted Red. Eager to be moving, Red snorted a protest at being held in check.

Another voice drifted their way. He couldn't make out the words, but he recognized Jackson's Southern drawl. His involvement complicated the matter. Amanda wouldn't forgive him if they captured Jackson. But then Jackson was the sort to go down fighting.

"I only hear two, sir," Jo whispered.

A horse splashed into the water. "We'll wait until she reaches this side. No shooting unless absolutely necessary." He heard the labored breathing of a swimming horse as it struggled against rough waves. Sam's muscles tensed. Night crossings on the Rappahannock were often risky, but with the cold and waves, this night was downright dangerous.

The horse reached the middle, and he could make out a shape. Jo looked to him for a cue. He signaled to wait. The horse swam closer. Sam tightened the reins, and Red stamped his feet.

As Holly neared the bank, Sam let the leather slide through his fingers. Cold water slapped him in the face. After a few strides, Red reached Holly. She headed for deeper water, but Jo blocked her avenue of retreat. Holly reined around, whipping her mount toward the Rebel side of the river.

"Your horse is tired," Sam said. "You won't make it."

"Sam," Holly hissed. "I should have known it was you." She cracked leather against the horse's flank and continued toward the opposite bank.

Another horse was in the water. Damn—Jackson was after them. Sam hoped his former commander was alone. Red struck a deep spot and started swimming. Icy water hit Sam full force, yet he managed to grip the reins of Holly's horse.

Holly swatted his forearm with her riding crop. The sting forced him to let go. She sent her horse for deeper water, and Jo moved toward her. Sam swung Red after them, only to find himself staring down the length of a pistol barrel.

"Prescott," Jackson said. "Fancy meeting you here." He holstered the pistol, and Sam let out the breath he hadn't realized he was holding in. Jackson glanced over at Holly and laughed. "She's yours. You should have brought a brigade along to hogtie her."

"Jackson, was Amanda involved?"

"Involved in what?"

"Smuggling supplies."

"We have a different perspective about *smuggling* in the South."

"Captain," Sam said, finding that he still resorted to Jackson's former rank.

"Not since summer. You can thank Mrs. Prescott for appealing to Amanda's kind heart that time. I wouldn't have risked her life during a campaign. Rest assured, both have been justly paid."

Before he could respond, Holly shrieked. "Major Prescott! I expect
your sergeant to be severely disciplined."

Sam sent Red after her. "Why?"

Holly pointed an accusing finger at Jo. "He ravished me."

Jo handed him several Rebel bills. "She had the Reb money tucked
in her dress, sir."

In spite of the cold, Sam laughed. He looked back to thank Jackson,
but his former commander was already heading for the opposite bank.
"I thought you had the sense to be paid in greenbacks or gold, Holly."

"All you men are alike. Wil Jackson cheated me. I should have
shot him when I had the chance. And you're no better, Major. Always
pretending to be a gentleman. Some gentleman. Amanda carries your
bastard child."

Ignoring her rant, he led her horse to the Union side of the river.

"You shall be facing battle soon, and your child may never have a
name. Poor Amanda—"

"Shut up."

"Or you will...? Sam, I know you well enough. You would never
strike a lady."

"But I ain't got no such reservations," Jo said. " 'Sides, you ain't no
lady."

Holly sent Jo a scorching look.

Sadly, Holly was right about one thing. Amanda could face being alone—again. Her good reputation would be ruined because of a
thoughtless indiscretion. With her in his arms, the war hadn't existed—
only Amanda had. Foolish thinking—the war always returned, and a
child was the result.

He would send Jo with a message. If he fell in battle, at least
Amanda might take some comfort in knowing he had taken measures
to provide for her.

Yankees were most definitely on her side of the river. Earlier in the
morning, Amanda woke to cannon fire. After breakfast, she discovered the Yankee guard shooing foragers from the chicken coop. With
food growing scarce, she didn't know whether he was a blessing or a
hindrance. In return for his protection, he expected free meals.

Wagon wheels entered the lane. She refused to take chances and sought the Colonel's rifle. She lifted the lace curtain and peered out the window. A wagon rolled closer. When she saw that it wasn't military, she breathed in relief.

Alice jumped from the seat, wearing a plain brown frock for a change. Amanda returned the rifle to its resting spot and grabbed her shawl from the peg on her way out.

"Amanda, the Yankees are getting ready to cross the river. For our safety, Colonel Jackson warned us to leave town. Mama's sick. We can't travel any farther."

"I have a guard. You should be safe here."

Alice raised a skeptical brow. "Your Yankee *friend*?"

"Sam sent him."

"It's the least he could do after all you've done to help him." Alice latched onto Mama's arm as she climbed from the wagon. With sunken eyes and sallow skin, Mama had never looked so old or frail.

Amanda grasped her mother's hand and led her from the wagon. "Mama, let's get you out of the cold. I shall have Frieda make a nice, hot broth."

With Alice on the other side, they helped Mama over the cracks in the brick walk and up the steps.

Once inside, Amanda showed her to the green wingchair near the fire. "How long have you been sick, Mama?"

"Ever since she found out about you and that *Yankee*."

"I will thank you kindly to refer to Captain Prescott by his name. You had best get used to the idea, Mama. I love him."

Alice latched onto Amanda's arm and nearly dragged her to the kitchen. "Amanda, what has got into you? You fuss at me for flirting, yet you proudly declare your love for a Yankee. Can't you see that Mama is ill?"

"I refuse to shelter her the way you do."

Like a spoiled child, Alice stamped a foot. "But a Yankee? Mama was hoping you'd marry Colonel Jackson. He's from a good Carolinian family."

If Wil had possessed the courage to mail the letter, declaring his feelings, maybe things would have turned out differently. There was no sense dwelling on what might have been. "That's not possible now.

And Sam is from a good family. It just happens to be a Northern one."
Amanda returned to the parlor. "Mama, I'm very fond of Colonel
Jackson, but we're friends. Nothing more."

Mama patted her hand. "I'm not in favor of you courting a Yankee..." Mama put a hand to her chest. A deep hacking cough came
from her lungs. "But I shall try to get to know him as a person."

Amanda shot an I-told-you-so glance at Alice.

Alice smoothed the folds of her simple cotton dress. "I see the two
of you are going to get along just fine. Now, if you shall excuse me, I
need to remove the valuables before the Yankees arrive. I'm sure they
will make me swear that stupid oath to cross the river."

"Alice! It's too dangerous to return home."

Alice sent her a glare, and Frieda entered the room with a steaming
cup on a platter.

"Frieda," Amanda said, "if you will tend to Mama, I'd like to speak
to Alice."

"Yes'm."

Alice's pretense vanished when Amanda escorted her to the porch.
"Amanda, I didn't want to say anything inside, but most of the refugees
have gone to Richmond. Yankees are guarding Bank's Ford. At first,
they weren't going to let me cross, but I pleaded that Mama was sick
and wouldn't survive the trip to Richmond. They taunted me, but I
agreed to take the oath. It's not in my heart, but I repeated the words
of loyalty."

Amanda squeezed her arm. "You said them for Mama's sake."

"Why doesn't that make me feel better? Amanda, if you're really
in love with that..." The word Yankee formed on Alice's lips. "...
Captain Prescott, I hope he's not one of those waiting on this side of
the river."

"Why?"

"The Yankees are building pontoon bridges. It looks like they'll
strike Fredericksburg."

"That would explain the cannon I woke to this morning."

Alice nodded. "Yankee artillery is trying to keep our sharpshooters
from making easy pickings of their engineers. Since we hold the high
ground, it's a game of cat and mouse. Colonel Jackson says if they

attempt a main frontal assault with their infantry, it will be the same thing on a larger scale."

Amanda's legs wobbled. "Sam's infantry."

"I'm sorry."

"He sent the guard, but why hasn't he contacted me?"

"He probably hasn't had the time. I'll fetch Ezra to see to the horse." Alice went down the stairs. "Amanda, I shall say a few prayers for your Yankee captain."

"Alice, wait. I'm carrying his child."

Alice's eyes widened in disbelief. "What?"

"You heard me. I'm going to have a baby. Judge me if you must, but I need my sister right now."

Alice cast her gaze to the brick walkway. "I won't judge you, Amanda. It comes as a surprise. You were married to the Colonel for such a long time. How come you never had any babies then?"

"I didn't think I could. Frieda says doctors conveniently forget that it's not always the woman's fault."

"Do you want the baby?"

She pressed a hand to her abdomen. "Yes."

"Does your Yank—Captain Prescott know?"

"I don't know. I sent him a letter nearly two weeks ago, but I haven't received any word."

"The letter may not have got through yet."

If at all. No need to say the words. Alice finally looked up and opened her arms. Amanda threw hers around Alice's shoulders and hugged her. They headed to the house.

A rumble shook the ground. It was too late in the season for thunder, but Amanda glanced to the sky, hoping for a freak storm. Cold air and billowy clouds hinted at snow. *Cannon fire.* Dread pierced her heart. The battle drew near, and she feared Sam would be in its midst.

They reached the front porch, and pounding hooves entered the bottom of the lane. *Sam*—her breath caught in her throat, but she mustn't take chances. "Alice, fetch my rifle and call the guard. He's warming himself by the kitchen fire."

"Why?"

"Just do it." Hooves galloped up the lane, and Alice rushed inside.

A brown horse bounded into the farmyard. The rider in blue brought it to a halt, stirring up mud and dust. With a boyish build, he was most definitely not Sam.

"Hurry, Alice," Amanda said under her breath. "We don't have any food. You Yankee thieves have taken everything you're going to get."

The soldier slouched in the saddle and spat tobacco juice. "Ma'am."

Not only were some Yankees cowardly thieves, but this one was downright rude. Amanda broke a branch from the poplar tree near the gate and raised it over her head. "Skedaddle! You heard me, I said get!"

He held up his hands. "No need to get riled. I got a message for Mrs. Graham. As I recollect, that's you."

"A message?" Dumbfounded, Amanda lowered the branch. A message—from Sam. She rushed through the gate and recognized the soldier. Her face was blackened with charcoal, but she was none other than the girl soldier. The fact that she might have been responsible for the Colonel's death made her hesitate, but only briefly. "Corporal Tucker . . . "

The girl soldier cracked a grin and pointed to the stripes on her sleeve. "Sergeant, but I 'spect you to call me by my given—Jo."

"Jo, please tell me the message is from Sam and that he's all right."

"He's fine, ma'am. 'Cept for a bit of trouble with the wounded leg, he's fine. Don't bitch about it none. Beggin' your pardon, that wasn't polite." Jo withdrew an envelope from her woolen overcoat.

With the letter finally in her hands, Amanda felt Sam's love. She hoped he wasn't angry.

"Should I wait 'round, so you might send somethin' back?"

"Yes, please wait."

Lugging the rifle under her arm, Alice joined them. The guard smiled at Jo in recognition.

"Alice," Amanda said, "show Sergeant Tucker to the parlor so that *he* may warm himself by the fire."

"But he's filthy."

"Then I suggest you sweep after he leaves. He's a guest, and I will have him treated as such."

"What will Mama think?"

"I don't care what Mama thinks. The sergeant is doing me a favor."

Jo dismounted and tied her horse to the rail. She spat again.

Amanda admitted to herself that she had never met such an unrefined woman. It must be a result of living with men all the time. Either that or pretending to be one had gone to her head.

After they returned to the house, Alice and Mama began arguing about Jo. Disregarding the heated voices, Amanda dashed to the privacy of her room. Seated on the bed, she tore open the envelope, nearly ripping the letter in two. Her hands shook, and she spread the paper on the bed to Sam's familiar handwriting. Tears filled her eyes.

My dearest Amanda,

On this brisk, clear night, I stepped into my tent and thought of you by my side. That thought brought a fond smile to my lips. I recall you in my arms, sharing kisses and caresses. Foolish us, for not stopping to think a child might be the result!

Amanda, my intentions have always been honorable. I beg forgiveness for any shame or embarrassment I may have caused you. Nothing will make me happier than returning to you and having you become my wife. If you will have me, I am forever yours.

My watch tells me that it is late—nearly 2 o'clock. The bugle will summon me early. As you are probably aware, we are likely to engage in battle soon. I don't live in fear of what I must do, but I am restless and cannot sleep. My greatest wish is to see you again, but if I am among the fallen, I have arranged for your well-being. Under the circumstances, I sincerely hope you don't find that presumptuous.

If these words bring you comfort, then remember that absence does not diminish my love for you, and death will never sever it.

All of my love,
Sam

"Jo!" Amanda snatched the letter from the bed. The girl soldier met her at the bottom of the stairs. "Take me to him."

She shook her head. "We'll be engagin' the enemy soon. Matter of fact, I'm carrying orders for your guard to return to camp."

If Jo had any notion to the contents, she would understand the importance of her request. "I need to speak with Sam. Step outside, and I will tell you why."

"I *know* why. His brother's wife spilled the beans. Womenfolk and kids have been sent to the rear. I'll play messenger, but I won't take you. It ain't safe, and he'd have my hide if I did anythin' so loony."

"Then I have no message."

The bowlegged girl soldier crossed the parlor to the door.

Amanda clutched the letter to her breast. As soon as Jo was gone, she would have Ezra saddle her mare. She would follow the girl soldier and find Sam herself.

Winter wind moaned through leafless branches. As arctic air sent icy tendrils around her neck, Amanda wrapped her cloak tighter. Snow was beginning to fall, and a white dusting covered the road. She had lost all traces of Jo, but a Federal picket lay ahead. Judging by the length, the line must span several miles along the Rappahannock River. Men, many still boys, looked her way, but she failed to recognize any familiar faces. She arrived at the line.

A soldier in faded blue stopped her. "No civilians are allowed to cross the line."

"I don't wish to cross. I'm looking for a friend, Captain Prescott."

"Ma'am, it's not safe."

Farther down the road, a cannon roared. The mare jumped. Amanda tightened the reins to hold her under control.

"Captain Prescott wouldn't want me to let you go mulling around looking for him."

"But I need to know if he's here."

"You don't know?"

She shook her head. "The Yankee army doesn't make a habit of letting Southern citizens know where loved ones might be."

His impatience changed to sympathy. "If you will wait here, I shall see what I can find out."

"Thank you. I appreciate your help." After relaying Sam's regiment, Amanda dismounted. While she waited, another soldier invited her near a fire where two other men had gathered around. She tied the mare to a tree and joined them, stretching her hands before the flames. The warmth felt good, but the men shifted on their feet as if they were uncomfortable by her presence.

"We don't usually get many Southron visitors," said a soldier with a graying beard.

"I suppose not." In an attempt to make conversation, Amanda asked, "Where are you from?"

"Franklin County, Pennsylvania."

"My sweetheart is from Maine."

This fact broke the ice. "I haven't seen Stella since last winter. Our youngest won't even know his pa when I return. I thought we would be home in time for Christmas."

Amanda saw it in his eyes—in each of them—homesickness of being separated from loved ones as Christmas drew near. Maybe next year they would all be reunited. But with battle imminent, how many might not see this Christmas? Such a waste. They must have sensed her thoughts, for the gray-bearded soldier fell silent.

Cannon roared in the distance.

One man with reddish peach fuzz broke the silence. He pointed downriver toward Fredericksburg. "Do you have kin over there?"

"My mama and sister live there, but they're staying with me."

"I'm glad they're safely away." His youthful blue eyes and cracking, high-pitched voice made her nearly choke—almost as if Frieda was looking over her shoulder, telling her that he wasn't going to make it home. She gently squeezed his arm.

"Ma'am."

Amanda turned to the soldier who had greeted her at the picket line.

"Captain Prescott will see you."

A lieutenant on a dun horse waited to escort her. After remounting the mare, she followed him up a steep hill. Covered by snow, the path had become treacherous, and the mare slipped a couple of times. At the top, the lieutenant led her through rows of tents. Seemingly oblivious to continuing cannon fire, men huddled around warm fires, watching her as they passed. The lieutenant came to a halt before an officer's tent and showed her inside.

The man behind the field desk stood. "Fetch Major Prescott," Charles ordered.

With a salute, the lieutenant ran. "Yes, sir."

Delighted to see Charles, Amanda grinned. "Charles? I hadn't realized you were in the field, and Sam—"

"Is a major now. He always was an achiever. I presume he's the reason you're here?"

"I was hoping he wouldn't be."

"I know. He's been busy, so he hasn't had a chance to call on you."

"I see."

He smiled broadly. "You look positively radiant."

Holly had probably spread the news of her condition to everyone she could think of, but Amanda hoped he would remain gentlemanly enough not to mention it. "Thank you."

"Since we have a few minutes before Sam arrives, make yourself comfortable."

He motioned to a camp stool, and she graciously accepted. These days, she was relieved for every opportunity to get off her feet.

"Amanda, I was hoping you could talk Sam into sitting this one out."

"For what reason?"

"He's not fully recovered. I could report him to the colonel, but—"

"You know he'd protest."

Charles nodded. "Exactly. I knew you would understand."

He had such kind eyes that he reminded her of Sam. He certainly deserved better than Holly's abusive treatment. "I shall do my best," she said.

"That's all I ask."

The lieutenant returned. "Major Prescott to see you, sir."

"Captain, this had better be important," came Sam's voice.

Amanda barely recognized him with his thick, scraggly beard. "Sam?" Forgetting about the others, she threw her arms around his neck.

Charles cleared his throat and snatched his hat from the desk. "Would you venture to say it was important?" He and the lieutenant made a hasty retreat.

"I didn't mean to embarrass him," she said, stepping back.

"Amanda, you shouldn't have come."

Had she detected anger in his voice? "I had to see you."

"I'll fetch the chaplain."

"I didn't come for that reason. I wanted to see you before—"

"The battle." As he crossed his arms, his blue eyes watched her thoughtfully. "We were foolish for disregarding any thought for tomorrow."

"Maybe—but I wanted you to know I don't expect you to marry me out of duty. After all the years I was married to the Colonel, who would have thought?" Her voice cracked. "I don't blame you for being angry."

"Angry? Amanda, I'm not angry." A gloved hand went under her chin, and he tilted her head until her gaze met his. A twinkle appeared in his eyes. "I was surprised but never angry with you. I meant every word." He drew her close and kissed her on the lips.

His whiskers tickled her nose, but it felt good to be in the comfort of his arms again. For a long while, they were content holding one another.

He stepped back. "There's not much time before I must return to my duties." He rubbed his eyes. When he started to pace, she detected a noticeable limp in his right leg. "How have you and Rebecca been?"

At least he had finally begun to ask about Rebecca. "We're both fine. Is that why you returned to Virginia? Holly said you had been ill . . ."

He raised a hand for her to slow down. "Charles has never seen the elephant. I need to be here," he said, as if that should explain her question.

"Charles wants you to sit this one out. As do I."

His eyes locked onto hers. "You'd want me to sit all of them out."

"Do you blame me? I lost the Colonel, and you were wounded." Amanda grasped his hand and felt it tremble beneath her grip. She opened her cloak, placing his hand to her belly. "I want you to see the baby—our baby."

Sam wrenched his hand free. "Is your family safe?"

Military men had that knack of purposely changing an uncomfortable subject. "Mama and Alice are staying with me."

"Good. Now let me show you something." Taking her hand, he led her outside. Snow had changed to flurries, but he helped her across the slippery spots. After passing several rows of tents, they came to a precipice. Through leafless trees and falling flakes, she spotted the white-covered banks of the Rappahannock. Sam pointed downriver toward Fredericksburg. "While the bridges go across, the Rebs are entrenching. They have the high ground on the other side. It's a foolish move."

Another cannon boomed, and she jumped. "That's supposed to comfort me?"

"We're in reserve. The first lines across won't break through. When Burnside sees how foolish it is, he will withdraw. Now, I shall see you to your horse. If you stay any longer, I won't be thinking of getting sleep."

Warmth rose in her cheeks. "Sam, I wanted to tell you about Holly."

He halted. "Because of Charles she wasn't arrested."

"I don't understand."

"Apparently Holly bragged about her involvement with Jackson to Charles. He knew that her dealings were usually more than personal, so when he accepted the field command, he brought her along to keep an eye on her. Holly's never been the sort to take on social responsibilities. She tried getting the money for the last supply run from me."

"From you?"

He nodded. "She got to your letter before Charles. Almost didn't release it to me, but I told her that Jackson was across the river. Charles alerted me when she took the bait."

The night Holly had been at the benefit suddenly made sense.

"By the time she returned," Sam continued, "Jo and I were waiting for her. Holly was in possession of Reb money."

"Wil paid her in Confederate dollars?"

"He said both of you had been justly paid."

Amanda covered her mouth, stifling back her laughter. "He had guessed what she was after. The same night he paid me in gold—more than the supplies I had salvaged were worth."

"I'll give Jackson credit, he knows when to bail out of business deals." He gripped her hand. "Never mind them. Amanda, I missed you."

"Kiss her, Major." The girl soldier stood behind Sam, grinning broadly. "Don't mind me, sir. I've seen a right many repugnant things in life. Pleasanter ones don't bother me in the least. If the lady wants you to kiss her, by all means, you should. Ain't nothin' worse than a scorned woman. I should know. I used to be one."

Low enough for no one else to overhear, Sam mumbled, "You were scorned or a woman?"

"Very funny."

Amanda couldn't help but laugh. A first—Jo's role in the Colonel's death had been a secondary thought. She must have been too worried about Sam to care anymore. "Good to see you again, Sergeant, even if it has been a matter of hours."

"And you, ma'am." Jo tipped her hat. "I had a feelin' you might try to follow. Tried to hide my trail. Must not have done so good. If the Rebs don't shoot me, the major will."

"I did lose your trail and got stopped by the picket. I think the major will go easy on you, if you answer a question I've been curious about."

Jo smirked as if she knew what was coming.

"How do you, well, hide your sex?"

Jo's cheeks reddened as she exchanged a glance with Sam. "I've learned some tricks. Don't even think twice about passin' water standin'."

Sam gripped Amanda's hand as a signal to come along with him.

"About that kiss."

He shot Jo a warning look.

"Right, I'll return to work, so I don't get double picket duty."

Sam and Amanda passed through several rows of tents and stopped by her mare. "I'll see you soon," he promised.

An artillery wagon rolled past, followed by the creaking axles of an ambulance. Amanda bit her lip until she thought she had drawn blood. "Sam—where is the regiment setting up hospital?"

"Amanda, there's no—"

"Sam!"

"There won't be any need to find it. I have no intention of requiring its services."

That thought brought her no comfort.

He must have seen her worry. "Down the road about half a mile in a yellow house."

"I know the place."

"I'll try and call on you by Christmas." His hands went around her waist, and he helped her mount the mare. His left hand pressed against her abdomen. "We shall make plans."

"I'll look forward to it." She forced a brave smile and bent over to kiss him. Her throat constricted. As she straightened in the saddle, their gazes met in a silent goodbye. She would keep her promise and not say the word. "Remember, I love you." Before he could respond, she reined the mare around and trotted down the road to the river. Tears froze to her lashes, blinding her way.

Chapter Twenty-Four

THE MORNING BROUGHT MORE CANNON FIRE. It was no longer an occasional boom as on the previous day, but a constant roar—thunder tearing apart the stillness of winter. Continuing through the day and into the following morning, cannon pounded without letup.

Amanada surrendered to any pretense of knitting and laid her needles aside. Rebecca whined like a colicky baby and curled in her lap. Near the fire Mama rocked, while Alice kept glancing in the direction of the rumble. When the house swayed, no one broke the silence.

Finally weary of the senseless waiting, Amanda dropped Rebecca into Alice's lap. "I can't sit here and pretend everything is all right."

"Amanda," Mama said, "you're not thinking of doing something foolish?"

"No, Mama. The hospital will need help."

"But we're on the Yankee side of the river."

"Yankees bleed and die—same as our own." Wounded men were usually thirsty. Amanda collected an earthen jug from the pantry. What else should she bring? The wounded were often left to fend for themselves on the cold, bare ground. She wished she had some spare blankets. In her sewing kit, she'd find some material that could serve as bandages.

"Amanda . . . " Alice joined her in the kitchen with Rebecca slung over her hip. "I'll go with you."

Amanda shook her head. "Since you've never been married, it wouldn't be proper. Besides, I need you to look after Mama and Rebecca." She planted a kiss on Rebecca's forehead. "Her papa's out there,

Alice. I can feel it. And I need to keep busy or I shall go out of my mind."

"What about your baby?" Alice asked in a low whisper. "You could lose it if you're not careful."

"I'm just as vulnerable sitting here fretting. This way, I can be useful."

"Miss Amanda . . ." came Frieda's voice. "He be fine."

With the quaking cannon, even Frieda's reassurance did little to comfort her. "Even if Sam is all right, there are others who aren't."

"Lots of dem die today. Even more goin' to before dey finished. Ain't nothin' you can do 'bout dat."

"I can lessen the suffering for a few." Amanda poured water from the bucket into the jug. The mare would be able to carry several jugs. "Frieda, Alice—if one of you could get my sewing kit—my dress too."

"You was makin' dat dress to surprise Mr. Sam."

"He'll understand." She filled two more jugs and collected her burgundy cloak on her way to the barn. Rumbling cannon shook the ground as she crossed the farmyard. At least the day wasn't quite as nippy as the past few, but many wounded would likely freeze to death before being transported to nearby hospitals. The air suddenly seemed colder, and Amanda pulled her cloak about her.

Inside the barn, she saddled the gray mare. Frieda brought her sewing kit and unfinished dress. Amanda touched the dark gingham fabric, envisioning Sam's eyes lighting up when he saw her wearing it. Best not to think about new dresses. It wasn't meant to be. She stuffed the material in the saddlebag and led the mare outside.

After mounting the gray, Amanda trotted down the lane in the direction of quaking cannon. When she neared the river, the roar of shells and rattling guns became deafening. The acrid scent of gunpowder stifled the air. On a distant hill, a mustard-colored farmhouse flew a red flag. She kicked the mare toward it. Near the top of the hill, a low moaning warned her, but even the sound couldn't prepare her for the sight.

Men sprawled across the yard, many missing limbs. Most had no blanket. Amanda felt queasiness in the pit of her stomach. What had she let herself in for? Sam could be among them. With that thought, she slid from the mare's back and secured her to a nearby tree. She unstrapped a jug and her sewing kit from the saddle. As she passed prone shapes, a bloody hand tugged on her skirt.

"Water . . . " The soldier, a corporal, licked cracked lips with a blackened tongue.

Amanda bent down and placed the jug to his lips.

"Thank you, ma'am." He sank to the ground and shivered. "So . . . cold."

Without blankets, she felt helpless. No use fretting about supplies she didn't possess. There were others to tend to.

She stopped by the next man—the boy with the reddish peach fuzz. Only a couple of days earlier, he had been full of life. Now a red stain spread across his chest. Glazed eyes stared at her in peace. "Mother," he whispered.

"I'm not . . . " He was dying. What harm was there in giving him that small measure of comfort? Amanda knelt beside him and took his hand. "I'm here."

With a contented smile he lay his head to the frozen ground and gasped a final breath.

Tears were hot on her cheeks, but she needed to keep her wits. She could grieve later.

Inside the farmhouse, every room contained wounded. Agonized moans came from everywhere, and the nauseating scent of blood assaulted her nostrils. A red river flowed across the floorboards. As she brushed through bloody pools, her skirt became edged in crimson. An animal-like wail came from beside her. Near her feet, a soldier thrashed a stump where his right arm should have been. Amanda clutched his shoulders, but he was too strong to restrain.

An orderly pinned his wrist, but the soldier flung his stump, hitting Amanda in the ribs, nearly throwing her to the floor. The orderly latched onto his shoulders, and the soldier let out a piercing scream. Already covered in blood, she inched next to him and held down his good arm. "Stop," she said. "Please stop. You've split your stitches."

"I don't care! Don't you understand, I don't care!"

The orderly strained against the soldier's struggles. Then, by some miracle, the soldier ceased fighting. Satisfied that he wasn't going to start thrashing again, the orderly let go. Amanda unpinned the empty sleeve and placed gingham cloth over the bleeding stump. "You're going to be all right," she said.

"Why would Sallie want me this way?"

"Sallie will be happy you're alive."

"I'm half a man."

"Two arms doesn't make a man whole. My Sam was wounded in the leg. If it had come down to him or his leg, I would have chosen him."

He calmed slightly, but his eyes filled with tears.

The orderly straightened. Missing a leg, he leaned on a crutch. He wasn't an orderly, but a soldier like the rest. "Thank you," he whispered. With his ashen face, he looked like he might faint.

She placed a hand under his arm and broke his fall.

He sat with his back against a wall. "You're an angel."

"Not really, but I try to do my share."

"You're Southron. Why?"

"I live near here. If I lived on the other side of the river, I would help there."

"An angel."

"Why didn't you tell him about yourself?"

"He needed to get the anger out. Nothing I could have said would have made him feel better—yet."

"You need rest. I would rather you didn't add to my work."

As the hours wore on, Amanda noted that many of the wounded were carried to and from the kitchen. When the men returned, minus limbs, it took little guessing what job the surgeon's saw had performed. Making a special effort to avoid the room, she continued tending those in need of comfort. Water jugs emptied, and dress material disappeared. She barely noticed that day had given way to night. Before dawn, cannon resumed its rumble. Only with the new onslaught did she realize the constant bombardment had stopped.

Toward midday, she located a vacant spot under the stairs. After gathering her skirts around her, she closed her eyes for a few minutes of rest. A familiar voice woke her. *Jo.* She had distinctly heard Jo's wheezy voice. Amanda searched through pain-ridden faces, looking for the girl soldier. Outside the kitchen door, Jo supported a wounded officer. *Oh dear God.* She clamped a hand over her mouth. *Sam!* Careful not to step on any wounded, she crossed the room as swiftly as possible.

"Sam . . ."

Pain-shrouded eyes looked in her direction. Familiar blue ones, but they belonged to Charles, not Sam. She didn't know whether to be relieved or not. His left hand cradled his right arm. *Don't look.* Blood dripped to the floor. His hand dangled from thin threads of tissue and bone splinters. "Amanda," he said in a weak voice.

"I'll stay with him," she said to Jo.

Without looking at his hand, Amanda drew his left arm over her shoulder, while Jo supported him on the opposite side. He clamped his eyes shut. "I don't know what happened to Sam."

She couldn't think about Sam—not now. "You worry about mending."

"He went in to fill a hole. After the shell hit, I didn't see him. If anything's happened—"

"Everything will be fine. Wait and see." If she repeated the words often enough, she might believe them.

The surgeon yelled from the kitchen. "Next!"

Jo stepped forward, but Amanda hesitated. She should run home and fetch Frieda. Yes—that's what she would do. Frieda could help Charles. But there was nothing left of his hand to save. While Frieda was a powerful healer, even she had no magical cure.

Amanda went inside. Blood trickled from the kitchen table, and a lifeless foot hooked its toes over the tub on the floor. Two men carried a wounded soldier away on a litter. Sick to her stomach, she reminded herself that Charles needed comfort. She drew on an inner reserve and remained calm for his sake.

The surgeon wiped his hands on a bloody apron and waved for them to hurry. "On the table."

Charles tightened his grip on her arm.

"It will be all right, Charles," Amanda said.

A cone went over his face to administer chloroform. Wild-eyed, he made guttural cries. He struggled to rise, and then he closed his eyes. As the stench of blood overpowered her, she gasped for breath. The walls suffocated her. Ready to retch, she covered her mouth. She bolted for the door and heard a saw make contact with bone.

"Mrs. Graham—Amanda." Outside the front door, Jo caught up with her.

More wounded filled the yard.

"You weren't supposed to be in the fighting! Sam said you were being held in reserve."

"He said that so's not to worry you none."

"Charles lost his hand for nothing. There was nothing gained by this fight, and all of these boys are dying for nothing." Where was her mare? In every direction, wounded soldiers covered the ground. Amanda went across the farmyard to the barn. More wounded—more prone forms, with barely any space between them.

"Amanda . . ." It was Jo again. "It's for what they believe in. Your Reb husband understood. I don't 'spect forgiveness."

With the mention of John, Amanda halted. Always suspecting the truth about his death, she had pushed Jo's involvement to the back of her mind. She met Jo's gaze. "I can forgive. Just find out what happened to Sam—please."

"I will. I swear to you." Jo vanished from the barn.

Her mare—where was she? Someone might have stolen her. Beside her, a soldier groaned. Unable to ignore him, she bent down to help.

The bodies were the only protection from the wind. To keep from being weighed down, Sam had left his overcoat behind before the regiment had crossed the river to Fredericksburg. Sometime after midnight the ambulances had arrived for the wounded. He wondered if Charles was among them. For all he knew, Charles could be one of the bodies stacked in front of him.

In the icy gusts a loose shutter blew on a nearby house. Only a few yards away the Rebs crouched behind the stone wall. No fires were allowed. They would have been sitting targets. Morning would arrive soon enough for that. He pulled a dead man's wool jacket over him and tried thinking of Amanda.

His fingers and toes had gone numb hours ago. He could barely concentrate. His teeth chattered, and he closed his eyes. Focus on her face—the way she smiled and how her emerald eyes lit up a room. He laid his head on his pistol and felt himself drifting. The cold could kill a man as easily as a Reb's bullet. He fought to stay awake.

When Charles woke, a woman with hair the color of golden straw had her head slumped on the bed. Amanda. Another officer with a swathed chest occupied the bed across from him. He recalled being brought to a farmhouse by the underage sergeant, Tucker, but drew a blank after that. Pain—he suddenly remembered more pain than he had ever thought possible.

He looked at his bandaged arm and wiggled his fingers. *Thank God*—his hand was still there. "How did they do it?" he asked.

Amanda rubbed sleep from her bleary eyes. "Do what?"

"Save my hand. I just moved my fingers."

"No, Charles."

"Amanda, I can feel my hand."

"Charles, I stayed with you until you went under. The surgeon amputated your hand between the wrist and elbow."

Charles snapped his eyes shut to choke off the flow of tears. His hand *was* there. He could feel it.

A cloth dabbed his face. Cool water revived him, and he opened his eyes to Amanda's gentle face. "I know why my brother loves you."

Wincing, she rung the cloth in a tin basin.

"I'm sorry. I didn't mean to make your wait worse. Has there been no word?"

"No."

"Amanda, you don't need to nursemaid me. I'll be fine, and Sam—when he has the opportunity, he'll be looking for you at home."

Her neatly pinned hair had long given way to stray locks, and she brushed them from her face. "I shall stay a while longer."

"You need sleep."

She forced a slight smile. "So do you, Captain."

"Then go home. You should know by now that the Prescott men can't sleep if there's a beautiful woman near."

No longer forced, her smile grew suspicious. "Exactly what has Sam told you?"

His arm hurt. If he let on, she would never leave his side. "Nothing that comes as a surprise. I know how he feels about you."

His fingers—he *could* feel them. Without warning, he clawed at the bandage.

"Charles!"

Amanda clutched his hand, but his determination won. He peeled the cloth free. The fabric fell away, and he could see the neatly sewn stump. He held up his arm. The stub didn't look quite real—like something foreign and no longer part of his body. "My hand *is* gone. I don't understand. I feel fingers. Amanda . . . " He gritted his teeth against the pain.

Cool metal went to his lips. "Drink this," Amanda said. "It will help the pain."

When his thirst was quenched, he went to shove the cup away with his right hand. "This is going to take some getting used to."

"I know."

The pain was turning to a dull ache. "If Sam had lost his leg—"

"I would love him anyway. Right now, I just want to see him alive."

"Amanda . . . " Amanda straightened her shoulders and faced Holly standing at the top of the stairwell. "If you will fetch material for another bandage, I shall tend my husband."

Suddenly drowsy, he nodded for Amanda to go ahead, and Holly's face hovered over him.

"Charles, I don't expect you to change your mind about us, but I shall see you through this."

"Why?"

With unexpected tenderness, she held his stump. "I owe you that much. I behaved poorly. Will you let me tend you?"

For the first time in their marriage, Charles detected sincerity. Too tired to reply, he nodded. Lying back, he closed his eyes. He hadn't expected war to be quite like this. Sam had tried to warn him. After a silent prayer for Sam's safety, he would rest. When he woke, the pain would be gone.

Chapter Twenty-Five

"SIR, DID WE HOLD THE LINE?"

Wil lifted the wounded private to help him breathe easier and touched the boy's shoulder. "It held."

A bucktooth grin reminded him of the boy who had wondered if he was kin to Stonewall. So eager to join the fighting, no doubt, he had probably got his wish by now.

Outside the hospital in the moonlight, among groans and sobs, he heard a soothing voice. He mustn't think too much about how many were dead. They hadn't taken the beating the Yanks had—not this time. He should have been rejoicing.

After the brigadier fell in battle, Wil had taken command and regrouped the line. His boys had fought the Yanks back. General Hill would most likely see that he got a promotion. A hollow achievement. He strode over to Poker Chip. Whoops of joy came from a tent near a small campfire. The boys danced and sang, pointing at the victory banner hanging in the sky.

Red, white, and blue flashed across the sky like patriotic colors in a flag. He stood in awe as he gazed upon the northern lights. He'd seen them once before in the Northwest.

Peopeo had said they were souls of departed friends lighting torches to guide those who followed. Many souls would follow the lights on this night, and Peopeo and Benjamin would be leading the way.

"Goodbye," he whispered.

* * *

A scratching of bayonets in the muddy soil surrounded Sam. The regiment had spent most of the day entrenched. With nightfall, they had set to burying the dead in shallow graves. He hadn't located Charles and hoped that was a good sign. But groans filled the hillside, reminding him of those in need of evacuation. *Keep searching.* The Rebs would only allow them until daybreak before opening fire again.

"Sir..."

At the sound of the soldier's voice, Sam froze. All were aware that he was looking for his brother. Instead, the soldier pointed to the sky.

Red and blue lights glimmered, spreading to a dazzling display of filaments throughout the night sky. He hadn't seen the aurora since leaving Maine and couldn't think of a more fitting tribute to honor the dead.

More than an homage, the aurora was part of home. He had crunched through fields of freshly fallen snow with the lights reflecting from a blanket of white. But this was Virginia, not Maine. To the grief of their families, many Northern boys would find the red clay their final resting place. As Virginia became a part of him, he no longer ached to return to distant northern regions. The northern lights had shifted, and so had he. They were calling him home—to Amanda.

"Amanda, come quick!"

But Amanda had spotted the lights in the sky before Alice's shout. Bright colors formed a Fourth of July display from the heavens. She ran to the middle of the farmyard where she could watch the dancing lights in the open.

"What do you suppose it is?" Alice asked.

Blues, reds, golds—all colors, all shapes formed striking banners and vibrant columns. She had never seen anything so magnificent and couldn't take her gaze from the fireworks in the sky.

"It's the northern lights," Amanda said, "Sam told me about them on the night we met."

Stragglers in blue had warned them of mounting Federal casualties. She had offered each a drink from the well and asked if they knew Major Prescott. With a shake of their heads, they continued their journey.

One man recognized Sam's regiment. According to him, it had been in the thick of the fighting.

Sam could be among the dead on the Fredericksburg hillside, and the lights—a warning.

"If they're the *northern* lights," Alice said, "then he's being watched over."

"I wish I could believe that." Amanda clutched her shawl in the evening chill. On the night she had learned about the lights, she had been safely dancing in Sam's arms. When the music had stopped he wanted to kiss her. She had known it then. Both were too proper to carry out an impulsive desire. A night of innocent flirtation—only to be fulfilled during the pangs of war. Innocence had long disappeared and waiting was all she had left. "When he told me about them, I don't think either of us could have fancied the times we live in."

Alice gave Amanda a reassuring pat on her shoulder. "He will come back."

The lights began to fade until only a flicker here and there remained. Finally, they vanished. As Amanda turned, she hugged her sister. War had robbed them of dignity, and oftentimes hope. She couldn't allow all hope to slip through her fingers, even though she had the feeling that someone close was about to die.

Fredericksburg lay in ruins. Shells from both sides had battered the buildings. Broken furniture, clothing, books, even a piano had been thrown wantonly in the streets. In the freezing rain, Sam limped along the picket line on the edge of town. His leg hurt like hell. The regiment had expected to receive orders to withdraw hours ago.

A stray Rebel shell burst in the air and hit a tree. Debris rained with the sleet. Sam heard a scream. Another man was down. Musket fire broke out farther on down the line. With ammunition low, he reminded the boys to hold their fire. Thankfully, they were dug in. Losses would remain minimal.

Across the way, a dark-haired woman appeared in the road. Sam caught his breath and thought of Kate. Through the mist and sleet, the woman ran. "Kate . . ." He blinked and realized that she wasn't Kate.

She chased after a small child. *Damn.* He thought all of the citizens had evacuated. She must have hidden in some corner of a cellar.

Another shell flew overhead. The woman fell to the ground, clutching her head, but the child kept running. Whether the child was running for the fun of the chase or panic, he couldn't tell. The child was too young to know better, and he thought of how it could have been Amanda chasing after Rebecca.

Sam charged into the open, hoping the rain would conceal him enough from the sharpshooters in the heights. He caught up with the dirty-faced child and returned him to the woman.

Tears filled her eyes as she scooped the boy into her arms. "I hope there's a cooler place waiting in hell for you, Yank." She ran for cover inside the house.

Unable to lay blame with her response, he turned. The entire line was firing now. Through rain and smoke, he couldn't see much of what was happening. A soldier waved. Nearly two days had passed since he had last seen the girl soldier. He had given her up for dead during the battle.

Sam crossed the road, and she hurried to join him. "Your brother's been wounded," she said.

"How bad?"

"Ain't good. Lost a hand."

A hand? He had seen men with worse injuries survive. At least Charles was alive, but a hand? He had meant for his presence to help.

"I know one lady that'd be mighty happy to know you're fine right about now."

"Amanda?"

"She was helpin' in the hospital."

As she had promised, and he took comfort that Charles had been in good hands. They were nearly back to the line when his leg finally decided it had taken enough abuse from the past few days. It buckled, and he drew his sword to help him walk.

Someone shoved him from behind, knocking him to the ground. The searing heat of a bullet grazed his arm.

A shell exploded, shaking the ground. Horses screamed. A wagon was on fire. On the cold day, the heat was gloriously warm. Shelling and musket fire stopped almost as suddenly as they had started, with only a stray shot ringing out. Sam got to his feet and vaguely remembered giving orders to attend to the fire, when he spotted Jo crumpled at the bottom of a rifle pit.

Ignoring the pain, he jumped down to her. Blood seeped from her right shoulder. Her breathing was raspy, and her eyes filled with pain. "Ask her if she can forgive me now."

"Who?"

"I killed her husband."

He fingered the sleeve where the bullet had grazed him. "Hang on, Sergeant. We'll get you to a surgeon."

"You can't."

"Jo, your secret isn't worth dying for."

"Ma would lose my pension. She ain't got no one else. You swore you wouldn't tell."

Jo closed her eyes, and he clenched her hand. Promises—what good were they? He had also promised Amanda. What honor was there in letting another die to keep a promise?

Chapter Twenty-Six

A s SAM RODE THROUGH the familiar bottomland, he wondered if the white farmhouse surrounded by a picket fence would be standing. He rushed Red up the final hill at a gallop. A plume of smoke rose from the chimney. War never seemed fair, but at least Amanda was inside and safe. He reined the stallion to the barn and tied him in an empty stall. In the next stall was Amanda's mare. He patted the gray on the neck, and she nickered to Red.

"Hold very still, Mr. Yankee," came a bitter woman's voice from behind him.

Sam froze. Not in the mood for further delays, he started to turn but heard a rifle hammer being cocked.

"I said don't move!"

He raised his hands. "Where's Amanda?"

"I will ask the questions. Are you Captain Sam Prescott?"

"Major Prescott."

"Go away. Don't come back. Can't you see what you're doing to her? Her reputation is ruined on account of you. I will tell her a messenger sent word that you died a hero's death—if that's possible for a Yankee."

Slowly, with his hands remaining in plain view, Sam turned around. Gray streaked the woman's otherwise reddish-brown hair. She was most likely Amanda's mother. He pointed to the rifle. "Do you intend on using that?"

The rifle wavered. "If you don't get. Now get!"

"Not until I see Amanda."

"Don't you Yankees care about anything? If you heard the whispers of what they call her in town. I pretend I don't hear when they call my own flesh and blood Yankee strumpet."

He *had* hurt Amanda, but he was here to remedy that. "The last thing I want is to hurt Amanda."

"Then ride right back out of here. She doesn't need the likes of you hanging around."

"I intend on marrying her."

Her brow wrinkled, and she sent a piercing glare.

On the other hand, his admission had been unwise. Best to save his arguments for later. "If you will allow me to get to my horse, I shall leave."

She motioned with the rifle for him to go ahead.

Over by Red, he untied several canvas bags from the saddle. "These are some things I thought Amanda could use."

"We don't need Yankee charity."

After dropping the bags in the straw, he led Red outside. As he was about to mount up, Ezra swung around the corner. The old man grinned. "Mr. Sam—"

"He was just leaving," the woman snapped.

Ezra's grin vanished. "Yes'm."

"You will not breathe a word that he was here. As far as my daughter is concerned, he's dead."

"Yes'm."

Sam mounted Red, and Ezra coughed through a fist. The Negro cast a glance over his shoulder. Smoke poured from a log cabin in the walnut grove. Ezra coughed again and shot another look to the cabin.

Sam nodded that he understood. "Take care of that cough, Ezra."

"Yessir." Ezra smiled in a happy-go-lucky manner, and Sam reined Red toward the bottomland. Once out of sight, he circled back to the slave quarters and tied Red around back.

Before he could knock, Frieda met him at the door and pulled him inside. "I bin expectin' you, Mr. Sam. Here—sit by da fire and warm yourself."

After tossing his hat and overcoat on the floor, he eased into a well-worn rocking chair.

Frieda shoved a hot drink into his hands. "Da supplies much appreciated. Miss Amanda's been frettin' fierce. She afeared dat you kilt. I keep tellin' her dat you fine, but when she saw da lights in da sky—"

"The lights?"

"Da northern ones. She say dat you dead."

He sipped the sweet apple cider, and warmth spread throughout his body. "I saw them too, but someone else died."

The old woman frowned. Her clouded eyes acted as mirrors. She already knew.

She patted his arm near the spot where the bullet had grazed him. "You bin through hell. Miss Amanda be out afore you know it. I got to help with supper. Me and Ezra will stay to da other room, so you make yourself to home."

Two tiny rooms with a ladder leading to a loft—the quarters must have been tight when Dulcie lived there.

The blind woman added, "We used to fit two fam'lies in. I bring you some supper."

Uncanny how she always knew what he was thinking. He thanked her for the hospitality, and she shuffled to the other room. After gulping down the cider, he set the tin cup on the floor and stretched in front of the fire. When was the last time he had truly felt warm? He couldn't recall. His shoulders slouched, and he closed his eyes.

A tapping sound . . . *Musket fire.* He sat bolt upright and reached for his pistol.

"Miss Amanda know your here. I don't mean to startle you, Mr. Sam."

He was in the slave cabin—not on the line. Breathing out, he leaned back in the chair. "That's all right, Frieda. I must have dozed off."

Frieda held out a bowl. "Miss Amanda relieved dat you safe and sound."

Sam smelled fresh meat and broth and gladly accepted the bowl. Chicken stew—nothing fancy, but real food. "Thank you, Frieda."

The lines around her mouth wrinkled as the old woman grinned. "My pleasure. Miss Amanda will be out when she can get away. You get some rest." She motioned to the straw bed against the far wall with her walking stick.

Famished, he gulped down the stew and barely noticed that Frieda had left. With his hunger finally satisfied, he set the empty bowl on the floor. Too much had happened—the battle, Charles, and Jo. So many dead. He shook his head to keep his mind from sinking. Think of Amanda. Even with the prospect of seeing her, he relented. Sleep was the stronger need. No wonder, there had been little time for rest in the past week.

Sam stretched his arms. Once over by the bed, he unstrapped his weapons belt, keeping the pistol handy just in case. He tugged off his boots and climbed beneath the patched blanket. Clamping his teeth against the chill, he closed his eyes. The cold passed, and he drifted.

The bed creaked, and someone moved in beside him. He smiled with fond remembrances but couldn't break the stranglehold of sleep. "Amanda . . ."

As Amanda snuggled next to him, he felt a light kiss on his forehead. "You sleep. Having you safe beside me is all I need."

He murmured her name and fell into inky blackness. When Sam woke, he cracked open his eyes.

The cold was definitely gone, and emerald eyes stared at him. Amanda's hair glowed against the fireplace's light. He stroked it and pulled her closer.

With a smile she said, "Normally, you're such a light sleeper. I don't think an entire Confederate brigade marching through could have woken you."

Her lilting Virginia accent. Her sweet scent. He felt a stirring, but the names—he was the reason for her being called a whore.

"I'm sorry about Mama," she said. "She doesn't understand that I love you. I was so worried. After what happened to Charles, I thought for sure you were among the fallen."

Charles. He couldn't think straight. Nothing he could do would change things. Amanda was next to him. He unpinned her hair. It dropped past her shoulders, and blonde locks tickled him in the face. Thankful for her gentle warmth, he touched and kissed her. He had witnessed far too much death lately. She was the essence of life itself.

Their clothing dropped to the side, and finally they were together, naked. He wanted her. He needed her. He ached to be a part of her.

A metallic clatter came from the next room. Sam jerked his head around, but Amanda threw her arms around his neck and drew him back to her. "It's Ezra or Frieda," she whispered. "They only take notice of things important to them. Love me, Sam."

She trembled, and the distraction became a distant memory. Clinging to each other, almost desperately, they came together as one. When his energy was spent, he rolled to the side and fell asleep.

Amanda snuggled closer. In the safety of his arms, all the days and nights of worry had ended. Bad times were behind them now. She watched him breathe—in and out. Listened to his heart beat. Savored his warmth. Hours passed. Embers in the fireplace grew dim, but morning hadn't yet arrived.

His eyes opened. "You never answered whether you would marry me."

Except for the letter, he hadn't formally proposed. "What did you say?"

He cleared his throat. "Amanda, I'd be honored if you would become my wife."

She drew the blanket over her body and sat up.

He grasped her hand. "I thought you would be happy."

"I am, but—"

"But what?"

"I always imagined us living here—in Virginia. We can't marry—not until later."

"What about the baby? Townspeople already whisper unkind words."

Suddenly suspicious, she asked, "Sam, what did Mama say to you?"

"Does it matter? I love you."

"I haven't told Mama about the baby."

Under the blanket, he lightly touched her abdomen. Although her belly was rounding, she could conceal the fact that she was in a family way. "You can't hide much longer."

"I know, but I wish to wait until this foolish war is over before we marry."

"You're likely to birth before then. Amanda, during war is a hell of a time to make plans, but knowing you're here gives me focus to face each day. I have a reason to survive."

Like a scared child, she hugged him close. "I'm so afraid that I'm going to lose you."

"You won't lose me—not ever." A meaningless promise during war, and he hadn't focused on her when saying it.

He lay back, pulling her atop him.

"Here I am pouring my heart out to you, Major Prescott, and all you can think of is seducing me. How do you think I got into this fix in the first place?" He kissed her throat, and her resistance faded. "Is this how you intend on getting me to say yes?"

"If it works. You will let me know—won't you?" He kissed her again.

In spite of his levity, she detected something amiss. The stories from town were about the Yankees marching up the hills of Fredericksburg— to their deaths. A suicide mission, some called it. Yet, he had survived.

He buried his head in his hands.

"Sam? Forgive me for not asking sooner—how's Charles? Holly surprised me when she came to tend him. Do you suppose she feels guilty for the way she carried on?"

"He told Holly that several men spoke of an angel at the hospital." His voice had wavered, and he kissed her lightly on the lips. Sam couldn't hide the lines of grief. She covered her ears to shut out his words. "He died before I got there."

"When I left, he was fine. Charles can't be dead."

"That's the way it is sometimes."

She should have trusted her judgment and fetched Frieda. Why hadn't she? Nothing would have saved Charles's hand, but Frieda's medicine could have prevented the complications from surgery. "Why didn't you tell me earlier? You ride in here and make love to me as if nothing has changed. Your brother is dead."

"I should have told you," he agreed, his voice barely above a whisper. "I told him not to resign his post in Washington. God damn his competition—he saw everything that way. He had to prove himself in battle. He proved himself all right—a hero's death. Why wouldn't he listen just this once?"

In her arms, his head rested on her breast. Why had she lashed out at him? He was already hurting enough. "You did everything you could."

He clutched her so tightly that his fingers dug into her back. He was shaking. She felt dampness on her skin and knew he was crying. So many lives wasted and families torn apart. While they clung to each other, their tears mixed. As his heart beat against her chest, she tasted salt—the man she loved. "I will marry you."

He wiped the tears away. "Forgive me."

"There's nothing to forgive. I want to marry you."

Seemingly empty of life, his eyes no longer held the haunted frenzy of a battle-weary soldier. He retrieved his faded blue jacket from the floor. On the right sleeve was a distinct bullet hole. "Jo took the bullet."

Not the girl soldier too. "Is she . . . ?"

"She wouldn't see a doctor. Holly is looking after her. The bullet made a clean exit. With a little luck, she'll be fine. She wanted to know if you can forgive her."

She pushed a finger through the hole in the sleeve and hugged the jacket to her breast. "I already had."

Sam's eyes no longer flickered a void. So much grief, yet everything to be thankful for. Together—they were stronger united. The war couldn't last forever. He rose above her, and the bed creaked to their rhythm, no longer with the intensity of a fearful separation, but with a quiet calmness and the joy of being together.

After making love, Amanda lay cradled in his arms while he stroked her cheek. "What are you going to tell your mother?"

"She promised she would get to know you as a person. I will hold her to it."

"Hide the rifle."

Amanda detected his sense of humor returning. "Papa never taught her how to use it. She was just as likely to shoot herself."

"Now you tell me."

"We shall tell her our plans—today." Her fingers went through his unkempt beard. "You might try shaving."

"You really don't like it? If I let it ripen a little longer, it would be like your Reb boys."

"Sam, I really don't care whether the *Confederates* wear them or not. Mama doesn't like them, and your whiskers tickle when you kiss me."

"Beard or not, I'm still a Yankee."

"She's less likely to point a gun if you have the proper appearance of an officer and a gentleman."

"I'll shave this morning." He kissed her again, and she scratched her nose to prove her point. "Amanda, I will come back to you—always."

Amanda pressed her fingers to his lips. "Remember, no promises. They're bad luck. And no goodbyes. They become permanent. That's our bargain."

"Then I need to keep telling you how much I love you."

"And you, sir, know exactly what I like to hear."

He drew her into his arms, finally realizing that they both needed to be strong, for each other's sake, or neither would survive the war.

When Amanda woke, sunshine streamed through the cabin window. She reached to the other side of the bed. Empty and cold. Sam must have left some time before. With Mama and Alice in the main house, he would likely remain discreet. All this time, she had been fooling herself that Sam was the only one suffering from the effects of war.

Braving the morning chill, Amanda slipped from under the covers. She broke out in goose flesh and snatched her rumpled dress from the floor. The faded frock was now her only day dress without bloodstains. Mended and patched several times over, it was becoming threadbare.

She dressed quickly. Before the tiny mirror hanging over the bed, she twisted her hair into a knot and started to pin it. Soon there would be no more pretending. Sam and she would be married. As Frieda had said, everything would be nice and proper.

But what of Holly? Amanda never thought she could feel sorrow for such a self-centered woman. The stress of war had proven her wrong. She would call on Holly later and pay her respects, which would lend Amanda the opportunity to check on Jo at the same time.

No one stirred from the other side of the cabin. Frieda and Ezra must have already left for the day. A hammer tapped in the farmyard. She pulled the tattered curtain away from the window and saw Sam mending fences. He was clean shaven, except for a moustache and chatting with Alice. With her sister as an ally, Mama might accept the news of the upcoming wedding a little easier. She could hardly blame Mama.

The day before, Sam would have been a sore sight—dirty, bearded, and wearing a tattered uniform.

She picked up the blue jacket with gold oak leaves on the shoulders and fingered the hole where the bullet had gone through. Her mood brightened. Amanda wrapped her cloak around her and stepped onto the porch, watching Sam mend the broken rails.

Each hammer stroke was powerful and fluid. The war might not be over, but they had so much to look forward to—a life together and, come summer, a baby. A baby she hadn't thought possible.

Alice pointed at her, and Sam finally looked up. His blue eyes looked on in approval. "Good morning, Mrs. Graham. I trust you slept well."

Amanda strolled across the farmyard and blinked back her astonishment. "You already know the answer to that, Major Prescott."

"A shame . . . " He shook his head. "Not very much." As he returned to work, Amanda felt her face flush, while Alice giggled like a schoolgirl.

"Alice," Amanda said, hushing her. Alice wiped the grin from her face, and Amanda continued, "I'm pleased to see the two of you getting to know one another."

"Mama's still not going to like it, Amanda. She has no love for Yankees." Alice whispered the word as if it had been a curse, and Amanda shushed her again. "It's the truth. Mama is set in her ways."

Amanda opened her mouth to protest, but Sam dropped the hammer and held up a hand. "There's enough fighting these days. Don't say things you may later regret."

His face darkened, and she thought of Charles. "You're right."

Hooves galloped across the bottomland. Amanda climbed the bottom fence rail for a better view. The rider, waving his hat, wore gray. Alert to danger, Sam wrenched her clear and reached for his pistol as a blue roan sailed over the final fence.

She seized his hand before he could draw. "It's Wil!"

Wil swung Poker Chip around, bringing the gelding to a sliding halt.

"Just like him to make a grand entrance. You're on the wrong side of the river, Jackson!"

"Are you going to be the one to arrest me, Prescott?" When Sam made no comment, Wil grinned. "I thought not. Morning, ladies."

Alice shuffled her feet and cast a shy glance to the ground.

"I have come bearing news for Mrs. Graham's lovely sister. She may return home. Except for a few dead ones, the Yanks have vacated Fredericksburg."

"Wil," Amanda said. "Sam lost his brother there."

Wil placed his hat over his heart. "I'm truly sorry. Forgive me."

Sam and Wil exchanged gazes. For a moment, blue and gray stood still. There had always been respect between them, a bond that she supposed only soldiers completely understood.

Sam saluted to his former commander in appreciation. When Wil returned the gesture, Sam broke the silence. "Perhaps you should warn them what to expect before they return home."

Amanda raised a hand. "Enough war talk. We can wait for the details. Wil, we were just about to sit down to breakfast. Would you care to join us?"

Wil glanced at Sam.

Sam shook his head. "I don't mind, Jackson. I hear Reb rations are sorrier than ours. You could probably use a decent meal."

In one swift motion, Wil jumped from Poker's back, and Alice ran toward the farmhouse. "I shall set the extra plates. I can't wait to hear what Mama says about a Yankee joining the family."

Half expecting to see pigtails flying behind Alice, Amanda wondered when her little sister had become a woman. "I think Alice is glad you're staying," she said to Wil.

"Amanda, you needn't distract me with a pretty face. I have accepted that you and Prescott are mates."

Warmth returned to her cheeks. She should have known Wil wouldn't show discretion. Not about to give him the satisfaction of knowing that it bothered her, she said evenly, "I wasn't attempting to distract you. I was dropping a hint."

With a laugh, he tied Poker to the rail.

"And remember—she is my sister."

He only laughed harder. "I assure you, I won't forget."

As she started toward the house, Sam caught her hand. "I get the feeling you know something I don't."

"Why do you say that?"

"He's certainly not the sort I would encourage to court my sister."

She would tell him about Wil's Indian wife later. "Why Major Prescott, when you threatened that your sister would make the journey from Maine to collect Rebecca, I presumed she was already married."

Blue eyes twinkled in amusement as he held up two fingers. "There's a lot you don't know. I have two sisters."

Laughter filled the air as he swept her off her feet. With her cloak swirling around them, the brisk morning seemed warm and delightful. He set her down and kissed her. Stepping back, Amanda met Wil's dark eyes—staring coldly at her. He blinked. Crossing his arms, he broke into a broad grin and winked. His sword clanked as he turned and walked toward the house.

Hand in hand, Sam and Amanda crossed the farmyard. An icy gust moaned through leafless trees as if echoing the dying cries from the Fredericksburg maelstrom. Amanda gripped Sam's hand tighter. Virginia's rivers continued to run red. Separate but united—in two weeks time was the dawn of 1863.

Historical Note

On September 11, 2001, the world watched in horror as the events of the day unfolded. We sat glued to our television sets until we were numb with grief. A similar experience took place in New York, 1862, as people gathered in Matthew Brady's studio, viewing an exhibition of what is still the bloodiest day in American history—the Battle of Antietam (or Sharpsburg, as it was called in the South). Daguerreotypes created the first war images from the Mexican War, but photographs from the Civil War brought the destruction of the battlefield home to civilians.

None of us can satisfactorily explain the reason for September 11, and it is with the same lack of understanding that I set out to write *Promise & Honor*. While seeking solutions for unanswered "whys," the more I read, the more troubled I became. My original draft played true to stereotypes. Stereotypes are a design from Hollywood based on minorities and caricatures. Victorians were far from prudish. Most Southerners did not own slaves, and few Northerners fought for righteous reasons. Real people lived, loved, and died in the Civil War. What is more, they had a sense of humor that carried them through such trying times, and it is the same spirit that sustained us through the difficult days following the aftermath of September 11.

Like most Civil War writers, I have read diaries and letters from the era, and I have navigated the miles of trails on the battlefields. I went so far as to locate the ford in the Rappahannock River that Amanda would have crossed to visit her family in Fredericksburg. Only remnants exist today, but by finding it, I knew Amanda.

Many historians concentrate on the *big* picture—the battles and generals. I see the scope of the era more like a jigsaw puzzle. By centering on the big picture, the individual pieces making up the whole can get lost. While the smuggling of supplies as depicted in *Promise & Honor* did occur, I have found no evidence of organized efforts. Small-scale operations undoubtedly took place, but during the opening stages, only seasoned officers foresaw a long, bloody conflict. When reality sunk in to the masses, organization became a necessity.

Several hundred female soldiers are documented to have served in the Civil War. On the grand scale, they were a minority. Most were detected early, but some kept their secret hidden and died alongside their male comrades. In the twentieth century, one soldier's gender was discovered after an auto accident. Another female soldier wrote about her experience in a diary. The number who left no record is anyone's guess.

Many skirmishes and small battles took place along the Rapidan and Rappahannock Rivers before the armies converged on Manassas in August of 1862, but the skirmish Amanda finds herself in the midst of is fictional. Except for General A. P. Hill, all characters are also fictional. While he is a known figure in the "big" picture, I chose him for his personal qualities. In several places, I alluded to General Hill's Light Division. This was intentional, but my representation of any given battle is a fictional recreation and not meant to be an accurate account of the actual events.

Although the exact date is in dispute, the northern lights did appear after the Battle of Fredericksburg. Finally, while it was considered a fact of life in the mid-nineteenth century, I made no intentional effort to bypass the slavery issue. There were individuals on *both* sides who abhorred it. Yet, I found little evidence that most soldiers were willing to fight for such a cause. I hope my characters reflect this successfully. I did recreate the slave dialect, found it difficult reading, and refined it. Any errors in doing so are entirely my own.

Best regards,
Kim Murphy

Acknowledgments

A special thank you goes to my editors, K.A. Corlett and Catherine Karp, and my cover designer, Mayapriya Long. My deepest appreciation also extends to Charles Holley for providing the battle scene photograph to make stunning cover art. Most of all, I would like to thank my family: my son, Bryan, and especially my husband, Pat; both of whom are often wondering if I might be from the nineteenth century.